LIFE'S FORTUNE

ROY WORRALL

LIFE'S FORTUNE

ROY WORRALL

DoctorZed
Publishing
www.doctorzed.com

This second edition published 2021 by DoctorZed Publishing.

DoctorZed Publishing books may be ordered through booksellers or by contacting:

DoctorZed Publishing
10 Vista Ave
Skye, South Australia 5072
www.doctorzed.com
61-(0)8 8431-4965

ISBN: 978-0-6452497-1-2 (sc)
ISBN: 978-0-6452497-0-5 (e)

A CIP number for this book is available at the National Library of Australia.

Cover image © catiamadio | Dreamstime.com.

Printed in Australia, UK & USA

DoctorZed Publishing rev. date: 11/11/2021

For Alicia

ACKNOWLEDGMENTS

I would like to take this opportunity to thank all those who helped with this book.

First and most definitely foremost, my lovely and loving wife Alicia, who assisted with many helpful ideas, proofread the manuscript as it got closer to completion and put up with the many long periods of my absence from her loving arms. I love you, my darling, for always and in all ways.

Next, to the many kind members of the historical representation group of which I have been a proud member since 2001 – the KNIGHTS' GUILD OF WESSEX & MERCIA, based in Brisbane, Queensland, Australia, who research and present English lifestyles during the period AD 1150 - 1220, the Renaissance period of the High Middle Ages. They have given me many helpful suggestions for historical details and encouraged me with their critiques of the work in its many stages of development.

I would especially like to thank Dr Joseph Goodall, for his historical piece on the historical Knights' Guilds, which appears in the appendix to this book.

There are several characters in this book who are named for, or at least fashioned around, some of the members of the said modern Knights' Guild. I am sure that you will all recognise yourselves when you read the book. Thanks for your help, boys and girls.

There are countless other people, far too many to mention individually, who have helped me immensely in this project. You may not even realise that you have helped, but you did.

Thank you, one and all.

INTRODUCTION

This story is intended to be read as the work of fiction that it is, although it can also be used as an educational book. It grew out of an idea, put forward by the Knights' Guild of Wessex and Mercia Inc., that every member of the group should have a small story – one or two paragraphs – that they had made up to describe how they each came to join the 'ancient' Guild, for their play-acting. Over the years my paragraphs grew very large indeed.

While most of the characters and events in this book are intended to be entirely fictional, I have utilised some actual mediæval individuals and occurrences, as well as real places, to aid in setting the book in the proper historical and geographical context, although some of these real people and events may be deliberately misplaced in time.

Research into the Domesday Book, various atlases and many other physical reference materials, along with numerous sites on the internet – especially www.british-history.ac.uk – has turned up the names of these real people, places and events, which I have woven into the fiction that is this book and for which I give due reference and deference wherever possible.

"If anyone threatens those near him with cruel misfortunes, or if someone wicked cruelly holds sway over his neighbours, kicking and clawing, and cultivating wickedness among them, stand up to thwart his evil violence alongside the neighbours."

Urbanus Magnus

CHAPTER ONE

My name is Rolf, son of Ranulf and Switha. I was born in Portsmouth in the year of our Lord 1206. Thanks be to God, I have led a full, rich and varied life, which, at the age of eighty-seven, I know is now rapidly coming to an end. Therefore, the time has come for me to record some of the events of my life and those of my friends, family and other people besides, so that future generations may learn how life was lived by ordinary people in my time, in this part of the world.

An entry in the Anglo-Saxon Chronicle for the year of our Lord 501 claims that "Portesmuða" (meaning 'mouth of the harbour belonging to a man called Port') – as our town was known long ago – was first settled by an ancient Saxon warrior named Port. The entry states that: *'Her cwom Port on Bretene und his twa suna Bieda und Mægla mid twa scipum on þære stowe þe is gecueden Portesmuða und ofslogon anne giongne brettiscmonnan, swiþe æþelne monnan.'* When translated into the common tongue this reads, 'Port came to Britain with his two sons, Bieda and Mægla and two ships, to a place called Portesmuða and killed a young Welshman, a very noble man.' This Welshman is thought by some of the storytellers to be Geraint ab Erbin, a noble warrior from Dyfnaint, who battled King Ine of Wessex in the Eighth Century.

People have conflicting ideas about whether or not any of this is true, not least because there are some two hundred years difference regarding when the supposed battle took place. Either way, people have been living here for a considerable time. Sometimes there may have been as few as twenty villagers, at other times it was recorded that there were as many as a thousand or more.

The weather in Portsmouth is mostly mild and clement and, although it rains occasionally, we are not overburdened with days on which we do not see Father Sun. The water that surrounds our island in the channel is – according to travellers and troubadours who passed through our town – quite a bit warmer than that which flows past many other parts of the country. This gives us a warmer climate than most of the rest of the land.

We are also told that there are parts of England and beyond that hardly ever see a day without rain. In some places, freezing winters last for more than half of the year. I am glad that our Lord God sees fit to allow me to live in such a pleasant part of this land.

My earliest memories are of my family and friends. During my childhood, we lived in a two-roomed cottage made of wattle and daub. The building was twelve paces across the front and six paces deep. The roof was thatched with reeds and inside, at its highest point, was twice the height of a man. The house was coloured a pale green on the outside. The insides of the walls were a pale shade of yellow and were hung with several of my mother's tapestries and drawings.

The small bedroom in which my parents slept occupied one end of the cottage. It was separated from the rest of the house by a wooden door set into a thin wattle and daub wall. My brother and I had our own beds, small pallets of straw, in the main room. They were set on a small shelf, running along one wall inside the house, near to our parents' room. During the day our mattresses were rolled up and the low shelf was put to use as a long bench. In this main area, there was a table on which we took our meals, with my brother and I sitting on the long bench and our parents on another bench on the opposite side of the table.

In one corner of the room my mother's drop loom leaned against the wall. She used this for weaving her tapestries when she could get the wool. There were stones – about the size of a man's hand – with holes through them, which were used to keep the warp threads

2

straight and taut to make the weaving easier. When the weather was fine, mother would paint or embroider or do some other craftwork outside, to make use of the sunlight. If the weather was too cold or wet to work outside, the table and bench would be moved nearer to the door, where the light inside the cottage was better to work by.

My father built his own tools and furniture. My brother and I would gather the wood chips to use as kindling to light the fire, which was a sunken pit surrounded by large stones, located in the middle of the room. The fire was used for food preparation and also for light and heat. Starting the fire was easy by using a flint and steel. With flint being plentiful in this area – due to the chalk hills and small pieces of steel readily obtained from the blacksmith – everyone in the community was easily able to make a fire.

Almost as soon as a child was able to walk, he learned how to make fire. Tinder was small, dry sticks, animal hair from dead beasts or small pieces of old rope. Each of these were formed into a small 'nest' for the fire making. The sharp edge of the flint was struck onto the steel to produce a spark, which landed on a piece of char cloth, that had been heated until it was black but not completely burnt. When the spark landed on the cloth, it was placed into the 'nest,' and slowly blown upon, to increase the heat of the glowing spark and causing the tinder to catch alight. Once a flame had been produced, a taper could be lit to preserve the flame if you wished. The ball of flaming tinder was shoved under the shavings of wood and kindling and the fire would roar into life. Once in a while, the whole process had to be repeated if the 'nest' burnt out before the tinder could catch. The floor of the house was packed earth, with a small amount of straw to cover it, for warmth, comfort and to keep our feet clean. We were careful to watch for sparks from the fire, in case the straw caught alight.

There was a small, fenced area near the house, which contained a covered pen for our two asses, a small roost for our chickens, a pigsty and a small shed for my father's tools – a long handled axe, three shovels, a hoe and a large, flat-based hand-barrow. My father built the cottage and shed himself, with the help of a few of our neighbours. Once the buildings were completed, he held a small celebration to thank those who helped with the construction.

We were not well off, but we were a free family and my father held a parcel of land, about two hides, near a small isle called Whale Island. It was not a real island, as you could easily walk over to it at low tide, provided you did not mind being covered in slimy mud up to your knees. For as far back as I can remember there has been talk of laying down a causeway made of rocks from the mainland to the island, though it is still just talk. Almost every person in the village had fallen over in the mud on the way out to the island. We laughed at each other when it happened, but we did so kindly and without doubt that it would soon be returned.

Many people went there to the island to graze their sheep, but only one person lived out there – Osbert, our tanner. However, every now and then a number of enterprising people would decide to spend several weeks, digging mud from the middle of the channel at low tide and carrying it up to deposit it on the beach of the island, slowly reclaiming more of the land from the sea.

As time went by, Whale Island grew and was able to graze more sheep. The shepherds would lay down long wooden boards for the sheep to walk across, and when these boards were lifted the sheep had to remain on the island until their owners came to retrieve them. Whale Island was lightly wooded, with several varieties of trees growing there. Osbert had cut some of them down in order to build his hut and workshop. No one went near to Osbert's hut who did not need to do so, because the terrible smell which arose from his leather-curing vats was enough to curl your toes. At least the grazing sheep did not complain about the aroma.

The tidal flow in the channel between Portsmouth and Whale Island was known to be dangerous at times. Twice a day, the water level rose from absolutely nothing but a mud flat to a depth twice the height of a man almost in the blink of an eye and then sank back to nothing before you'd had time to turn around. I heard tell of folk who were dragged away by the rushing waters. Their bodies could – by the grace of God – be washed up somewhere on the shore at a later time. Sometimes they were never found.

When the tide was out, the channel between our land and the isle was laid bare. The people from our town would then go out onto the mudflats and gather mussels, cockles and winkles. When lightly boiled, these small, snail-like creatures were a tasty meal. There were clams in the channel also, which the Normans called '*escalope*' and some folk had developed small oyster beds there. When we could get them, the oysters were another delicious source of food. Fish of many types were plentiful, as were waterfowl, which were delicious when salted and roasted. The salt the village used came from the large saltpan in the nearby village of Cosham.

But not all of the villagers obtained their food from the sea alone. Most had other means of supporting their families, as the ocean could sometimes be treacherous. Once in a while, not every fisherman made it home after a heavy storm at sea.

Most people of our village grew grains and fruits on the small patches of ground that they dared call their own. In truth, the King owned all the land in the country. Some grew only one crop and bartered with others for the balance of their diet. A few grew a variety of crops and fruits, as did my father.

Grains were taken to the miller to be ground for bread, although the largest of each year's grain was kept for next year's planting. This was to ensure a better harvest than the previous year, provided the weather was kind. Fruits were eaten fresh, as they were picked, but if a glut occurred then any excess was stored or dried for the winter months. The summer brought strawberries, raspberries, redcurrants and blackcurrants and with the autumn came apples, plums, pears, elderberries, blackberries, sloes and many others. Meats were readily available with the many pigs, sheep, fowl and a few cattle. Offal was a cheaper option if that was all you could afford to barter or pay for, but for the richer citizens in the community, the better cuts of meat were plentiful. Nuts came in a great range too – chestnuts, walnuts, hazelnuts, pine nuts and many more. All in all, if we lacked variety in our diet, it would be of our own choosing.

CHAPTER TWO

The island of Portsmouth did not, for the most part, support a great deal of vegetation. The soil was either sandy or full of gravel in the south and primarily thick clay further north. Only vegetables such as beets, turnips, swedes, parsnips, carrots, peas, beans and some others were grown here in any great measure and all of our wheat was imported from other towns. Several of the townsfolk grew a small quantity of grain plants – these were mainly barley and oats – as well as some varieties of fruits such as apples, pears, plums and so forth.

My father grew several of these grains, fruits and vegetables on his portion of land. With careful nurturing they grew easily enough to feed our small family and all twelve pigs and the asses that we had tamed. Even with all these hungry mouths we were left with enough produce to trade with others in the town for the things we needed.

One thing that we grew in our community that most towns in the surrounding vicinity did not have, were grape vines. A young Italian woman named Marissa had learned all that her father could teach her of the vintner's vocation before she was taken as a wife by Joshua, a man from our town.

Marissa was an attractive, slender, dark haired woman, with eyes of a brown so dark they were almost black. Her accent had softened over the years that she had been in England. Sometimes when she grew overexcited, her accent became so thick that her speech was almost impossible to understand.

She had met Joshua in Tortona – a city in the far north of Italy –

while he was returning to England from the Crusades. It was while in Tortona that Joshua had met and fallen in love with Marissa. He had been receiving treatment for injuries sustained in the Holy Land, when he had been stabbed by a Saracen. Joshua had been unwell for quite some time since that incident.

Marissa helped the sisters of the Franciscan order who cared for the many sick and injured travellers. The convent was one of very few buildings left standing when Frederick Barbarossa levelled the town in 1155. It was very nearly abandoned, but the people living on the land in the surrounding vicinity needed somewhere to have their wounds and illnesses treated, so the convent stayed where it was.

Over time, Marissa acquired some amount of skill at preparing simple medicines for the patients. The medicines they used were grown in the grounds of the convent or gathered from the surrounding countryside. She used these medicines to tend to Joshua, and over time as he recuperated, he convinced her to spend pleasant hours simply walking and talking with him.

When Joshua's health had improved enough for him to travel home, he gathered the courage to ask Marissa's father for her hand in marriage. There were some grave discussions among her family as to whether she should be receiving permission to marry this Englishman. Joshua made a good case, however, for an expansion of the family wine trade into England. He had also proved his strong love for her by promising to allow her to inherit his property and the rights and privileges held for it – should she outlive him – and he willingly signed a legal document to that effect.

Joshua also promised to have the document ratified when he returned to his native England. He held quite a sizeable piece of land at home with many servants, so that Marissa would never need to be concerned for her finances. Impressed by his generosity and deep love, her family consented to the wedding. Joshua was indeed a very charismatic and persuasive man.

As a wedding present, her father had given Marissa and Joshua as many varieties of vine cuttings as they and the servants who would accompany them to England could carry, so they could at least make a good attempt at starting a wine industry in England.

Her father also sent many barrels of wine from his vineyard on the trade ship with Joshua and Marissa when they sailed to Portsmouth. The wines were well received by the lords around the area and were a fine introduction for the new vineyards to be planted. There was a promise from Marissa's parents that more wine would be forthcoming, so that they could begin to set up a wine trade between Italy and England through Portsmouth.

When they had finally settled on Joshua's land in the north east of Portsmouth, they took great pains to grow the grapes. They planted, fertilised, watered, pruned and harvested the vines, both of them working very hard to keep the plants alive so that they could build a good business from the wine and table grapes. It was not easy, but with patience, care and good weather, the vines grew well. They were cultivated both as table fruit and for pressing for wines.

Over the years, Marissa's wines proved to be as sweet as honey and very popular with many of the people in the town. Unfortunately, Joshua died only about five years after arriving back home. He had suffered many bouts of illness during those years, as his wound had never healed properly. As these years passed, he became more and more an evil-tempered individual, subject to bouts of sudden rage. On one occasion, his fury was so potent that he put his fist through an inside wall of his cottage. Whether this change of temper was indeed a result of the injury or for some other reason, no one ever had the chance to find out. It is God's truth that he was never beforehand known to be a violent man. Had he been an aggressive person, Marissa would likely have had cause to fear for her life.

One day, while harvesting the grapes, too impatient to wait for help, he attempted to single-handedly hoist a very heavy basket of grapes from the ground onto his cart and his wound burst open. He cried out, first in agony, then for his wife, who at once dropped what she was doing and came running, guessing some misfortune had befallen her husband. She did not realise how serious the injury was. Marissa sent one of the labourers to fetch the physician at all speed and, although she tried her utmost to staunch the flow of blood, Joshua bled to death in her arms before the physician could arrive to save him.

After his funeral, Marissa donated a large cask of wine to the church each year, as payment for prayers for the soul of her dead husband. Her wine was also used in the Holy Eucharist. Of course, as only the priests partook of the wine during this service, this meant they had quite a lot of wine left over for their own use, to accompany their meals or at other times. Marissa was careful enough not to allow these donations to cause her cellar stocks to drop too far. She also rationed the amount that she sold to the taverns and inns, so that if there was ever a bad year for the grapes, she had sufficient to last until the next vintage.

Due to this husbanding of her reserve, there was almost always a reasonable quantity of wine to go around in the town, so that no one who could afford to acquire his own portion of the vintage, was ever likely to go without. Most villagers made do with a smaller share mixed with water. How much water was added to the wine depended upon the status of the drinker. Similarly, the quality of the wine varied, according to how much one paid for it. Those with small means either drank a lower standard wine or used more water to stretch the wine further, using the better wine only for special occasions, such as weddings, births and so on.

CHAPTER THREE

Another unusual fruit to grow in our town was oranges. They were here because one man, Thurstan, had somehow managed to obtain a pair of oranges while on his way home from travelling in Spain and France. After eating his first couple and very much enjoying them, he was intelligent enough to keep the seeds and, once he returned home – with extremely careful nurturing – managed to grow two orange trees.

He was disappointed not to have more trees grow, considering he had had over thirty seeds to hand. Despite his best efforts, he could never keep more than four trees alive at any one time; quite possibly because the weather in this part of our country was not really favourable to the good growth of oranges.

These trees were, as you would expect, zealously protected, as they were the only oranges we had ever seen growing in this area. Thurstan had even built a high wall around the trees and placed a trusted guard near the trees at all hours of the day and night, in case anyone should try to steal the oranges. The fruits were, by all accounts, delicious, though I believed I was unlikely ever to experience them for myself.

None of us common folk had any idea what they tasted like, though there were some who boasted that they had indeed sampled one. How much truth there was in those boasts was for anyone to guess, though there might have been some clue in that the so-called descriptions of the taste varied quite considerably. These oranges were destined only for the tables of the well born or for those others who could pay the high cost he put on them, and for Thurstan's family and close friends, of course.

By the sixth anniversary of my birth, our community comprised one hundred and three people, one hundred and nineteen pigs (including the twelve being raised by our family), two hundred and forty-seven sheep, thirty-seven goats, eleven cows and three bulls, two ploughs, each with two oxen, countless chickens, pigeons, geese and ducks. We were in no great risk of starving, unless the weather turned very bad, which it rarely did for any great length of time.

Most people in our village had a cat or two. The miller had at least three. These were useful for catching the rats and mice that ate the grain. Most people, as they relaxed after the day's work was done, liked to have a cat curl up on their lap, purring softly. About one house in ten had a dog. These dogs were hairy beasts, of a breed known as lurcher. All the dogs had to have their dewclaw removed, to ensure that they would suffer no injury from twigs or roots as they ran through the woodlands. These dogs were used for rounding up the sheep and other herds. Some men used them for hunting, which was a very dangerous thing to do. If the shire reeve caught them, the dog would have three of its four toes cut off on each foot, if they let it live. Any dog caught chasing animals without its owner would certainly be destroyed. The man might be put to death too for hunting in the King's forest.

Marissa's dogs were unusual. They were all black, smooth-haired greyhounds. Most greyhounds in our country were owned by people of higher class, but she had brought them with her from Italy. She had started with a breeding pair, which meant that she always had one or two by her side at all times. Whenever a bitch had whelped, there was never a shortage of noblemen to buy the pups. This supplemented her earnings from her vineyards and she lived quite comfortably on this income.

Besides the normally domesticated animals, there were about four dozen asses in the area, some running wild and several tamed and penned by those who had need of them, such as the smiths, the priests and the miller. While these animals could be bad-tempered, they were extremely easy to look after, as they did not need a great deal of food stored for them. They could graze on the meadowlands and would happily eat whatever food scraps were given to them.

The asses were quite hardy beasts, well adapted for harsh, dry conditions, but they lived well in our town where they were well cared for. The only thing we had to provide for them, besides food and drink, was some sort of shelter from the rain, as the fur of an ass is not waterproof, as is a horse's. Many were the times that we young children tried to capture and ride the wild asses for play. They were difficult to corral, but with five or more energetic children working together, the job of rounding up one or two asses was manageable.

Riding an untamed ass with no bridle was an adventure in itself. Very often we would fall off, skinning ourselves on the hard ground, to the derisive laughter of our friends. Once they were tamed and put between the traces of a cart, however, they became quite easy to guide, which was why their cousins were tolerated, running wild.

Our miller, Roger, owned both of the mills in the village. He was a large man, though not quite as big as my father. He was well versed in the art of sword play, as he had been on the Crusades with my father. This intimate and proficient knowledge of swordsmanship made him a formidable opponent if anyone rashly decided to chance his arm against him.

Roger and my father would occasionally practise their sword craft in the small paddock behind the northern mill. Whenever these sessions took place, there was always a crowd of young men watching, attempting to learn what they could from the spectacle, after which they would collect some strong sticks and practise for themselves. While Roger and my father were great friends, the practise sessions sometimes became rather serious, though there was never any great injury suffered by either man. Once in a while, one or the other would receive a small cut to their hand or arm, but these were soon easily healed and neither man begrudged his friend the injury.

Roger held the mills from the abbey of Fontevrault in Anjou. The mills were granted to King Richard, the first of that name, by His Holiness the Pope and then King Richard, in his turn, granted one to the abbey. They were located on the southern half of the western shore of the island, as there were no rivers running anywhere through our town. The mills were partly driven by the tide, running through what was known as the millstream, as it rushed in and out through the narrow and shallow strait between Portsmouth and Alverstoke. This was an empty area of land occasionally used by our sheep and cattle for grazing.

Within Alverstoke was an area known as God's Port, which eventually became known as Gosport. It was generally accepted that this was where the first settlement had been on that side of the harbour. It was, like Portsmouth, not a place for prolific growth of crops, although people managed to survive quite well on what they grew there, as we did on our side of the harbour.

Roger always had several asses, which he used to power the mill when the tides were still or too low to move the wheels fast enough to grind the grain. Roger lived in the more northerly of the two mills. His young son, Henry, was not the most intelligent of men, but he was, like his father, thoroughly honest. So much so, that when he reached the age of only fifteen years, he was entrusted to operate, manage and dwell in the southern mill, some two hundred and fifty paces from his father's building. Henry knew every single part of both mills as well as he knew the back of his hand.

Henry was, like most people, not very good at reading, but he was clever at sums – as he needed to be if he was to avoid being duped by some of the more unscrupulous villagers. He understood mechanical things, so that if either of the mills needed any sort of repair, Henry was the man to carry out the work. He could make any part he needed for the repairs, no matter how large or small. It seemed to us that this skill was almost an instinct.

Roger, in addition to being the miller, was the shire reeve – or sheriff, as the position became known – and he was notorious for his ability to be on the spot whenever anyone made the mistake of being dim-witted enough to be doing something against the law. Any minor crimes committed within the parish were swiftly punished. The people of our town knew far better than to do anything that was likely to disturb the peace while Roger was anywhere in the vicinity.

For some reason, neither cats nor dogs liked Henry, and he hated them. They would bark or hiss at him whenever he approached. In fact, not very many animals were fond of him. Even the asses brayed continually whenever he approached. He could not operate his mill without the constant sound of the asses calling out. The cats in both of the mills avoided him if they could. Henry's arms, legs and face were perpetually covered in scratches from cats that were in a room which he entered. They would jump at him with claws flying, and then run from the room. Henry soon learned to enter rooms carefully, if he thought that a cat may be in there.

Although the men were unwilling volunteers, the miller was sometimes able to give his asses a rest and use manpower to grind the grain. He used his authority as shire reeve to force any petty miscreants in the area to power the mills by chaining them to a capstan and having them push the large grinding wheels around by hand. The townsfolk knew what Roger had in store for them if they broke the law. It was mainly incomers who suffered the indignity of replacing the asses in their jobs. In such a way, these petty criminals came to benefit of the town through their labour and served as a reminder to all that it was best to keep on the right side of the law.

CHAPTER FOUR

In Portsmouth we had the good fortune of having an honest miller. Such a person is sometimes hard to find in that profession. We heard tales of millers in other towns and villages who, when given grain to grind, would find many dishonest ways of keeping most of the meal for themselves, or they would charge exorbitant fees for the milling. These fees were known as 'multure.' Normally they were not high, but with those millers whose hearts were filled with greed, the villagers would suffer greatly.

Roger was also one of our town's most prominent churchgoers – he was almost always elected to the council of elders. He generously took it upon himself to pay for and supply the bread for the Holy Eucharist each week. He ensured that the loaves he gave were always of the very highest quality. Marking him out further as a man of great importance in our town was the fact that he was one of the very few men to possess his own horse. This was due to his position as shire reeve. Sometimes he had to travel outside the town, his duties taking him far and wide and he would often regale the townsfolk with stories of other places he had visited, the people he had met there and the strange ways of speech they had. He was a gifted mimic so he amazed us with the strange accents from other places – some nasal, others throaty, all different.

Alongside Roger the miller, the town had eight bakers, several seamstresses and tailors, two undertakers, three chandlers to supply our candles and sixteen taverns and alehouses, seven of which had sprung up since the new church started construction. These alehouses ranged in quality, from a place to which one could take one's family for a pleasant afternoon's relaxation and entertainment, to something resembling a den of robbers, where men would slink in and out as if they had committed some crime by going there. It was the latter sort that proliferated after the commencement of the building of the church.

There had been, when I was young, a man who bore the lonely task of charcoal burning. He lived in the woods to the north of the island, in a small shelter made of large sticks and straw. Two hundred paces from this shelter was where he built his mounds to burn the wood that made the charcoal. He gathered some small sticks to make a fire and then surrounded it with ever larger sticks and logs, until he had a pile about as tall as he was. He would then cover the top with peat, moss or mud, light the small fire inside at the bottom, then stay watching it for up to four or five days. The fire had to smoke in a particular way, so sometimes he pulled the pile down and began again. Once it performed to his satisfaction, he would wrap himself in his cloak, lean against a nearby tree and prepare to watch the burning pile for days until he deemed that the flames had done their work. He had to be there, for if any sparks flew from the fire, they could set the whole woodland ablaze, ruining his livelihood and putting people's houses in danger. Thankfully, he only had to light his fires once every month or so.

I went to see him once, with Gor and a few of my other friends – we were curious about how the charcoal was made. He was friendly enough, although I guessed he was not greatly concerned for company. He told us about his work and even gave us some charcoal sticks so we could practise drawing and writing. Although we knew not how to write, we could draw. For the next few days, we drew everywhere we could make a mark, until our charcoal was worn down to a tiny piece.

For those of our town who had letters that they needed to read or write, we also had three scribes. They were kept busy, as almost everyone was illiterate. This was true for most of England at this time and even King John, the brother of Richard, could neither read nor write. This meant that there were always wills, business letters and legal documents that needed dictating and so the scribes rarely had a day in which they were unemployed. The scribes lived at some distance from each other, although they would come together and discuss the merits of new writing styles. Sometimes they would train themselves in them to diversify their skills.

One of the scribes, Heleward, was married and had a young son. Heleward had been taught to write by his father who had died from the pox. Heleward could read and write in French, Spanish, Latin and German. He had a beautiful hand, so long as he did not rush. Another scribe was Anselm, a man who had suffered a fall from the top of a small cliff when he was young and had injured himself so badly that it looked as though his face had been twisted halfway around his head. He was blind in one eye; the skin having healed over it. He was not likely to marry, but had been taught to read and write by Heleward. People did not care what you looked like when you could read and write for them, and besides, he was a very likeable man with a kind heart. Once he had earned enough money as Heleward's apprentice to pay him back for the cost of his lessons, he went into the scribe business on his own and gained sufficient funds to support himself.

The third of our scribes, Peter, had entered an abbey nearby when he had grown old enough to decide for himself that a monk's life would be better than begging. As he had no family or manual skills his choices were few. He had spent almost five years in the abbey and had learnt to read and write effortlessly before deciding that abbey life was not for him. So late one night he left by climbing over the abbey wall and roamed the countryside before settling here, as we were short of scribes at the time.

I loved to watch the scribes as their pens flew over the pages. It seemed almost magical that a few scratches of a goose feather could carry thoughts, emotions and wishes across vast distances and could be read time and time again for many years. I could almost imagine these ideas were being trapped upon the page, to be explored by anyone with the skill to read them. I longed for that ability, but my family could never afford the cost of the lessons. We had far more important things on which to spend our money.

However, by occasionally pestering the scribes to write some things for me, I did learn to recognise a few words, including my own name. Even though I knew I would never be likely to have the chance to write for myself, except with a stick in the dirt. Or so I thought at the time.

CHAPTER FIVE

There were four blacksmiths supplying and mending tools; shoeing horses for Roger, the nobles and travellers; producing and repairing armour and weapons, including arrowheads; and making the steel bands for the cooper, who made our barrels and buckets. In fact, anything that was needed and could be made from iron, steel, copper, tin, brass, or any other metal, the smiths did it.

Two of these smiths, Gregory and Eustace, had apprentices working with them. The other two, Alan and Robin, had, not long ago, started out in their own smithies, having learned all they could from the older men to whom they had been apprenticed. One advantage to being a smith was that once you had the raw materials – fire and iron – you could make the tools for your craft. They may be crude at first, but as your supply of materials grows, the quality of your tools improves. Apprentices usually make a set of tools as their first learning project.

When swords, arrowheads, knives, horseshoes, or other iron or steel objects needed to be hardened, they were heated until almost white hot, then dipped in oil to quench the steel. This quenching made the metal quite hard without becoming too brittle. The metal was then beaten into the shape needed, which meant that it had to be reheated and dipped again. This process was repeated until the metal was brought to the requisite shape and hardness for whatever its use might be. If the quenching was repeated too often, without the intermediary step of beating it into its required design, the metal would become too brittle to use. The smiths had to learn to use their judgment, so as not to make this mistake.

Gregory's apprentice, Troy, was a married man, and his wife, Mary, was known for her excellent work with silver, gold and precious stones. Troy had made the many small, intricate instruments for Mary to use for her jeweller's trade. She made beautiful pendants and brooches of all descriptions, as well as circlets, rings, crosses and many other objects for the people of the town and for the travellers or pilgrims who passed through on their way to holy sites in England, France and beyond. One year after they had married, Mary had given birth to their first son, John.

Alan, the youngest smith in the town, had only recently buried his father, who had also been his master in the trade. Alan's father, Alard, had suffered terrible burns over most of his body when he fell asleep one evening without first banking his forge's fire. Alard had been one of the best customers of the nearby tavern, the Pied Merlin. He often took home a large container of mead or of good ale to finish off his day. Alard was known throughout the town not only as the best armourer and animal healer, but also as a prolific drinker, regularly drinking himself to sleep. Alard and his son had, besides two asses, an old destrier – a knight's war horse – which bore a terrible scar on his left front leg and across his side which caused the animal to limp.

An old friend of Alard's, who had been raised to knighthood, had been involved in a tournament and his opponent's lance had dropped too far downward and speared the horse through the leg. The lance hit the bone and shattered; the sharp end opened a wide gash on the flank of the beast. The destrier's injuries were roughly bound and the animal was brought to Alard. While Alard was examining the injured horse, the knight had said that he would prefer that the animal be destroyed to put it out of its misery.

Alard asked, "Would it not be better if I purchased the horse from you?" The knight declared that the animal was no longer of any use as a war horse, not only because it would shy at the very sight of armour and lances, or even the lists, but any great exertion would likely break open the wounds and make him bleed. This being the case, the knight declared he would exchange the horse for a new breastplate and helm for his son. Alard agreed heartily and found himself the proud owner of a lame destrier.

The horse, which Alard renamed Jack, was about eight years old at the time of the accident and, through the tender ministrations of the smith and his young old son, had become a great deal stronger, a much-loved member of the family and a useful part of the community. While he would never again be a fighting horse, he was quite able to draw a cart, due to some clever work by Osbert, the town's only leather worker. He created a padded harness that did not stress the animal or aggravate his injured leg and chest.

On the terrible day that the fire killed him, whilst Alard was still hungover from the previous night's drinking, the smith and Alan had been arguing loudly in the smithy about the store of iron ingots becoming so low. "You are a lazy good for nothing!" Alard yelled at his son. "I have been reminding you for the last week to keep up the store of metal for our work. How do you expect us to make a living without iron? Where is it? Why have you not gone to get it?"

Alan had shouted back at his father, "How can it be my fault? I told you yesterday that the ship is not due to arrive until tomorrow. All this morning I have been getting the cart ready to travel to the dock, so that on the morrow I can go to collect the metal."

He then stormed out of the cottage, went to the stable and selected two of the strongest asses to hitch to the wagon. He went into the house and decided to leave for the wharf that day rather than wait for morning. He collected his parcel, containing some bread, cheese and onions, as well as some ale so that he would not have to pay the high prices at the wharf while he waited for the ship to arrive. For the rest of the day, all sorts of things went wrong for Alard. He hit his thumb with his hammer; he bumped his head on a low beam and many of his nails bent as he hammered them into hooves. By the time Nones had come and gone, he was in a foul temper.

Late that afternoon, Alard had been shoeing a pilgrim traveller's horse. The first three shoes were nailed to the hoofs with no significant effort. However, when the last red-hot shoe was being held near to the fourth hoof, the pliers had slipped and the hot shoe landed on the horse's leg, causing the poor horse to scream in pain and to kick and buck. In its pain and panic it kicked over the oil bucket, shattering and spilling oil everywhere. The smell of burning hair and the noise of the agitated horse were too much for Alard. He took time to attempt to soothe the scorched animal, then, once he had regained some control over the creature, he led the burnt horse away from the rail where he had been secured. Despite the horse throwing his head against the halter, he managed to open the gate to the outside pen so that he could secure the beast out there in order to tend to the burn.

He then yelled out for his son, "ALAN! There has been an oil spill. I have to tend to a burn on a traveller's horse. Come in here and clean up the oil, will you?" Receiving no reply, he shouted again, "ALAN! ALAN, where are you? Get your lazy backside into the forge and clean up the oil. ALAN! I'll tan your hide if you don't answer me when I call you!"

He presumed that Alan had been ignoring him because of the argument they'd had earlier that morning and continued with his attention on the injured horse, forgetting that Alan was away. Cursing his son for his ignorance, Alard tied up the horse in the holding pen while he went to search for some spare cloth with which to tie on a healing poultice, but there was none to be found in the house. His neighbour was his best chance for some cloth scraps, as she was a seamstress, so he went there to collect some rags. After obtaining the cloth, he treated the injured animal and then went back inside the smithy to get a drink of ale to calm his frayed temper, still swearing oaths against his ignorant son. Regrettably, he could find no ale, just a half-empty container of mead, left over from last night's revelry. So he sat by his anvil and settled his rattled nerves with a few large mugs of that instead, drinking considerably more than his usual afternoon portion.

That night, after Alard had fallen into a drunken sleep in the smithy, some of the townsfolk were walking home from an evening of dicing, singing and table games and had seen the glow of a fire and smelled the acrid smoke. They realised that the smith's fire should have been banked by that time of the evening and, quickly moving in the direction of the smithy, saw the inferno inside. They bravely dashed over and their shrill cries of "FIRE! FIRE!" brought the near neighbours out of their beds in a hurry. Some of the would-be rescuers noticed that the flames were not going out easily when water was thrown and guessed that it may have been an oil fire. While many of them tried, unsuccessfully, to douse the flames from outside the building, a few people rushed to the animal pens to ensure that any beasts were safe. The animals were, as expected, quite agitated by the smell of the smoke, but once they were moved far enough away from the blaze, they settled quickly.

The thick, black smoke soon threatened to overcome the rescuers who called out to Alard. Someone spotted his badly burnt body just inside the door and, at the same time, the corner of the roof creaked and groaned, threatening to fall in. They hastily rushed in and managed to drag poor Alard out of the flames. However, they could not save the burning structure, which collapsed in a shower of sparks and smoke almost as soon as he was hauled to safety.

Roger, the shire reeve, arrived on the scene just as the body was being removed from the fiery shell of the building and immediately took control of the dreadful situation. He ensured that the fire was kept under control and then angrily rounded on some young men, onlookers who were merely enjoying themselves by watching the spectacle unfold. "You there, you idle good for nothings, this is not a show for your entertainment! Go and find buckets, fill them with water and see to it that the neighbouring buildings are in no danger of fire from these sparks flying through the air. Be off with you now, quickly and take these other lazy dolts to assist you!" And to encourage them to be on their way, he kicked as many of them as he could reach on their backsides, as many times as he could.

As soon as the spectators and idlers had been dealt with, Roger sent another villager to get the physician out of bed while he inspected Alard's body. He also sent for the local priest. He guessed, though told no one, that Alard would not survive for very long as he was so badly burnt. As Roger was examining him, Alard abruptly awoke from his stupor and screamed. He saw Roger and spoke, gaspingly and in great pain. He gave him a message to pass to Alan, before lapsing back into unconsciousness. Roger had him carefully lifted and taken into the house and laid on his own bed in a room lit with lamps, so that the physician could better examine him when he got there.

Sadly, Alard never again rose to consciousness and breathed his last, just moments before the physician arrived. "There was nothing I could have done, in any case," he said to Roger. "He was far too badly burned. The pain alone would have been sufficient to kill him. May God have mercy on his soul." The physician and all present at the time crossed themselves as he said this. The priest arrived not long afterwards, administered the last rites and made many long prayers for the repose of his soul

It was later supposed that a spark or an ember had fallen from the fire onto some of the oil which had not been mopped up. The oil, it was guessed, was the reason the fire had spread so quickly and so widely. Alard did not stand a chance once the fire caught hold. The smoke would have almost suffocated him, so that he did not awaken during the blaze. The smithy itself was totally destroyed.

Alan returned from the wharf early the following day, only to be met by Roger and told of what had happened. Roger passed Alard's message to Alan, saying, "Your father told me to tell you that he forgives you your dispute. He did not wish for you to regret your last words to each other. He said that it was his fault you argued. Or, at least, as much his fault as yours. He wants you to take over the family business. He also told me to make sure that you understand that he has always loved you." Alan was almost inconsolable but, some time later, he was able to face up to the fact that his father was dead and that the smithy would have to be rebuilt from the ground up, with the help of some of the men of the village. Alan was now an orphan. It took him nearly a month before he could even begin to take up the business again. In the meantime, Roger looked after

Alan's animals and the other villagers fed Alan until he was back on his feet again. Regardless of his father's last words, Alan fervently wished that his final words to his father had not been made in anger.

Alard's wife had died several years ago. She had been brutally raped and murdered by a gang of outlaws, which explained, though did not excuse, why he was such a heavy drinker. As Alan had neither brothers nor sisters, it would now be up to him to carry on his father's trade. Thanks be to God, Alan was able to rescue most of the tools from the aftermath of the fire. The iron and steel parts of the tools were all still solid and useable, with only the wooden handles in need of replacement. The bellows, being made of leather and wood, had been burnt to nothing. Many townsfolk offered to make these objects at no cost, to show their sympathy for his loss.

The only thing that could be said to be good about the events surrounding the death of Alard, was that neither the house nor the animal pen was directly connected to the smithy, so they were not damaged. Jack, the asses and the other animals were safe, God be praised.

Alan went on to make of himself an excellent smith. When he married and had sons of his own, they were all taught strict fire safety from a very early age. Not one of them suffered so much as the smallest burn, once they understood that metals and fire could be extremely hot. His workshop was the safest smithy for many miles. There were buckets full of water in every corner and several more outside. As if that was not enough, he dug a deep well between the house and the stables. He also hung a bell outside, so that if there ever was a fire, this could be rung to alert the villagers to come to his aid. He vowed that he was never going to suffer the same fate as his father.

CHAPTER SIX

Along with being a good drinker and an excellent animal healer, Alard had been well known for making the steel hoops for the cooper's casks and buckets. A great many of these barrels made by the cooper, who went by the name of Thomas, were used to hold Marissa's delicious wines, as well as the copious amounts of ale and mead brewed by Francis and his family. Francis's ale was considered by most people in the town to be the best drink available for quite some distance. He supplied many of the taverns with his products and made quite a tidy profit from the sales of his excellent brewing.

Other local brewers had been trying for years to learn the secret of his outstanding ale, but with no success. He guarded his recipes extremely jealously – even in his own family, each member only knew some small part of the process. Everybody, including his relatives, hoped that he would pass on his secret before he died, as it would be a terrible shame to lose the best ale in Hampshire. We all knew that, at fifty-five years of age, he might not live much longer.

Envious detractors and resentful and incompetent brewers, whose ales were less well made, alleged that he wiped the insides of his barrels with animal dung or urine to give his brews their distinctive taste. He laughed off these ridiculous suggestions and rightly so. I often wondered that Francis did not have these people taken to the courts for their vicious slandering. I believed the reason was because he was kind-hearted enough to want to spare them embarrassment for something so blatantly ludicrous. His family thought him a fool for not doing so, but to his credit he maintained his moral stance and kept on pouring out his most excellent brews.

Some of his best customers were the fishermen, who drank his more potent concoctions while out on the cold, wet seas. They swore that these drinks were all that was keeping them warm and happy while out there. Several fishermen lived on the north part of the western shore of the harbour formed by the triangle between Portsmouth to the east, Fareham to the north and the empty land on God's Port, on the west side. It was well protected, both from the weather and from attack, due to the narrow channel at the harbour's entrance.

The fishermen often had quite large wooden boats, able to carry up to ten or fifteen men. They were busy the whole time they were out. They came almost daily to the shorefront market with their catch, so that we had fresh fish of great variety most of the time. Of course, anyone with a net or trap could catch fish for themselves if they chose to do so. A few people had made their own coracles. These small, bowl-shaped boats – as wide as a man is tall – were constructed from a framework of thin, flexible but sturdy branches, covered with the skins of whatever animals they were able to trap, layered and stitched together, then covered with pitch or resin. The coracles were propelled by a single oar and, with the aid of these little boats, several members of our community became part-time fishermen in the shallows off the coast.

There was a beekeeper named Timothy, who had numerous beehives spread over quite a large area. To tend his hives, he travelled by donkey for many hours each day, making repairs and building new ones as needed, collecting the honey and separating the unborn queen bees for the new hives. He supplied almost all of the honey in our community, for use in mead and as a treat to spread on our bread and for the apothecary and healers to use in their ointments. Timothy also supplied beeswax for candles and for waterproofing leather. His house always had the most delicious smell.

His wife Kate bore him two sons, William and Stuart, both of whom helped with the hives from the day they learned to walk and had learned everything their father would teach them about beekeeping. Timothy had discovered that if he wore a pale-coloured tunic, the bees showed less interest in stinging him. It was this chance finding that determined what he wore any time he went to his hives. People in the town soon learnt that whenever he wore his pale tunic, honey and beeswax would shortly be available for sale or barter.

CHAPTER SEVEN

We had a few spinners in the town. Some spun wool, others spun flax. With so few sheep there was not always much spinning to do, even when the flax was harvested and stripped. Quite a sizeable portion of the cloth we used came from neighbouring villages, as did much of the leather we used. Of course, this meant few fullers and even fewer tanners to stink up our town, for which we were thankful. The majority of the more expensive imported cloth goods was paid for by villagers doing piecework in return, or even, in extreme circumstances, selling themselves or their children into indentured slavery for a term.

Those spinners that we did have were also our dyers. The first thing they would do each Monday was to go around the village, collecting the urine from the tuns and buckets people left out behind their cottages. This was used for bleaching the cloth, and when we could get it, the leather. The stale urine also took out all the oils left in the wool after shearing, making it clean and almost white, once it was thoroughly rinsed with fresh water. The wool could then be combed to take out all the impurities, such as prickles and burrs, or lumps of wool matted with dung. It was then carded so as to bring all the fibres into the same alignment and from there it would be spun.

For the best dye work, the wool or flax would be dyed before spinning. They could be dyed in an almost unlimited range of colours, using dyestuffs such as madder or red lead for red, woad or indigo for blue and a variety of other materials for yellows, browns, greens and so on. With additional materials such as walnut husks or tree bark, almost any colour you can think of could be produced, from crimson to the palest of greys. If black, or at least a very dark brown, was required, rust dust or iron scraps were obtained from one of the smithies and allowed to sit in the dye mixture. The five principal mordants – namely copper, alum, tin and iron – would fix the dyes in the wool or flax, or even on leather. The amount of mordant used in the dyes determined the depth of the colour. The more concentrated the mordant, the darker the colour became. The mordants were available from mines in Sarum, Cornwall and Devon.

Once the wool or flax was dyed, spun and wound into skeins, it was soaked in a vat of very heavily salted water to set the dye, so that the colour would not run or fade too quickly. The dyed and salted yarn was then rinsed in fresh water and hung out to dry. Once it was completely dry, it could be woven into almost anything, such as clothing, blankets, bags, hats and many other objects besides.

Many generations ago, some of our cleverer weavers learned from travellers that if several of the warp threads – those running vertically – were a contrasting colour from the rest and set at regular intervals, a striped cloth resulted. Similarly, if several weft threads – those running horizontally – were also treated in the same fashion at the same time, a checked cloth was the end result. This interesting discovery allowed for a wide variety of patterns in our cloth, using two, three, or many more different colours.

If one wanted a pattern that could not be simply woven, then embroidery was one answer. However, this work was time consuming, and so became vastly expensive. This meant that most people resorted to a simpler and faster method for patterning cloth – block painting. A piece of wood was carved into the desired shape and dye or paint was placed into a dish. The carved end of the wood was soaked with the colour and then carefully stamped at regular intervals on the cloth to produce the pattern. This treatment could be repeated with many different colours and designs for more complicated effects. To create more intricate designs, great care was needed to place the prints in the correct position, otherwise a skewed pattern could result. The painted cloth could then be treated in exactly the same way as any other dyed cloth.

Wool would often be felted, so that it formed into the required shape, then wet and rubbed until the fibres knitted together to become a tangled mass. This meant that the wool would be much warmer than ordinary knitted cloth, as the gaps between the stitches would be closed. This method was used for socks, hats, small bags and any other tubular item. It also made very warm cloaks.

In order to make woven belts or braid, card-weaving or tablet weaving was employed. Although a lot of people tried to make their own, David the weaver was our best person at this task. His braids and woven bands were the finest and most colourful for miles around. He was also, by far, the most prolific producer of braids in the village. For a single braid that would take anyone else a day to make, David would have produced two or three of the same size. These braids were used for decorating our tunics. They were stitched around the necklines, hems, cuffs, or anywhere necessary to dress up anything from shoes to bags to clothing. They could also be used as straps for pouches and satchels.

David was also very skilled at finger loop weaving. This involved making long loops of thread and, by using nothing but one's fingers, weaving the threads into a wide variety of patterns. The braids produced using this method tended to be rather thin, which made them suitable for draw cords, or small decorations on all kinds of items. Occasionally, if the number of loops used was larger than the number of fingers he had, another person was required to assist him. Almost all of the people in our town wore some of David's braids somewhere on their clothing.

Inkle looms were also in use to make braids. They could make lengths of braid up to two or three times the height of a man, although it often took almost as long to set them up as it took to actually do the weaving. These decorative bands could be as narrow as a small child's finger or wider than a man's hand. They could also be sewn together, side by side, to create large expanses for clothing, blankets, or the like.

Karen, the daughter of Thomas the cooper, was intrigued at an early age by the patterns produced on these inkle looms. She determined that she would become skilled in using one, as well as making the looms themselves, both of which she did in a very short time. When her father had cut up the wood for his barrels, there were often enough scraps of wood left over for Karen to make small objects such as inkle looms. She frequently made other items from the wood she had collected and shaped of her own accord, such as the thin wooden cards used for tablet weaving, or toys for the local children. Her husband, Daniel, had been the forester, collecting the wood from which his father-in-law had made his barrels. Daniel was killed just before the baby was born. He was on his way back into town with an ass-drawn cart loaded with wood, when he was attacked and beaten to death by a gang of bandits. He had had no money or any other valuables in his possession, merely the fallen branches from the trees in the forest. All they stole was the ass and Daniel's life.

Karen became quite adept at both loom and card weaving and, by watching her father, woodworking. She only stopped the strenuous tasks when she was too large in her pregnancy to properly use the tools. Once she had borne the child, Karen went straight back to producing wooden toys and other articles. When he was old enough, her young son, Tomas, played with many of the wooden toys Karen made. If he could not break them, they were considered strong enough to sell or trade. Quite often, a wheeled barrow, a chest, or some other object would appear outside the cooper's hut. They were also Karen's work. They would be expertly made and sold for a good price to the villagers or to passing travellers. In this way, she knew she would be able to support herself, when eventually she should suffer the loss of her father. She always doted upon her son and never re-married.

On the northern end of the island of Portsmouth, our potters had their workshops. The clay for their work came from the swamps near the narrow channel, known as Port Creek, between our island

and the mainland. The potters made our ewers, dishes, goblets and oil lamps and many other items for the villagers. Most potters had a wheel on which to throw their work – the wheel was spun by kicking a smaller wheel at foot level, driving the working wheel on top.

Most children in the village had, at one time or another, enjoyed trying to make a bowl or some such item on one of these wheels. The results were often tragically misshapen, not that the children cared. They were happy just to have produced something, no matter how ugly, to show off to their parents. Those few who actually managed to consistently make something in a close approximation of the correct shape might be offered an apprenticeship to a potter, though the children were rarely serious enough at the task to accept the offer. Sometimes, their parents would be too proud of their own family businesses to allow them to leave and become what they saw as members of a lowly, dirty trade.

The potters never thought of themselves as lowly or dirty, especially as they made some of the decorations for use in the new church, such as the gargoyles around the roof and arch bosses for its ceiling. The potters also supplied earthenware amulets and pilgrims' badges to the many religious or superstitious travellers who came through our town. There were some potters who, rather than use a spinning wheel to shape their work used flattened lumps of clay, forming their artefacts by pushing the clay into a variety of shapes. This was the usual method for making flatter items, such as trays, platters and the like.

Whether the pottery was thrown or formed, every piece had to go through a kiln to cook the clay. If this was not done, then the dried clay would remain brittle and porous. Glazes were put on the inside and often on the outside of the pottery vessels, making the cups, bowls and other utensils waterproof wherever the glaze stuck. Some glazes were as simple as dropping a large amount of salt through a hole in the top of the kiln onto the pots. Some were painted on. Other glazes were applied by dipping the vessel into a liquid. If the potter did not want his pot to stick to the kiln, which would ruin the pot and, possibly also the kiln, he dipped the part of the vessel which rested on the shelf of the kiln into molten beeswax, supplied by Timothy, so that the glaze would not stick to the pot in that place. That left bare clay under the wax and the wax melted out in the intense heat of the kiln.

The kilns were made of mud and they were hot almost all the time. Two or three times a year, the potters would build a new kiln from the plentiful material at hand – the mud flats close by. This was necessary if one of the ovens developed a crack in its side. The heat would escape from this fissure and the pottery would not cook properly.

There was always a need for new pottery, as breakages happened almost every day. This was not to say that the workmanship of the earthenware was poor, it was just that some people were not so careful as others. Besides, our potters exported their wares to places as far away as London, Dover, Exeter, Shrewsbury and the Isle of Wight, proving their good quality.

CHAPTER EIGHT

Our one tanner and leather worker, Osbert, had his workshop on the western shore of Whale Island, far enough away from the rest of us that the smell did not bother anyone too often. The smell of tanning is so bad that not many people can stand it.

Animal skins were removed from the beasts, stretched over a frame and then scraped with a knife or sharpened bone to remove the fat which lay on the flesh side of the skin. The skins were then taken down and soaked in a mixture of water and dog fæces or the pulped brains of the animals whose hides were being tanned, to help remove the hair and to prevent the skin from rotting. Once the tanning process was completed, the leather was again soaked, this time in stale urine, to remove any fatty deposits not taken off in the scraping process. This also bleached the leather somewhat, so that dyes could then be applied in whatever colour the customer required.

Apart from the very rich, who could import shoes any time they wanted or needed a new pair, people went barefoot a lot of the time or wore felted woollen shoes or wooden shoes, much like Flemish clogs, saving their leather shoes for special occasions.

Osbert lived alone and the whole village was concerned that he could never keep an apprentice long enough to properly learn his trade. This was a worry, because if he died, we would have no other leather tanner for many miles. We would then either have to travel quite a distance to obtain our leather goods, or someone local – preferably someone with little or no sense of smell – would have to learn the trade from scratch. There were very few people in our community who had the stomach for the smells produced in the leather making processes. We all fervently hoped that someone would step forward before Osbert died.

Osbert was kept busy enough, supplying shoes, purses, belts, scabbards and many other leather items for the town – everything from armour, laces, hats, reins, arm braces, balls, quivers, bow handles and bowstrings, straps, headbands, bracelets, coin purses, bottles, mugs and cups, sundials, hinges, arrow rests, tool handles, horn holders, toolboxes, jackets, blankets, lanterns, bowls, pouches, buckets, scrips, seats, sheaths, plates, shields, tankards and trousers.

Of course, he could only work when he had enough leather or was paid enough to make something in preference to anything else. While most people could and did, make their own small, simple leather items – pouches and the like – Osbert was the one who made complicated items such as shoes and drinking vessels. Osbert knew well how to make all of these things and many more, but he occasionally struggled to find enough leather for all the work he had to do. Almost any animal which could be skinned could supply some sort of leather. Cats, dogs, rabbits, deer, sheep, even some fish and birds could be used, depending on the object to be made.

Osbert set many traps around the countryside, primarily to feed himself, but he also used the skins for his leatherwork. Roger the shire reeve pretended that these traps did not exist, otherwise he would have had to prosecute Osbert for poaching the animals. Besides, Roger occasionally discovered a brace of rabbits lying by his door. He was well aware that this was his payment for looking the other way. Most villagers knew of the arrangement, but no one cared to do anything about it. Life was hard enough without the shire reeve on your back with revenge in his heart.

Rabbit, cat, or squirrel pelts made excellent purses and pouches, due to the size and shape of the animals. Even badger pelts would do, if one was brave enough to attempt to trap one of these ferocious beasts. A trapped badger was indeed a fearsome opponent. Once an animal was killed, the skin had to be carefully removed in one piece and, once the meat and the insides were removed and the skin cleaned, it was the easiest of tasks to simply sew the tanned skin back together. When the neck was used as the opening, a purse virtually formed itself.

Osbert was very sparing with what leather he had. He charged a reasonable price for his works, as good as they were, even though he had the only market for leather goods for a great distance. His shoes were amazingly comfortable and long lasting, especially as they were not worn every day. The shoes were made in a variety of styles, from slippers to knee-high boots, all crafted with exquisite care and skill. He even occasionally made shoes with hooks in the soles, for Matthew the thatcher, when Matthew could afford to pay for them.

Matthew was kept reasonably busy, too, even though he had three apprentices working for him. His work was well regarded. He knew that some villagers preferred to have him decorate the tops of the thatched roofs with birds and animals, which a few people believed brought luck to the house. His reed birds looked almost lifelike, sitting up there on the rooftops. One had to tread carefully whilst on thatched roofs, with almost no hand holds to grab if you fell, it was why he needed the hook-soled shoes.

On one occasion, one of Matthew's apprentices, Owen, was assisting with thatching a roof on a building situated right next to a pigsty. He was carrying a bundle of reeds up the narrow ladder laid on the lower thatch, when he slipped and lost his footing. He slid down the roof, scrabbling for a non-existent handhold and landed on Mog the sow, who was suckling her new-born piglets. He bounced off her, into the mud and the reeds he was carrying landed on top of him. The bundle burst, spraying the reeds all around, one poking the sow in the eye and another landing in her ear, irritating her even more. The sow had been known by all in the town to be a most cantankerous beast, attempting to bite or butt anyone foolish enough to come within reach.

Gor, one of my younger friends, seeing this happen, immediately ran to get the rest of us children, as he knew we were playing not far from the pigsty. We ran with all possible speed, in case we missed what promised to be a memorable show. As we ran, Gor explained what had happened so far. We got there in time to see Owen and Mog both struggling to their feet. As we might have imagined, Mog was not the least bit pleased with what had occurred. She snorted loudly at Owen and started to move menacingly in his direction. Owen made a great effort to remove himself from the sty, but the sow would have none of that. She raced up to him and butted him, whereupon he fell over again. She nipped hard at his heels, his head and his backside every time he tried to climb out and chased him around the pen, with Owen slipping over every now and again, which gave the angry beast yet another chance to attack him. Owen was finally able to clamber over the wall of the pen, but he was a terrible mess – mud and muck from top to toe and bite marks and bruises up and down his body. Fortunately, he had not suffered very many large wounds.

Many people had heard the noise Mog was making, as well as Owen's cries. Some had seen us running and had followed to see what was happening. Owen had provided a great show for many people of the village. We had laughed until we had tears streaming down our faces. Some of the adults, though still laughing, were sympathetic enough to take Owen to the physician, to ensure he was well looked after and that there were no serious injuries. He was obviously embarrassed, and he was fated to be the butt of all sorts of pig jokes for many weeks to come. He continued in his profession and became a most excellent master thatcher who, it was reported, never again fell from any other roof. Although, he steadfastly refused to work on any building that was even remotely near a pigsty, no matter how placid the animals were reported to be.

CHAPTER NINE

Of carpenters we had our share. There was always a need for beams for housing, repairs to wheels and carts, as well as boats, seats, chests, tables and many other wooden objects. Stephen was acknowledged as the best in the town. He could make anything from even the poorest wood, and it would often be of far higher quality than anything made by any other carpenter in the community, even if they had used the best wood they could find. Stephen had been contracted to make a pair of seats for the high table of Hugh de Warenne's dining hall. They were polished so well that not a single rough spot could be found on them. The joints were constructed so beautifully that a very close inspection would be needed to distinguish between the joints and the grain.

Stephen's wife, Anne, and their daughter, Rochelle, had moved into our town with him when he had returned from France. Anne and Rochelle had set up their own profitable business as seamstresses. Their work in sewing and embroidery was quite without equal in the town. Rochelle had been named for the port of La Rochelle. Stephen had travelled to France to learn polishing techniques and had met his wife in the town where the ship docked, fallen in love, married her and stayed long enough for their daughter to be born, before moving back to England, bringing his wife, child and knowledge of the French polishing techniques with him. He was the only person in the county who knew how to treat wood in this way.

Stephen's house was decorated with many examples of his craft. He had even hung a sign outside his house, beautifully carved, to show his expertise. On this sign there were all sorts of animals, as well as people and mythical beings. The carvings were all quite exquisite.

Stephen and several other carpenters and apprentices were working on the new church. Their wood came from the many species of trees growing on the island and the mainland. They were given a special dispensation from de Warenne, who held the land from the king, to be allowed to cut down a certain number of trees each year, in order to carry out their work. This allowance included the yew, ash and elm trees used for longbows and arrows. These were among the preferred woods for these items, though most of the yew wood came from Spain, Portugal, Switzerland and elsewhere. These yew staves were part of a tax payment on other imported goods – for every ton of goods brought into the country from overseas four bow staves must be brought in as a levy.

The yew bows were constructed so that the heartwood of the yew was on the belly of the bow, toward the archer, while the sapwood was on the back, away from him. Yew's natural properties are that the sapwood is elastic and allows the bow to stretch, while the heartwood is able to withstand compression. Both tend to return to their original attitude when the tension is released. This means that the yew wood forms a natural spring, so that, when drawn, both parts of the wood act in concert to allow the bow to work efficiently.

Another of our woodworkers, Anthony, was also our finest bowyer and fletcher. His bows were finely crafted, with leather thonging wrapped around the middle for a handle – when he could get it. He bartered with travelling traders for pieces of deer antler for use on the ends of the bows' limbs, to protect the wooden ends. If deer antler was not available, cow or goat horn was used in its place.

Our archers were ranked among the best in the land. They practised every week, in accordance with the King's law, which stated that all males between the ages of twelve and fifty years must practise their archery for at least three hours each Sunday, following attendance at church.

Most of our men were used to shooting bows with draw weights starting at about fifty pounds for the youngest men, going up to over one hundred and eighty pounds for the most experienced archers. My first bow had only a thirty-pound draw weight, but I was only six years old at the time. I expected to grow into much larger bows as I continued to train. With years of practise, the muscles of the archers became stronger, allowing them to draw ever larger bows. The negative aspect of this constant training was that the bones in the bow arm became compressed and the bones in the right arm, which drew back the string, became elongated or sometimes even separated. Also, the spine became somewhat twisted due to the repeated actions of using the same muscles. This did not mean that the bones became weaker, quite the contrary. Many archers were rather large, solidly built men.

Most bows had a useful working life of about one to three years, as they tended to either bend so often that they stayed bent, which was known as 'string follow', or they would break after constant use for that amount of time. Before they broke, sometimes the archer would get some sort of warning. There could be a compression fault, when a ridge would appear in the wood on the belly of the bow. The other fault noted most often was a 'lifter' – a sliver of the grain would show itself proud of the rest of the wood on the back of the bow as it was drawn.

It was for these faults that each archer would inspect his bow before shooting, running his experienced hands up and down the smooth wood, seeking rough or sharp spots which would indicate where the wood might fracture. It was a sorry archer who held a bow at full draw when it suddenly gave way. He could be hit in both the head and the groin if he was not quick enough to react to defend himself. If this ever happened at a practise session, the poor injured archer could expect not only to be hurt, but to be laughed at as well, even though it could happen to any one of us at any time.

Every year on Midsummer's Eve, an archery competition was held within the town. Only our townsfolk were permitted to shoot in this contest. The butt would start at twenty paces from the shooting line, with each archer shooting three arrows at a small rope circle on the butt. With each round, those who did not hit wholly within the circle with all three arrows were eliminated and the butt would then be moved away a further five paces. This would continue until there was only one person who could make the shot with all three arrows. He would be declared the winner of the shoot – the town champion – and would be given a prize of a new bow and a quiver full of arrows made by Anthony. The prize was paid for and donated by de Warenne. In this way, de Warenne ensured that he had a standing force of competent archers, if ever the King decided to go to war.

The town also had, on regular occasions, battle training. This consisted of all the adult men bringing their shields along to a large open area for practise in forming a fyrd wall. They separated into two teams at each end of the field, with red or blue ribbons on their arms to identify each side. Padded sticks were used in place of spears and the men formed up in lines, shoulder to shoulder, dressed properly in their armour – what they had of it – for the occasion. Their shields overlapped, ensuring there were no gaps, as if it were real war. The ranks of men were then trained to advance in a straight line without leaving any openings at any time. If a gap should open up between any two men, they were repeatedly told, the enemy would be able to force their way through and kill the man on each side of the breach. This would make the breach wider, allowing more of the enemy through and they would then eventually be able to kill the whole line. Members of each team would often break through the other line and were told that when they did so, they should strike the slack defenders on the rump with their sticks, just to drive home the message of the importance of keeping the line in one piece.

Javelin throwing was another activity that was held on these practise days. The men would throw their spears at a man-shaped target stuffed with straw, situated some twenty feet away. Some of the men were completely useless at this task, while others hit the targets every time. Those who could not hit the mannequins were told that if ever they were called to go to war, they would be either shield men or archers. Those better at javelin work would become spear men.

Sword training was also held for those who might be wealthy or lucky enough to own one, or who were returned soldiers from earlier battles who had been able to pick one up from a battlefield. More than once a man would walk home from these training sessions with a cut to the head, leg or arm from an opponent who was a better swordsman on the day. Thanks be to God, serious or fatal injuries were few and far between.

Several of the town's children would come along to watch, though from far enough away to keep out of trouble, in the hopes that something interesting would happen. For instance, some of the men folk often took these practises rather too seriously and now and again injuries occurred, caused by the sticks jabbing into eyes or mouths. Sometimes one man would step on the toes of another, or a makeshift sword or spear would hit a head rather than a shield and a fight would break out. There was always a lot of angry shouting. I often wondered whether the trouble they went through was worth all the effort and I wasn't the only one who thought so.

Such was life in a small English town in the early Thirteenth Century. It was normally not very eventful, but on occasion, there was enough to make life quite interesting for the people who were living in and around the place. I enjoyed myself for the most part back then, as did the majority of the people I knew, both old and young.

There were, however, some very dull times too, when nothing, it seemed, could make life appealing. Life at these times felt like the same thing every day, 'round and 'round. Work, eat, sleep, work, eat, sleep. Thanks be to God, these times were quite rare. If daily life ever got to this level of boredom, someone in the town would do something – almost anything – to liven it up again.

CHAPTER TEN

In total, there were about two hundred and eighty individuals who were native to our town. These folks' parents, grandparents and so on seemed to have been born here since time before memory. Although our ancestors had been here for what appeared to be forever, there was no mention of our town in King William's Domesday Book.

I know this because some years later, I had the fortune to be permitted to examine this magnificent work very closely. I naturally searched for my hometown amongst the many pages. I was told that almost everyone who had the opportunity to see this work did the same. The entry reads – in the common tongue: *"In Buckland there were six villeins, two bordars, two serfs; in Copnor, five villeins, two bordars, two serfs; in Fratton, four villeins, four bordars, four serfs."*

The survey was an enormous undertaking, the largest of its kind that anyone has ever heard of. William wanted to know over what he now ruled; which barons and earls owned what lands; how the archbishops were using their lands; who was renting from whom; how many people lived on the land and so on. When the survey was taken, land people, tools and animals were all given an arbitrary value. It mattered not how much or how little you valued your own possessions, the valuers told you what they were worth. That was what went into the book and that was how the people were taxed from that moment onward.

Some parts of the book were quite hard to read, not just because it was written in Latin with very tiny handwriting, but because the scribes also used the vernacular, or commonly used words, as well as a sort of shorthand code. For example, 'Wm' represented King William, 'TRE' stood for *tempus Rex Edwardus* – in the time of King Edward – and so forth. Some said, with good reason, that the shorthand version was done to save space on the valuable parchment. This may well be so, as it is a plausible explanation. On the other hand, there were those who believed that the scribes did it this way so that the ones who compiled this work were almost the only people who could make any real sense of it. Why that should be, however, if it is indeed true, is yet to be guessed. It has been supposed that it was possibly an attempt to ensure their continued employment within the King's Court.

My mother's grandfather lived in Cosham when he was quite a young man and he, as well as all the men in the village, was questioned by William's clerks. They questioned the assets of the place, the people who lived there, who the landowner was, how much they thought the land was worth, who owned how many animals, fish and birds, what equipment was available and what legal rights they had. They wanted to know absolutely everything about everybody. My great-grandfather gathered the courage to enquire of one of the King's soldiers "Why does the King want all this information? What is he going to do with it?" He was frowned at and then brusquely told, "The King is taking a census of every city, town, village and hamlet in the land, so that he can take stock of his whole kingdom and so that his taxes," the soldier laughed sarcastically, "can be set in a *fair* manner." The soldier then cuffed my great-grandfather a few times around the head for his impertinent question, pushed him away and ordered him back to work. These soldiers appeared to believe that they were immune from retribution for this sort of treatment of the villagers. They were probably right. They were, after all, the King's men.

Some time after my parents married, my mother's grandfather talked with my father about the census, and how it seemed that the part of Portsmouth where we lived was never taken into consideration, as none of father's acquaintances or relations had been approached by the King's men at that time or since. There were, however, parts of the town mentioned, such as Fratton, Cosham and Fareham. From my reading of the Domesday Book, I could find absolutely no mention of our part of the town. This probably meant that it was either too small to be bothered with, or they missed this area. That, or there was just no one living on our land at the time of the census. The King, therefore, had no regular tax revenue from our part of the town until after King Richard paid us a visit much later in 1194.

For well over two hundred years there had been a small church in the area, but it was always too cramped for our needs. Baldwin of Portsea held a portion of land, called *Sudewede*, to the value of two knights' fees, from a wealthy Norman merchant, Jean de Gisors, who was also Lord of Titchfield in 1166. This same Baldwin gave a virgate of land to the abbey of Quarr on the Isle of Wight.

In 1180, he also gave a virgate of land in Portsea, within the town of Portsmouth, to the Augustinian monks of Southwick Priory so that they could build a modern, much larger church to the honour and glory of the one-time Archbishop, Thomas of Canterbury. Later, King John was to acquire the land surrounding the church from de Gisors and from then on, it was to be under his control.

Because of this gift to the monks, there were over one hundred and fifty incomers visiting our town, most of whom were involved in erecting this enormous new edifice. It was, when I lived there, nearing completion, with just the northern wall and the windows to be finished. Even without one wall or any windows, the building was utilised as though it were complete.

The partly built church attracted innumerable travellers and pilgrims from far and wide, who came to see the latest addition to the network of God's houses. The townsfolk soon became accustomed to seeing strange faces in the area, though not all were welcome.

Some of these travellers were charlatans, preying on the poor and gullible. They came to sell fraudulent medicines to the sick, who would believe their lies of quick cures for anything from a worm in the tooth to the plague. A few of the so-called 'medicines' were nothing more than a mixture of ordinary dirt, dung, urine, water and field flowers – more likely to make you sick to death than to cure you. Whenever one of these false physicians was discovered, his money was taken from him and given to the church healers who would be paid to heal the sick person properly, then all of the deceiver's belongings were confiscated or destroyed and he was soundly beaten and run out of the town. We found that we never had to reprimand the same fraudster twice. Occasionally, one of the incomers was found to be a thief or pickpocket. Were any of these caught, they would most likely be horse whipped or beaten by the aggrieved party, then taken to the sheriff who would convene a manorial court of justice to try the evildoers.

Adam of Portsea, the nephew of Baldwin, was appointed as a Justice in Assize for Hampshire in 1218, which gave us fairly regular access to the King's courts of justice without having to wait. This was to our great relief, for no one could say how long it would be until one of the King's Justiciars deigned to visit on their rather irregular rounds.

If those charged were found guilty and the crime was a petty one, the fools who attempted the crimes would be put to work, usually in Roger's mills. If the transgression was very serious, then they might have had to suffer the punishment of having their right palm branded and their left hand cut off. Thanks be to God, not all the people to wander into our town were dishonest or immoral. Most travellers came only to trade, work or entertain us, or to praise our Lord in His new church.

There was the occasional instance of a worker who would meet and fall in love with one of the young girls in Portsmouth. When this happened, the father – or another close relative – of the girl would question this man very closely to ensure that what he felt was really love, not merely lust. After all, what parent would want to find their daughter pregnant and with no man to stand by her? Most people thought that there was far too much of that sort of thing happening anyway and anything they could do to avoid more was always a good thing in their eyes.

There were, however, some few girls who had run away with a man they loved because their parents and family did not approve of him. Over the time it took to build the church, thirty-seven of our girls were married to workers on the building. In the earlier days of building the church, one of these girls had a son who eventually grew up to work beside his father on the very same church, both serving as masons.

The church was a magnificent affair, quite the largest building anyone in our town had ever seen. The architect had built a small, wooden model showing how it would look, which was displayed near the site of the actual building. All the townspeople had come to see it. The model showed a fine-looking cruciform building, with a central domed tower and an accompanying bell tower. As the building took shape, we could see that it differed slightly from the model. The architect had made changes to the number of windows and the size of the steeple before the construction started and the model was merely to give those who raised the funds an idea of what it would eventually look like.

Quite a lot of the stone for this building was imported from Caen, in France, and the rest came from Binstead, on the north coast of the Isle of Wight. There were six magnificent white limestone columns in the nave of the church, with four black marble columns in the sanctuary. Beautifully smooth, flowing Norman arches were everywhere and four large windows were positioned high up on each side wall, with two or three smaller windows under each large one. A rose window was situated above the western door and the vaulted ceilings were a marvel to behold. The church was consecrated in two stages – the chancel and nave were consecrated by Bishop Toclyve of Winchester in 1188 and the two transept altars and churchyard were consecrated on the twelfth day of March 1196, by Godfrey de Lucy, successor to Toclyve.

CHAPTER ELEVEN

The workers' appetites for food, clothing and leather created quite a significant drain on our town's sparse resources. We could not, by any means, begrudge them the food they needed while they worked, but we did go a little hungry ourselves at times. Most of the leather they used was needed for aprons. There were other essentials besides leather and food which were in short supply while the building continued. We knew that we were getting a splendid new church in exchange for the provisions and understood that this was a good trade by any account.

We knew that food would grow again, as would our stomachs, and when that happened we would have a grand church for the greater glory of God. Besides, quite a few young men of our town were selected to work with these craftsmen, learning their trades, becoming carpenters, stonemasons, tilers, glaziers, truss makers and so forth, in their own right.

Not all of the workers moved on when the church was completed. It was always the case that some decided to stay when any building project was completed. Those who stayed would either marry girls from the town or simply settle to continue their trade.

The ordinary stone worker occupied in building the church was paid two pence per day for his work. The more experienced and talented a worker, the higher the pay would be. A master mason could be worth as much as fifteen pence per day. In order to be appropriately recompensed for his labour, each person who applied to work on the new church was required to give his name and occupation to add to a roll, which was held by the church administrators, so that no worker would either miss out on being paid or be improperly paid for someone else's toil. As it happened, the wisdom of this arrangement became apparent all too often.

The church administration accommodated the master masons, master carpenters and other highly specialised workers and all of their families in church properties, so that the chief workers had comfortable quarters. Most of the other workers lived in lean-tos, shanties and temporary huts propped precariously around or against the church walls. With monotonous regularity, these flimsy homes would burn to the ground. The workers were frequently careless with fires inside their hovels and the result of this carelessness would see the occupants stumble out, blackened, scorched and coughing, while their belongings – such as they were – would have to be replaced when they received payment for their work. In the meantime, their tools had to be borrowed from co-workers or hired from our town blacksmiths.

If they were especially unlucky, the occupants would be too tired or drunk to get out and then we would find the charred bodies the next morning, when the ashes had cooled enough to search through. Most of the time, we could identify the body only by either asking whether anyone knew the victim or recognised any remaining belongings. Otherwise, if he was unknown or unrecognisable, a roll call would be taken from the list of workers to discover who was missing.

The taverns and alehouses were often very full at nights, with the many workers from the new church being their most regular customers. Some of them became quite drunk and raucous after they finished work for the day and quite a few of them would weave their back to their temporary homes, vomiting in the streets and fighting with any unlucky townsfolk they chanced to meet on their way. I am ashamed to say that I unkindly hoped that their fat, drunken heads would hurt horribly the next morning when they awakened.

On one dreadful occasion one of the church workers, Bardulf, was on his way home, reeling a little from drink, when he made an attempt to rape Edda, one of the young prostitutes in the town. Our townspeople do not actively encourage prostitutes, but we allow them to work because we see them as a necessary evil. It is known that towns without these working women have many more rapes and other sexual assaults on girls and women of all ages.

Some of these working women were young, in their teens or early twenties. They would pick up their partners from the taverns and alehouses and were not fussy about where they conducted their trysts. A neat room at an inn or a filthy alleyway – it seemed to all be the same to them, so long as their customers paid in cash. These women were indiscriminate and rather indiscreet. Although some of these women were local, several of them travelled from town to village with the masons and carpenters, going where the work went. Some of them were even the wives, sisters or daughters of these craftsmen.

Other working women were older and were most often women who had lived in the town for most of their lives. Occasionally they were widows who may also have been seamstresses or alewives and, with these more 'respectable' women, it was often a young man's father who would arrange the assignations, frequently bringing with them gifts of food, wine or game, rarely daring to offend with hard coin. These older women preferred that the men call upon them in the women's own homes, also requiring that they do so with a measure of discretion, to give a modicum of respectability to their vocation.

The differences between these two groups of women were not limited to their ages, how they were paid, or where and how they met their men. There were differences in the way they conducted their business. The younger girls were keen to have the transaction over and done with fairly quickly so they could move onto the next customer and make as much money as they could in one night. The older women often had what might be considered a more social aspect to their assignations, sometimes taking a short evening walk in the woods or enjoying a meal and a goblet or two of wine beforehand, but almost always saw only a single man on any night.

On the night Edda was attacked, Bardulf saw her walking alone along the road on her usual route, so he hid behind a tree and waited in ambush. Then, as she drew level with where he was hiding, he jumped out and grabbed her from behind, twisting her right arm up her back, then moving his hips in to hold the arm in that position with his body. He attempted to stifle her screams by placing his right hand over her mouth as he started to remove his braies with the other to reveal his readiness for the evil crime he was about to commit.

Edda, for her part, had the presence of mind to bite his hand, taking off a sizable chunk of his palm, which made him swear coarsely and remove his hand from her mouth rather quickly, allowing her to scream. He punched her on the jaw, rattling her teeth, which almost knocked her out. He threw her to the ground and ripped her shift from her body. He laughed madly as he saw her nakedness, fell on top of her, fondled her roughly, then lifted his tunic and clumsily attempted to rape her. She scratched at his face, instinctively aiming for the eyes, opening several long, raw wounds. There was blood everywhere, most of it his. She was also punching and kicking at him with all her strength. He was hit on his legs, head, body and occasionally in the groin. He apparently felt none of her attacks, shrugging them off as if she were but a small kitten patting him with tiny paws. All the time she was defending herself, she continued to cry out loudly for aid.

Thankfully, several of the town's menfolk were walking nearby, also returning home from a tavern. They heard Edda's screams and rushed to her rescue. The half-naked attacker was grabbed, lifted off her and beaten violently. Edda was covered with a cloak and both of them were taken to the sheriff's cottage. Following a brief interview with the sheriff, Edda was treated by the physician, who had been roused from his bed and brought to the house by the sheriff's son. She was then sent home to recover.

The next day, because the would-be rapist was a freeman, he was tried for his crime in a manorial court. As he was caught *in flagrante delicto*, he was found guilty. He was stripped of all his tools and other possessions, which were sold and the money given to Edda as a form of compensation. He was then sentenced to be whipped and castrated. That was the usual punishment in our area for this crime, as it satisfied the *jus talionis,* an eye for an eye. He also received a brand on the palm of his right hand, so that anyone who met him would know of his heinous felony. The branding helped seal and cleanse the wound caused by Edda's bite. His whipping and branding were performed publicly, so that all would know that justice was properly dispensed. His castration was performed by our physician behind closed doors, with three strong men holding him down – his screams heard for quite a distance.

About six days later, Bardulf was deemed to have recovered from his surgery and although he was still rather pale and stupefied, he was sent away from our town, never to return under threat of death. This punishment may seem barbaric, but it was good for the peaceful running of the area, as it would be quite a long time before a crime of this sort was committed in our town again. Still and all, it did not seem right that these men, who solemnly declared that they were working for God's greater glory when they signed on, should act in the way they did.

CHAPTER TWELVE

My father, Ranulf, was thirty-two years old when I was born. He was a big bear of a man, a head and shoulders taller than most men in our town, with quite a muscular physique. He generally preferred to wear a woollen jerkin, as this close-fitting sleeveless jacket allowed him to move his strong arms with freedom. His hair was thick, rather curly and very dark brown, as was his beard, which he wore in the Saxon style, full and untrimmed. He wore his hair long, tied back and always with a red leather headband, about twice the width of a man's finger, to keep it out of his eyes. The headband was decorated along its length with embossed gold lozenges, interlaced with vine leaves. His eyes were dark brown and, if you were unfortunate enough to incur his wrath, they seemed to shoot lightning at you as he glared. He was normally a gentle, even-tempered man, not quick to anger; though if his ire was aroused, he was quite capable of being a very dangerous man.

My father was very accomplished with his hands and marvellous at improvisation, so that he was able to make whatever item he needed for any project with seemingly little effort. He was also extremely skilful with a sword, axe, bow, or indeed any other weapon which would come to hand. Besides the jerkins and trousers, my father owned two long-sleeved tunics for important occasions. One was a deep blue, woven and dyed in wool from Flanders and came halfway down his calves. It had red and white decorative trim around the cuffs and hemline. The sleeves were half-length. The other tunic was white, with blue and red embroidered cloth sewn on the cuffs, elbows and around the neckline. This tunic reached down to the top of his feet and the sleeves were full-length. This was his very special dress for weddings and other important ceremonies. He kept both tunics, as well as his cream-coloured under-tunic, in a small chest that he'd made for that very purpose when he was a young man. Cedar blocks were placed on, above and beneath the clothing, to keep out the moths and worms.

The land my father held was on the western side of Portsmouth, in the Portsdown Hundred, not far from Portchester Castle. How he came to own the land in freehold, or 'in alod', as he was wont to say, I shall relate in good time.

Switha, my mother, was tall for a woman – taller than some men. She had thick, copper red hair that hung down below her waist. When she was working, which was most of the time that the sun was in the sky, she had her hair tied and braided into what seemed like a solid rope. She, too, wore a headband to keep her hair from her eyes. Hers was of green leather, stamped with oak leaves and acorns along its length. She was nearly five years younger than my father. Besides her wedding outfit, my mother also had another tunic for special occasions. This tunic was a light green, embroidered on the front with dark green oak leaves and brown acorns and with yellow trimmings around the elbows, cuffs, waist and lower hem.

While she was not muscle-bound, my mother was no waif, but rather a strong, well-built woman. Her eyes were emerald green and sparkled when she laughed, which was often and easily. No-one I know could ever remember seeing her without a smile on her face. Her skin was smooth and soft, with no wrinkles, but she had small lines by the sides of her eyes from smiling and laughing so much.

My mother was very good with all children and animals, able to calm them whenever they were distressed. Everybody trusted her. She was a wonderful listener, with a knack for being able to solve effortlessly whatever problems people brought to her. She was also very talented in weaving threads on a trollen wheel, which we employed for making ornamental cords for decoration around cuffs and collars, strong cords for drawstrings and many other uses. She was also an expert finger loop braider and an amazing artist with charcoal, chalk, paint or any other medium. Chalk was certainly plentiful in the area, with the huge hill across the small channel north of the town seemingly made entirely of the material. Chalk could be coloured in the same way as cloth, by dipping it into various dyes. My mother could draw or paint a picture that would have had you believing it was the real thing. Some of her painted works were still hanging on the walls of our cottage. They were the only decorations that my father allowed there after she died.

My father had gained his freedom by single-handedly protecting his earl, Hugh de Portcestre, from a night-time attack by bandits, armed only with a small hand-axe and a buckler. This was in the year of our Lord 1191, when he was only seventeen years old. He had accompanied his earl, along with a few hundred men, on a journey to the Holy Land to fight in the Third Crusade. They had camped for the night by a well near Arsuf, when some time around midnight my father was awakened by the harsh sound of fighting. It was the sentries being attacked and shouting a warning as they died. There was much screaming, ringing of sword on sword and clashing of shields. My father grabbed his buckler and axe, quickly ran out of his small soldier's tent into the centre of the compound and was instantly fighting for his life with two swordsmen.

While engaged in this fight, he saw a group of the attackers rush into the earl's pavilion, obviously intent on killing and robbing him. My father, having quickly despatched his two attackers, charged into the pavilion to discover that the earl was surrounded by seven bandits. Hugh was not the best swordsman in the land, but he was waving his weapon back and forth, keeping the attackers just out of reach. My father immediately set to and killed them all during a fierce struggle. Hugh was uninjured and my father suffered only minor injuries, but he lost his left forefinger in the fight, it having been cut off by an attacker's sword early in the contest. He always proudly displayed, above the hearth in our cottage, the sword which had cut off his finger. It still had his blood on the blade.

From all that my father had told me of his involvement in the time he was away on Crusade, this was to be the biggest battle in which he was to take part. However, for this single exhibition of loyalty, strength and valour, Hugh de Portcestre made my father a colibert – a freed man – and bestowed upon him a parcel of land consisting of two hides. Either of these rewards would have pleased my father immensely, but to receive both together was beyond his wildest dreams.

Father told me that after this incident, there was a long, arduous, but otherwise relatively uneventful journey to Jerusalem, during which several of the would-be crusaders almost died of thirst. By the time they arrived at the Holy City, however, peace had been temporarily restored and there was no fighting to be done. This also meant that there were no riches to be taken. Father was pleased that he had won his freedom and some land on the way to the Holy Land, as there was almost no possibility of doing so once he had arrived there and even less likelihood on the way back to England.

Six months after saving the earl, when he had finally found his way back home, he took my mother, Swilha, as wife and settled down to work the land bestowed upon him and to raise a family. My mother was also a freed woman and they had met and fallen in love two years previously, not long before my father left for the Crusade. He was away on Crusade for a total of nineteen months, but knew she would wait for his return, however long it took. She was very pleased to see him come home with little injury.

In just under three months after his return to Portsmouth, they were married. Father wore his white tunic, while Swilha wore a snow-white under-tunic, with a pale-yellow leather waistcoat over a pale-green overdress and new red shoes that she had made especially for the occasion. There was a garland of fresh field flowers on each of their heads in place of their usual headbands. For once, both of them had their long hair flowing free. Everyone in the village attended the wedding and there was a sumptuous feast laid on. Seven removes, consisting of more than ten courses each, were placed on the tables. If anyone went away hungry, it would have been their own fault. The feast went on far into the night, with many speeches and much gift giving. I understand that the last of the guests finally left well into the next afternoon.

CHAPTER THIRTEEN

I was the younger of only two surviving children. My brother, Ralf, was around eleven years older than me. He was a mixture of characteristics of both my parents, solidly built like my father, tall and red-haired like my mother and with her green eyes. He had always been a large boy for his age – not fat, just physically powerful. He preferred to play the rougher games with older boys. To have a brother much younger than him, as I was, meant that he and I did not often do things together. He had his friends, I had mine and while we could not be mistaken for anything but brothers, our two groups had wildly different interests.

When I was young, I had white-blond hair. My facial features were similar to my brother's, but there the resemblance ended. He was so much larger than I was. While I was indeed quite a small lad, I hoped that I might one day grow into a large man. I knew I would always be significantly less well built than my brother, but I had no doubt that I could be as tall, if not as wide or as strong. I was, after all, my father's son.

I remember hardly anything about my mother, as she died from an accident during a harvest when I was about five years old. I was often told that she was a very kind and beautiful woman and this is in agreement with my few memories of her. Not long before she died, my mother was, along with several other villagers, helping a neighbouring farmer with his harvest. An old man, Nicholas, almost blind but still eager to be of use in the village, swung his scythe too close to her and her ankle was cut. He could not apologise enough for injuring her, although the wound was not a very large one. However, the scythe was old and rusty and the physician was away in a nearby town. The cut became inflamed and infected and eventually blood poisoning set in. On his return, the physician was forced to remove her leg above the knee, but the rot had already spread to the rest of her body.

Tragically, she died within two months of the accident, at just thirty years old. My father was devastated. He moped around the house for two days before coming to his senses. After all, he realised that his wife would not have wanted him to act in this way. My brother could not talk to anyone for several weeks. For myself, I carried on as if my mother had just gone away for a time. I was far too young to understand. I was sorry to hear that Nicholas died about three weeks after my mother. I heard that he fell into a deep pit one night due to his poor eyesight. When the villagers discovered his body the next day, they found that he had broken his neck in the fall. I think, perhaps, it was a kindness for him that he would not have to carry the blame for my mother's death. Every person in the town, including my father, attended his funeral.

Two days before my mother died, she called out for me to come to her side. She had already spoken with Ralf. When I knelt by her bedside, she said to me, "My darling boy, I must speak with you. Rolf, my dearest son, do you know how long we waited for you to be born?"

"No, Mother," I replied.

"We waited many years for you. You are indeed your mother's boy, are you not? God bless you boy, you have brought so much joy to our lives." At the mention of the joy my parents had felt, I had to wipe my eyes and face, my tears running free. While I understood that my parents were glad I was born, I was too young then to understand any other meaning. When I later told my brother of the conversation, he explained what she had meant by it. He told me that three sisters and a brother had all died, well before any of them had reached the age of even half a year. It must have disappointed my parents terribly to suffer such losses, but they had never spoken of the matter. And so it was my brother, not my parents, who told me of the siblings I would never know. I do not believe that it was for spite, but merely as a matter of fact. I felt sure that my brother missed having siblings closer to his own age, to talk to and to share the many other things that families do together, but he rarely spoke of it.

Back at the bedside, my mother had continued, "It would make my heart glad to know that you will be free and happy in your life, and so before I leave, you must promise me two things."

"Of course, Mother, anything."

"I know you are a good boy, but you must promise me that you will honour your father. He only wants the best for you, just as I do, but you must do as he asks in all things. Will you promise me this?"

"Yes, Mother, of course I will."

"And always remember that God will be with you in all that you do. Will you remember what I say, Rolf?"

"I will remember always, Mother."

"Now go and fetch my satchel from the end of the hearth."

"Of course, Mama."

I ran to fetch her precious satchel. It was a beautiful piece of leathercraft, designed to carry everything you would need for a few days away. It had been made by an old priest from Ireland and brought to England by my mother's grandfather, about fifty years ago. She struggled to sit up, so I helped her. When she was upright, she carefully removed each of the things in her satchel, placing them all on the small table beside the bed, and when she had emptied it completely, gave it to my keeping. When she gave me her satchel, I was delighted but unsure of her intention. Then she took her oak leaf headband off of the table and gave it to me, placing it gently in my hands, at which point I started to cry again because she, too, suddenly had tears in her eyes. While suffering such sadness, I was at the same time so happy that she should give me these things that were so much a part of her identity.

She gently took my face in her hands and said, "Will you promise that you will take care of this satchel, as I have done? Promise me you will keep it close to you, so that you will always know where you came from when you feel this leather in your hands."

I told her that I would treasure it always. It would never leave my side no matter where I went or what I did. This bag became my most prized possession. Every single thing I owned that I held dear was stored inside it. After she gave me these things, she lay back down again and told me to go outside and play because she felt very tired. I did not feel like playing, but I went outside anyway. I ran far away from the house, away from everyone in the town and sat alone on a log, crying, hugging the old satchel to my breast.

I remember exactly what I was doing the moment my mother died. It was early in the afternoon and I was practising writing my name in the dirt with a stick, behind the cottage. I heard a cry of "NO!"

It was my father's voice, but in a tone I had never heard before. I can barely describe it now, but I remember that it scared me immensely when I heard it. I ran to the house but was intercepted by my brother, who prevented me from entering. I struggled to get free of his grasp, hitting and kicking, but to no avail; he was so much bigger than me. He suffered the blows I rained upon him and when I was calm, he told me that we should give our father some time alone. He took me to spend the rest of the day with Roger the miller. I was not permitted to return home until late the following day, when I was allowed to say goodbye to my mother for the last time. She looked happy and peaceful, finally out of pain, and that is how I choose to remember her. We all had to carry on with our lives somehow.

CHAPTER FOURTEEN

My father, on several occasions, had related to anyone who would listen that in May of the year of our Lord 1194, just a few weeks before he married my mother, there was a great visit from our beloved King Richard, son of Henry, the second of that name. "Lionheart", the Saracens called him – Richard the Lionheart. Richard was on his way home after being released from captivity in Austria, where he had been detained while returning from his Crusade.

While on this voyage home, the King sailed into Portsmouth. He had sent couriers ahead to give the town a week's warning that he was coming – which was what important people who travelled usually did. There was much preparation needed from everybody in the town. It was certainly a rare occasion that the King himself paid us a visit and so this was to be very special. Almost everyone who could afford to do so had a new set of clothes made and the rest had their best outfits cleaned and repaired. Roadways and houses were scrubbed, animals were groomed and their pens cleaned out, and many other things done to make the place as presentable as possible for the King.

When he had finally arrived and a Royal Court was set up, the King had his herald summon all the townspeople to gather together. During the court, he declared that he would set up a standing army for the country and he commissioned a Royal Fleet to be stationed here. This town would become an important military base with an establishment for the King's new navy. We were certain that this town could play a very significant part in the defence of the realm.

Along with the innumerable – and at times insufferable – nobles and servants who attended the King, many members of the best known and well-loved of the Guilds of Knights were also visibly in attendance. This was the Knights' Guild of Wessex and Mercia. These knights were the King's personal enforcers. Once, they had been two separate guilds – one for the kingdom of Wessex, one for the kingdom of Mercia. However, thanks to the casualties at the Battle of Hastings and the diminishing numbers of knights within each of the separate guilds, each had voted to amalgamate into one single guild to simply survive. The required standards for joining the guilds were high – a knight was required to show great prowess and leadership and to be invited by at least two current members.

Both groups had, at one time, worn a similar mantle, pure white, with their guild badge on the left shoulder. Once they had merged, however, they wore both badges on their white mantles, with their own badge in the upper position, showing their proud allegiance to their own section within the guild. There had always been several minor instances of disagreement between each division, but so far, none of these had escalated to the point of too much blood being shed or serious injury being suffered.

The whole of our town came out to see the King and his entourage. People cheered and clapped at everything the King said or did. In their normal, everyday life, the townspeople wore clothing that was mainly brown, green, or tan, those being the cheapest and easiest colours to dye the cloth. On this occasion, however, there were blues, reds, yellows, a few purples and many other bright and beautiful colours of clothing. The occasion amounted to a public holiday and the only people doing work of any sort were the taverners and cooks – kept very busy preparing food and drink for the King, his noblemen, the multitude of servants and officials and all the commoners who attended.

During the Royal Court, amongst the many other items of business, King Richard personally confirmed my father's freedom and the grant of land to him. He even stated that my father and his land would be free of taxes for one whole year. The King had ordered that an official document be prepared and presented to my father, to ensure this declaration would be known by all. This made my father extremely proud, not only that the land was now legitimately his, but to have met King Richard! My father considered it such a great honour to have been addressed by the King. The fact that he paid no taxes for a year was, for him, simply a bonus.

One particular item of business in the Royal court, with which the town's people were most happy and the sole reason the King himself came here, was the fact that Richard also granted the town a Royal Charter, giving permission for us to hold an annual free market fair, for up to fifteen days, commencing at the feast of St Peter *ad Vincula,* which is held on the first day of August. We were also permitted to hold a weekly market on Thursdays and were granted permission to set up a local court to deal with minor matters. As if this wasn't enough, the King also generously allowed our town quittance from passage, payage, pedage, pontage, stallage, talliage and toll, as well as many other tax liberties.

Alongside these most serious and wonderful decrees, there was much celebration. There was an official joust *á plaisance,* which included a tilt with blunted lances, in addition to displays of swordsmanship and hand-to-hand combat. Each of the knights participating had their own pennons flying on top of poles. It was, by all accounts, a very colourful affair. The town also held an archery competition and a village fair in honour of the royal visit. An area of the common had been fenced off, with seating for the nobles and special guests and standing room for the rest. There were separate arenas for the different disciplines of martial combat. Some of these sections included a list for the tilt, a square, fenced-off area for the sword fights, a roped ring for the unarmed hand-to-hand combat and so on. The town's people were very impressed with the tilting exhibition, most of them never having seen one before. I was often told about the joust when I was growing up. It sometimes made me wish that I had been born earlier so that I could have been there and seen it for myself. I was certain that I would have enjoyed it as much as the rest of the town had done.

The list was, when discussed later, by far the favourite display for most of the people in our community. Two magnificent horses, their eyes wide and glaring, draped with their knight's colourful livery, galloped at full speed toward each other on either side of a list fence. Each of the knights had his lance aimed at the other's chest. Suddenly, a crash of metal and one knight rode past with his arm in the air, holding a broken lance as the other swayed in his saddle before falling to the ground, defeated. Thankfully, the lances were tipped, with the aim of making them too blunt to cause severe injuries. Quite a few knights did, however, suffer serious blows to the head or body, or endure splinters of lance piercing an arm or leg. God be praised, no one was fated to die that day.

After the tilt, there were many sword fighting bouts and unarmed combats, either one-on-one or in mêlée. All in all, it was a grand display of skills from the knights of the kingdom. Each bout was conducted with rebated weapons and by scoring points rather than actually injuring the opponent. Many brave and skilled knights had come forward that day, but only one of them could be the ultimate champion. That title holder was William de la Colline. He was the champion of the Knights' Guild. A wonderful spectacle was beheld by the people in our town, thanks to the King's visit.

Many young men, whether they thought they were suitable for it or not, were inspired by the tournament to beg their fathers to ask the knights to accept them as squires or servants, so that they might work with the knights and earn a living travelling the country with them. Many men approached the knights, cap in hand, to speak of their son's strengths. Quite a lot of these youngsters were to be sadly disappointed. Only a few knights took our local boys with them.

It was this royal occasion, as well as his official grant, that prompted my father to finally ask for my mother's hand in marriage. Switha's father, very impressed with the amount of land granted to Ranulf, readily agreed and set about making plans for the wedding ceremony to take place as soon as arrangements could be finalised. My brother was born around the middle of the following year.

Six years later, at the turn of the new century, King John

reaffirmed the rights and privileges awarded to the town by his late brother, Richard, although he did not come to our town for the occasion. We learned about this confirmation when a messenger arrived to speak to our bailiff and pass on the parchment on which was written the charter of the town, sealed with King John's Great Seal.

King John also established a permanent base for the royal fleet and ordered that the building of the navy docks and a hospital be commenced. This latter structure was built to perform its duties as an almshouse and hospice for the relief of the poor. The hospice was founded by Bishop Peter des Roches and was known by the title of Domus Dei, or God's House.

CHAPTER FIFTEEN

For a young child in the village there was always something to do, although sadly, not all of it was fun and games. Household chores took up a fairly large portion of my day – collecting firewood and water, cleaning the cottage, carrying the night bucket and emptying it into the large tun for the fullers and the tanner, helping with planting, weeding and harvests, looking after the chickens and pigs, assisting with cooking the meals – the list seemed endless, but when I did finally get through these tasks, any time left was my own and I could do as I pleased.

Comical events, such as that occurring between Owen and Mog, were not as frequent as we would have liked, but they added much needed excitement when they did occur. At one time or another almost everyone had something happen to them that was humorous to everyone else. The laughing was good-natured, but had a visitor to the town laughed, we would have quickly banded together against the outsider in defence of the aggrieved party.

There were quite a number of young children in our town, about a tenth of the population and, for the most part, we all played together. Games were often as simple as riddling, hide and seek, catch, the old Norse wrestling game of Glima, bell the cat and even knur and spell. Equipment for the games was as we found or handmade. For example, someone would often draw a merrills square in the dirt for a quick game and gather some small stones of differing colours or bits of twigs, which became the playing pieces. Of course, dice games also formed a portion of our activities. These games could be played indoors or outside, as weather did not usually have an effect on the throw. Some dice were made from pigs' or sheep's knuckles or bone, others from stone, wood, antler, or whatever other suitable material was available. Most dice had six sides, although I have seen several with four, seven, eight or even twelve sides. Dice could be used as gambling tools, or as implements for determining how many spaces one would move one's pieces on a board game, such as backgammon.

The priests told us that, "Dice are the instruments of the devil!" and that they should all be destroyed. But no matter how often they stamped on the dice to crush them, or confiscated and burnt them, we always made more.

Almost everyone had some dice, because they were so easy and cheap to make. I had made several wooden sets, with the dots carved or burned into each of the sides. Sometimes I would use the paint left by my mother to colour the wood before I put the spots on. There were, naturally, some people who made dice so that they fell one way or another on a regular basis, in order that they might cheat at games or gambling. If any such swindlers were discovered, the dice were smashed and the fraudsters punished and often expelled from the town. These cheaters only tended to prove the priests right, but they still did not stop people playing with dice.

There was a large, mostly unused grassy area we called 'the common,' where we played our more boisterous children's games, such as catch as catch can, wrestling, field football, chase and the like. This was also the area where the fyrd training most often took place, due to the large size of the ground. It was also one of the popular places on which to graze sheep, so sometimes our games 'inadvertently' involved wrestling with the sheep, although the shepherds tried to dissuade us from this practise by attempting to catch us and beat us with their crooks. The shepherds were often not very bright, but if they were fast enough and managed to catch us, they would teach us a lesson or two.

The older boys and younger men would sometimes be involved in village football, a game played between two neighbouring villages. The object was to get the ball to your own village, while the other village would be trying to do the same. The ball was a heavy, dense object, made by sewing several pieces of leather or thick cloth together and filling the cavity with moss and peas, or small pebbles if peas were not to be found. Sometimes the ball would only have been carried to specially placed markers, if the villages were too far apart. A single game could take up to six days to finish and there were often hundreds of players on each side.

This sport was a dangerous pursuit, as there were very few rules and even fewer that were actually observed. It was the sort of game which my father vigorously tried to discourage me from taking part in. I remember several villagers who had been quite seriously injured and one or two who had died from head injuries. I must say, however, that our town had always excelled in the game, especially when the challenge came from a village along the coast, which until recently was called Hantune. Long ago, in the olden days, it was called Hamwic. It is known these days as Southampton. We always found that it was quite easy to triumph over them.

In addition to these pursuits, I also liked to watch the men and the older boys practise their archery every week after church. Every now and again, when I had no chores to do, I shot my bow for a short while. Occasionally, I was able to go hunting and bring home a rabbit or two for dinner. Archery training was not compulsory for someone of my age, but some of us younger boys would occasionally have our own practise times. Some of the more conscientious archers practised for two hours or more almost every day. They were, obviously, the much better shots.

I remember seeing one boy, Ulf, who was about fourteen years old at the time, shoot a squirrel out of a tree from a distance of about one hundred and thirty paces. When he suddenly swung slightly from the line of the targets to shoot at the trees, I wondered what he was aiming at. I did not even see the squirrel until it fell out of the tree with the arrow through its head. I do not believe he took as much as a single breath while aiming. Some of the men who were practising were very impressed with his shot and joked playfully about his accuracy.

One of them said, "The infidels in the Holy Land had better watch out if this one ever fights in the King's army."

Village life, while being pleasant enough most of the time, could also be dangerous. Hunting accidents or mishaps happened while simply gathering firewood. Although these events were rare, the injuries suffered could easily result in the loss of a limb, if not death. Wild boars could turn and attack in a wink of an eye. A more common threat was severe disease, which would sometimes strike with little or no warning.

Our village's one and only physician was kept quite busy – sometimes too busy for a man of his advancing years. If your injury did not look too severe, you would have to wait until he could get around to seeing you. He often had to treat someone far worse off than you, with your broken rib or knocked out tooth.

Every so often he had to travel to the nearby villages, as they had no physicians of their own. Sometimes he simply refused to treat anyone, complaining of illness himself, or just because he did not wish to do so. Very many people died simply because there were not enough physicians in the country to heal everyone who needed help.

There were quite a few women living in and around the area who claimed to have various degrees of skill in healing. One of these was Marissa, the wine maker. Most of these women used simple remedies, some of which were rather worse than the injuries or illnesses from which you suffered. They tended to live alone, well away from the rest of the village, often in a cave or in the middle of a forest clearing, where they could avoid the priests who repeatedly accused them of witchcraft. The priests always maintained that women had no capacity for learning such things as healing. I privately disagreed. After all, it was the mothers who always looked after the babies and children, so how could the priests suggest that they would not share information with each other about the health problems of their children? In doing so, surely the women would gain knowledge of many afflictions.

While one or two of the women had genuine knowledge of herb

lore, and often really helped your health improve, a vast majority of these women's supposed cures were nothing more than crushed stones, or boiled poultices, which were made from grasses and whatever herbs and flowers they had happened upon that day. Still, when the regular physician was away or indisposed and you found yourself in serious medical trouble, you took whatever assistance you could get.

There was one woman in particular, known to all in the village as Aunt Esme, though there was no one who knew her real name. She had good reason to be wary of the priest. Her antics were very strange indeed and as soon as she saw or heard anyone mention the priests, or anything else to do with the Church, she flew into a mad rage, throwing anything she could lay her hands on at whoever was around at the time. Most people around Portsmouth supposed that her behaviour was due to going mad because she spent so much time alone, but there were some who told a tragic story to explain it, which sounded to me as if it could be true. They said that it was because her husband argued with her about religion constantly. He was a believer, and she was a follower of Wicca. Her faith was in the natural spirits, as she called them – the divine character of trees, rocks and animals. One day, in a foul temper after a most vile argument, her husband had told her that he was going to leave her and enter the Church, and when he did, he took his two sons with him. However, on the way to the monastery, all three had perished when the bridge they were crossing collapsed underneath them, the rubble trapping them under the water. When she was told of their fate, she loudly and vilely cursed God and all Christians, left her house in the village and moved into an abandoned hut in the woodland of Hayling Island, east of Portsmouth.

Hayling Island was named for the two parishes of Hayling, originally called 'Northwode' and 'Southwode.' Over the centuries, as the trees were cleared and replaced by crops, the names were changed to North and South Halinge, which in the end became Hayling. This island is a true island, with no connection above water to the mainland, even at low tide. Portsmouth has only a very narrow channel separating us from the rest of England, but to get to Hayling Island, you needed a boat, or at least a coracle.

Only desperate people went to Aunt Esme, and everyone had reason to be scared of her. It seemed she could read the thoughts inside your head. No one believed that she could be lied to – she always appeared to know what you meant to say, even if you said something completely different. Regardless of how you felt about Esme, she could always cure whatever ailed you, provided you could manage to avoid mentioning the Church or anything to do with the Christian religion.

CHAPTER SIXTEEN

ne evening, just after the beginning of the new year of our Lord 1213, when I was nearly seven years old, my father sat me down and gravely told me, "I have some news for you. Though it pains me to do this, I will be sending you to Buckfast, where your mother's cousin Walt lives, in order that you should enter the abbey there and be educated by the Cistercians. It has cost me quite a tidy sum of money for this effort to get you into the abbey." When he told me how much it cost him, I was surprised. I had no idea he had amassed such an amount. He had sold several items of my mother's art, as well as her clothing and the plough left to him by his father. I knew he could barely afford to lose so much money.

He continued, "I will consider the investment a worthwhile one, as you will eventually be able to support yourself as a priest." He then told me, "I discussed this with your mother just before she died and she agreed that it would be the best course for you." He also said that he would give me a week to come to grips with this news. He did not, however, allow me the choice as to whether or not I wanted to go, he merely informed me that I would be leaving. I was devastated to think that I should have to leave the only home I had ever known, to travel who knew how far, to a distant unknown place and spend the rest of my life away from kith and kin, living with strangers and possibly never seeing anyone I knew here again. I spent the whole night crying, thinking that my father didn't want me. Throughout the night, I tossed and turned in my little cot, but could not sleep a single wink.

Over the next few days, I reasoned out my father's situation. My older brother was a brawny man, obviously well able to work the farm. I, on the other hand, had never been a strong child. I had, like so many of my friends, suffered through several of the usual childhood diseases and though I had overcome them, they had left me much weaker than my brother. I would not be much help to my brother on the family land. My father obviously saw no alternative for me if I were to make an honest living in this world. My father knew well, as did I, that I had no possibility of making a livelihood as a farm worker. Besides, my brother would then not have to feed, house and clothe someone he would be likely to see as a burden.

By the evening of the third day after he told me, I had come to the conclusion that my father was indeed right in his decision. I went to him and made the longest speech I had ever made, saying, "I am ready to go whenever and wherever you wish, if you think this is the only possible solution. I may not like it, but I have come to understand your decision and I will try to make the best of the situation. I will respect the promise I made to my mother, to honour you and obey you in all things. I know that you are much older and wiser than I am, therefore, I will trust that you know what the best thing is for me."

He hugged me firmly and solemnly thanked me for coming to the right decision. He told me that my mother's cousin's servants were coming to fetch me and warned me that cousin Walt and his servants were well known for being rather arrogant, even though they were only servants of the local baron and not lords and ladies themselves. Despite this, my father made me obey their instructions, unless their demands would demean or shame me. He told me to remember that they were no better than me and that I would only be with them for a few days. He then informed me that once I left, I would not be likely to see the family home again for many years, if at all. He told me to remember that no matter what happened, he had always loved me and always would. He promised to send word to me as often as he could and made me promise to send word to him also, to let him know how I was faring.

I spent the next few days saying goodbye to all my friends in the village. They were sad that I was going. I gave away some of my personal things, such as my sling and my bow and arrows. The servants arrived on the Friday of that week. My father insisted that they stay overnight and rest before returning. They begrudgingly accepted his invitation, and I was introduced. They took very little notice of me. For the evening meal, we had generous servings of the foods that father grew on his land, as well as meats such as pork, lamb and beef. The guests, however, seemed to treat the meal as if it consisted of the lowliest scraps that one would throw to a dog. My father showed great restraint by not losing his temper with them. I wondered how I would be treated on my journey.

On the day I left for the abbey, I promised myself that I would not cry in front of everyone who came to see me away. All my friends were there to wish me Godspeed on my journey. I hugged my father for what I thought would be the last time, shook hands with my brother and barely managed to keep the tears from flowing until we were out of sight of the small crowd who had gathered to see me off. Once I was no longer able to see those who had waved us off, I cried like a baby until my tears dried up. Walt's servants showed no tolerance for this display of emotion and berated me for being such a cry-baby. From shame, I managed to stop my tears. That was the last time I cried for many a year.

I often shudder when I remember what happened during the five days that the trip took. It involved a lot of walking, when I was not riding on a very cantankerous ass, which, for one of my small size, was not at all comfortable. There were times that I thought I would be either split in half, like a chicken's wishbone, or shaken to pieces when the beast moved at a bumpy trot. On one day, we rode on a dray and I was able to lie face down and rest my sore backside. Thanks be to God, we suffered no incidence of robbery or other attack. It was, in fact, quite a peaceful journey in relatively comfortable weather. I would have preferred that the weather was overcast and rainy, rather than the sunny times we had. It would have better suited my mood.

The children I met while on my journey were far too busy with their daily drudgery to spend even the least amount of time in playing games with a travelling stranger. Any that tried were severely reprimanded by their masters for wasting time that would be better spent working. It made me sad to think that these children were too occupied with work to have any time for laughter and games.

Alongside the travelling, a series of lower-class inns and taverns played a great part in our journey. They were large, noisy places, stinking of spilled ale, sweaty men and rancid straw, loud with the talk, song and raucous laughter of the patrons. The small sleeping rooms in which I went to bed were alive with mice, rats and other vermin, which would scurry away when we entered or lit a candle. The rooms contained beds with thin, stained mattresses, stuffed with old straw from the stables and riddled with fleas and bed bugs. I did not sleep much while travelling.

The servants who accompanied me slept in better conditions. While I awoke bleary-eyed from the little sleep I could get, scratching away the fleas, they seemed well-rested, having spent the night in the hostler's rooms. They also ate better than I did. I considered myself lucky to be given a small loaf of bread, sometimes soaked with meat juices and a lump of hard cheese. They ate bowl after bowl of pottage. While I drank small beer, they drank wine or porter.

I considered the fact that the journey was not to last forever, so I ate and drank what I was given, thankful that I was fed at all. Once we finally arrived at cousin Walt's house in Buckfast, Walt was standing in the courtyard, speaking angrily to one of his stablemen. As we entered, he curtly dismissed the man and turned to address those who had brought me here. The servants were immediately sent back to their normal daily tasks. They seemed glad to be rid of me.

Cousin Walt told me that I was not allowed to enter the house before I was taken on the next part of my passage to the abbey. He told me to wait inside the gate until I was collected. He then disappeared into the house. I was not given even the smallest drink or morsel of food for my comfort. I examined my surroundings while I was waiting. The house was large, with ivy growing over the front wall. I guessed that the building had been here for quite some time. I had seen ivy start to grow on one or two of the older houses back home.

A young barefoot boy, who I guessed was only a few years older than me, came running up to me from the back of the house and told me that he was sent to take me from the house to the abbey. There was to be no ass for this last leg of the journey, we were to walk. This latest servant also neglected to take any notice of my welfare as I was passed, just before sunset, into the hands of the brothers of the Cistercian Order at the abbey. His only concern seemed to be that I arrived alive, reasonably healthy and sufficiently presentable. I was just one more tiresome task to take him from his home and family for another day. He too was happy to be rid of me so that he could get back to his loved ones. How well I understood that. At that moment, I would have given anything to be back at home with my own father, brother and friends.

The entire trip from my father's house to the abbey passed without me learning the name of even one of my fellow travellers – not even the young boy would tell me his name. They, for their part, seemed not to care what my name was either. The only time they deigned to talk to me was to tell me where to go each night and to call me each morning so that I would not be lost or late. I had never met such uncaring people. I was glad to be finished with them.

CHAPTER SEVENTEEN

As we approached the abbey, I was struck by an unfamiliar sinking feeling in my stomach. I realised that this place was to be my home for the foreseeable future. I was very far from my family and friends, and I would be alone among strangers.

The first person to meet us at the gate of abbey was the prior, whose name was Mannus. The young servant introduced me to him and told him why I was here. While they were talking, I took the chance to look around. The walls were about twice the height of a grown man, constructed of carefully cut and placed stone. There was barely a space between the blocks to insert a knife blade. The stone had faded with age to a dull grey. The floors were of a flecked grey – a harder rock called granite that had been brought from Dartmoor. I was not too sure I liked the look of this place. It was dark, dank and seemed distinctly uncomfortable. When they had finished their brief discussion, I was commanded by the servant to accompany the prior. The very moment that the servant saw Mannus take hold of my hand, he turned and left without another word, simply walking away.

Mannus smiled down at me and welcomed me, kindly trying to reassure me, saying, "Welcome to Buckfast Abbey. Whatever misgivings you are having – and I am certain you will have quite a few – I assure you that they are not uncommon, especially in one as young as yourself. I have no doubt that you will soon learn to overcome these feelings."

Mannus was a man of small stature. He was fine boned, with a curiously small, round head. His eyes were odd – one looked at you and the other looked away, as if not to miss anything that happened around him. Not only that, but his right eye was brown and the left one was blue. His left eyebrow was completely white. These oddities were as a result of a childhood illness.

Mannus knew every single person in the abbey, no matter who it was, and he was able to skilfully assess each person while merely holding a conversation with them as to their abilities, strengths, and weaknesses. He had a fascination with history and could relate the entire story of the abbey from the laying of the very first foundation stone, through to the names of every brother and abbot who had resided here, no matter for how long or short a time. He took me inside the abbey to present me to the abbot, who was seated at a desk in his office. Once I was introduced, Mannus was gently dismissed and went back to his tasks, leaving me alone with the abbot, who I found to be a kindly man.

He spoke to me with a gentle voice, "My name is Brother Samuel and from now on, it would be better for you if you should try to forget your family and where you came from, as this is to be your new family and home." I was not best pleased with that concept and, with a surly tone in my voice, told him so, but he responded with a sympathetic smile and said, "Quite a lot of the new acolytes – even I, a very long time ago – felt rather the same way, but I and they, well, almost all of them, eventually came to accept and even enjoy their new lives here at the abbey."

I was not so sure about that for myself, but I told him that as I had nowhere else to go, I would try very hard to become a useful part of this community. Though I did not tell him, I think he knew that I had privately decided that I would give this place a short passage of time to prove itself before I left and ran away back home. Providing, that is, I could even find my way home from here, as I had not taken a great deal of notice of any landmarks on the journey. I knew we had headed west, into the setting sun, but when and exactly where did we turn north? I would not have to think about that until I came to the decision that I'd had enough of this place and wanted to leave. Thinking back on this conversation now, I laugh when I imagine that many young boys in the same position as I had been would have had the same feelings.

Abbot Samuel smiled his acceptance of the answer I gave him and rang a little bell that sat on his desk. As the bell's ringing faded, another of the brothers entered the office and was instructed to take me to the infirmary. As the abbot bade me farewell, he said, "This is Brother Vivien, he will look after you until you are familiar with the abbey and its surrounds. If you have any questions, find him and ask him. He will answer any query you may have. Tomorrow you will start your training. I bid you a good night. Sleep well, my son. I look forward to talking with you again in a few months to hear your views on our home."

I bade the abbot good night in return and was accompanied by Brother Vivien along many different corridors from the abbot's office to the infirmary. Here I was bathed in a large tub, which looked like a wine barrel cut in half. I was told that I was expected to take a bath once a week, on Saturday mornings, whether I deemed it necessary or not. After my bath, I was given an old robe to wear. Its length had been adjusted to suit my stature. It was a dark brown colour, although a little faded with age and wear and was made from a roughly woven woollen material. This habit, as I was told it was properly called, was a very straightforward piece of attire, just three tubes joined together, one for the body and two for the arms. There was a hood attached for warmth and to keep the rain off. A piece of rope served for a belt. These, with my new sandals, would become my only clothing. Each article of which would be replaced as and when they became too ragged or too small for me to wear any longer.

The clothes I had worn on my journey to the abbey were taken away and would be given to the poor of the neighbouring village, as was the rule here at Buckfast. Normally, any possessions one had were either locked away until the novice removed himself from the abbey, due to a lack of desire to remain within the walls, or they were handed to the Bursar, so that he might determine whether the items were better off being passed to someone outside who needed them, or sold so that other items may be purchased for the common good of the abbey and for the glory of God's work.

My satchel and the headband contained within, I was allowed

to keep when I explained that they were gifts from my mother just before she died. I had begged that I be allowed to keep them with me and for pity's sake, I was. At least, they told me, for the time being. I was informed that I could use the satchel for carrying anything I would need when working outside or if I ever went travelling with the brothers. I would not be permitted, however, to wear the headband at any time I was wearing the habit. This I accepted, so long as I could keep them both.

Only after I had been bathed and dressed anew was I asked, "Have you had anything to eat today?" To which I forlornly replied that it had been many hours since, just after sunrise, I'd had a meagre breakfast of a small, lump of dry bread, a handful of stale cheese and a mug of very weak ale. I was immediately taken to the refectory and told that this is where I would have all my meals. I was then handed a wooden plate, on which were some thinly sliced cold meats, large crusty lumps of warm buttered bread and a few pickled onions, along with a small goblet of watered wine. I was also given a nef – an eating kit – consisting of the plate from which I ate the food I had been given, a sharp knife in a thin leather scabbard, a spoon made from cow's horn, a pottery goblet, a small wooden bowl and a green cloth napkin. These were to be mine to use from now on. They were my responsibility.

I was told, in no uncertain terms, "These are yours to use while you are here. You are to keep them clean. If you do not bring them with you to each and every meal, you will go without or make do with your fingers. If anything breaks, we shall replace it, if there are any spares with which to do so." My nef was to be kept in a small cloth bag. I resolved never to forget the kit. When I had finished eating, I made sure that my eating utensils were cleaned, dried and repacked into their bag, then I was taken to one of the dorters, which some called the dormitory. There were four of these in the abbey and I was shown which bed was mine.

My bed consisted of a rough-hewn cot with a thin but clean and comfortable mattress and one warm woollen blanket. There were thirty such beds in this room and mine was not quite in the middle. It may not have been much, but it was clean and warm. One item

I was given that I did not understand was a Paternoster. This was a circle of fifty-six beads on a string. There were six large white beads, made of bone and fifty brown wooden beads. The beads were arranged thus: one white bead then a group of ten wooden beads, the pattern repeating, so that a white bead lay between each decade and at each end of the round. Attached between the two white beads at each end of the round was a row of three brown beads with a crucifix, made of carved wood, on the end. It was explained to me that this Paternoster was for my own personal prayer times.

It was expected that we work our way from the cross to the join, then around the loop back to the join then down to the cross again. When I started and returned to the cross each time, I was instructed to say the *Apostles' Creed*. The first bead next to the cross was to remind me to recite the *Paternoster* – the great prayer that was taught to us by our Lord Jesus in the sixth Chapter of the Gospel of Matthew. This prayer gave the name to the string of beads. The next bead meant that I should recite, three times, a prayer known as an *Ave Maria*, a prayer to Mary, Mother of Jesus. The third bead was for the *Gloria*. Then I arrived at a white bead. The white beads represented the times I would say the *Paternoster* again. There followed, as I mentioned, ten brown beads. Each brown bead in the round represented when I should repeat the *Ave Maria*. The whole round of prayers was known as a circuit. The beads enabled us to keep count of our prayers, although, since I first received that original set of beads, I have lost count of the number of circuits I have completed and the number of Paternosters I have worn down to nothing and had to have replaced. Although I already knew the prayer known as the Paternoster, as did everyone with whom I was acquainted, I took a few days to learn these other prayers. Reciting them many times daily meant that they were easy to learn.

The next few weeks were a constant amazement to me – that so much could happen within a single set of buildings. I quickly learned that the abbey was an efficiently run organisation, with a place for everything and everything in its place. I soon learned the fastest way from each corner of the abbey to any other. It took me a mere three days before I could accurately describe to any stranger how to get to any part of it from wherever we were.

The Abbey had become fairly wealthy due to fishing, as there was a river nearby – the River Dart – and through trading in wool from the many sheep we kept. While each individual brother took his vow of poverty, the abbey needed money to fund its many works of charity. This wealth was the only reason it was possible to give me my own personal kit of eating gear. Had I been sent to many of the other less well-funded Abbeys, I would have had to find or make my own, or to make do with my fingers at mealtimes.

The fact that we had the river nearby meant that we were never short of fish. We had trout and pike aplenty. Our cooks used a wide array of sauces to help stave off our cravings for more varied meals. The surrounding hills were lush green areas, on which the sheep, pigs and cattle could graze and grow fat and breed. Due to bequests from rich men who feared for the welfare of their immortal souls, the abbey had been granted a large amount of fertile land on which we grew many varieties of fruits and vegetables and bees were kept for their honey and beeswax. Once in a while, deer had been sighted near the abbey. Their cast-off antlers, when we could find them, could be used for tool and knife handles, spoons, needles, buttons, beads, combs and many other uses.

Over the next few months, I was passed from pillar to post, working in each different area of the abbey. I guessed, correctly, that the brothers were trying to determine where my strengths lay and where I would fit best into Abbey life. However, no matter in which parts of the abbey I worked there were always the standard daily chores and tasks for each of us to do, outside and inside, especially for the novices. My new life consisted of a regular round of worship, prayer, reading and manual labour.

And every night I was glad to fall into my bed.

CHAPTER EIGHTEEN

For much of the day we worked hard with our hands, washing, cooking, raising crops and performing all the other tasks required to maintain the running of a large Abbey. In addition to these chores, we would spend several hours in private prayer and meditation, as well as in reading or hearing others read from the Bible. Attendance at specialised duties and at chapel took up the remainder of our day. In all, we were joined in communal prayers for nearly five hours each day, while our private prayer and contemplation could take another four hours.

First and foremost of our obligations was the *Horarium* – the daily Offices. We were called by the bell into the chapel seven times a day. The bell also gave the villagers around us a rough idea of the time. I had heard that there were some self-important, high-ranking people who were mistakenly of the opinion that most villeins in the area were so ignorant that they could only tell the time of day by the ringing of the chapel bell. They were decidedly wrong. Telling the time was relatively easy if you were not too particular about how accurate you were.

If you were to hold out your hand at arm's length, the width of your hand would enable you to roughly determine the time. If the sun was, for example, two and a half hand widths above the horizon, then the sun had been up for about two and a half hours, which meant that the time was approximately half past the hour of eight of the clock. Six hand widths meant that it was near noon. Similarly, if the distance between the setting sun and the horizon was one hand's width, then there was something in the order of one hour left before sunset. All of this is only a rough guide, of course.

The first of the services for the day was *Prime*. We were woken about two hours after midnight and we would groggily shuffle our way by candlelight down the Night Stair, which led from the dorter to the chapel, for orison and chanting. We were grateful for the hoods on our robes at this service, as they kept in what heat we radiated, although they did not keep out the often-freezing draughts that crept up our legs.

Woe betide any novice or brother who fell asleep during this or any other office. He would later be expected to present himself to be disciplined for his crime of fatigue. Also, at any night-time office, he would be given the large candle as soon as he had been woken and was then required to amble around the choir stalls, while still participating in the singing of the office, watching for the next person to fall asleep. This person would then take over the candle walk. This office would continue for about an hour, after which we would go back to bed for a couple more hours' sleep.

Next came the service of *Matins*. Rising from our cots at sunrise, we would again attend the chapel for another round of singing and prayer, this time for only half of an hour. We would then go out into the garden or do other chores until it was time for another short service, *Lauds*, which took place just before breakfast. We would then go to breakfast, usually a gruel or thin porridge perhaps with cheese and bread. Possibly, if a nobleman had recently visited, there would also be some thinly sliced cold meats from the previous night's dinner. Often, there would be various fruits from the orchard.

Once this service was complete, we would return to our manual labour, study, healing in the infirmary or whatever our particular task was for the day. This would continue, generally without pause, until the bell rang for *Sext*, near midday. After this service we had a midday meal, commonly of fruits, bread and watered down wine or light ale. In the high summer months and then only on days with extreme heat, we would have a small rest for about an hour or so and then it was back to work again.

Nones came in the mid-afternoon – this too was quite a short service, which was over far too soon for some, because afterwards we went back to our daily tasks. *Vespers*, at sunset, was welcomed by most of the brothers, as it meant the end of the working day. Dinner followed this office. We ate, as usual, in silence. After dinner, we were free to study or get what sleep we needed. *Compline*, in the evening, before bedtime, at the eighth hour after noon, was the last office for the day. After this office, we were expected to maintain silence until we went to bed and fell asleep.

The whole round was played out at approximately the same times every single day that we were inside the abbey and usually whenever we were abroad with our work outside. Quite some time was required to become accustomed to the daily routine of monastic life, but once the body had become familiar with the rhythms of the day and night, it eventually became a lot easier to bear. Sadly, some people never did get used to it, which meant that they had to leave the abbey and return home. Fortunately, over a short period of time, I was able to accustom myself and, as Prior Mannus and Abbot Samuel had both foretold, came to enjoy the calmness and tranquillity of the abbey lifestyle.

CHAPTER NINETEEN

To describe the abbey itself in any great detail would take an immense amount of time. It was definitely the largest set of buildings I had ever seen – much bigger even than the new church they were building back home. I will, however, briefly describe some of the parts of the abbey to give an idea of the complexity of the buildings and its separate sections.

I have already mentioned the dorter, the infirmary, the refectory and the chapel. Not every one of the brothers slept in the dorter, some slept in separate cells, either by choice or for other reasons which were not yet explained. The abbot always slept in his own quarters, away from the rest of the community, as is the rule among the Cistercians.

After about seven years in the abbey, I developed a rather loud snoring problem. It was so annoying for the other members of our community in my dormitory that it was decided I should have my own cell, so that the other novices and brothers would not have their sleep unduly disturbed. This, it seemed, was only one of the reasons for having separate cells. Some men became almost hermits in their cells, saying that their path to holiness could only come from solitary meditation and complete separation from others. Their food was left outside their cells so that they could avoid meeting other men. I found that, at certain times, I rather preferred the solitude. In a place like the abbey, where everyone is thrown together almost all of the time, I had a small space where I could sometimes be alone, if I thought I needed to be, so long as my duties for the day were completed.

Near each of the dormitories was a garderobe. There was also one downstairs outside the refectory and one inside both the front and back gates to the abbey. They were situated so that any brother who had need of the 'small office' to take his ease would not have too far to travel, no matter where he was, in any part of the abbey. Of course, outside the abbey, there were numerous trees and bushes, so there was no shortage of private places of relief.

The infirmary was run by Brother Michael, the chief physic. This was the place where ailing travellers could be treated for their many and varied illnesses or injuries, as well as where the old, infirm or sick brothers were housed. If they were too feeble to do their work, they were confined to bed here and taken care of by the infirmarian, until they became well enough to go back to work.

Sick travellers were first washed to clean their bodies, and then fed, so that their bodies were made stronger. Then they were shriven – given Confession – so that their souls were cleansed. Only after these responsibilities were properly discharged did the infirmarian finally consent to examine them to discern their ailments and to treat them.

The frater, or refectory, was the place where all meals were taken, in strict silence, except for the nominated brother who stood in the reading pulpit. Each brother took his turn by roster. There were selected Bible readings for each day, including the Psalms and the brother chosen daily for the task would read them to us while we ate.

Because meals were considered as an essential element of Abbey life, monks were expected not to excuse themselves from the communal partaking of the meals without good reason. The refectory was a place consisting of one large hall, with long tables, around which we would all sit on benches, each bench seating six of us. As I have mentioned previously, each person eating would have his own nef. It was very seldom that a brother or novice would forget his nef more than once.

Because we were ordered to eat in total silence, apart from the designated brother who read a selected passage at each meal, hand signals were used to ask others to pass things like butter, salt, bread and so on. For example, to ask for butter we would hold one hand flat, palm up and, holding the first two fingers of the other hand together, make a 'spreading' motion over the flat hand. There were many different signals, enough to carry on a reasonably intelligent conversation. This was our way of conversing without breaking the Rule of Silence.

Of course, the kitchen was situated next to the refectory. The kitchen was larger than several houses in my town put together, but then it had to be, in order to feed all the brothers in the abbey. Some of the kitchen staff were engaged in peeling and chopping the vegetables, some were making sauces, others baking breads, while many more spent their time cleaning the multitude of kitchen utensils and pots and pans.

Meats, such as pork, beef, lamb and venison, were not often cooked – except when important visitors arrived. Small amounts of meat were, however, served to those brothers or invalids in the infirmary, who were in dire need of the strength it gave. Fish of many varieties, on the other hand, were available three or four days each week as it was not considered to be real meat. There were always pots boiling and bubbling, with brothers dashing hither and yon preparing the multitude of meals required. There were about one hundred and thirty souls residing in the abbey when I had arrived and so if all the pots and pans were collected together and melted down into one immense piece of iron, it would be more metal than most of the people from my hometown had ever seen in one place.

Before entering either the frater or the kitchen, all brothers passed through the lavatorium, where they would wash their hands and faces before sitting down to their meals, especially those who had been working in the stables. Nobody wanted dirt or dung dropped into their food, which would make it distinctly unpalatable, as would eating with dirty hands. So, a trough of water was supplied either standing or flowing, depending on the location of the abbey. If the water was standing, it would be replaced before each meal by means of a bucket from the well. If it was flowing, it was always fresh without the need for the additional toil of emptying and refilling the trough.

Thankfully, our Abbey had a small spring erupting into one of our courtyards, around which had been built a well. From this well we could carry or redirect water, so that it flowed through a system of troughs and pipes for our washing water.

We made our own soap, using ash from the fires or lye mixed with rendered animal fats. It was harsh on the skin, but it made us clean. The soap we made was used not only for our bodies, but also for our clothing, the dishes, the floors, the furniture and anything else that needed to be cleaned.

Near to the kitchen was the cellarium for most of the general stores, such as flour, spices, wine and herbs, as well as the granary where all the grains were kept. Another well was also dug near the kitchen, so that water was in plentiful supply without having to carry it for any great distance.

The chapter house was a room in which the brothers met on a daily basis, to discuss any Abbey business and to listen to a chapter of the monastic rule. This was so that any emergent problem could be dealt with immediately and so that we would be constantly reminded of the seventy-three Chapters of the Rule of St Benedict and the twelve Chapters of the Cistercian Rule, or *Charta Caritatis*.

Attached to the chapel was the sacristy, a small building in which sacred vessels and vestments were kept for use in the chapel. Some of the items in the sacristy had been donated by wealthy travellers, in order to show their gratitude for the cures and kindness that the brothers had given when treating their injuries or illnesses. There were some items that had been held by the abbey, or by its mother house in France, for over one hundred years.

Occasionally, during the first year I was there, the Master of Postulants, Brother Vivien, would take me and the other young boys on a walk around the cloister, which was a covered walkway within the abbey. Abbey cloisters were often situated around a quadrangle formed by the various buildings. They usually comprised either a plain wall or colonnade on the outer side and often a series of windows on the inner side, as did ours.

Brother Vivien took us on these frequent walks to ascertain what we had learned since arriving or to clarify some obscure point or other. If he judged that we had learned and understood enough about one particular part of Abbey life, he would report this to the abbot and we would, from then on, be learning something new.

If any novice, postulant or brother needed to be disciplined for any breach of behaviour, such as falling asleep during the Offices, he would be told to report to the Misericord, so that his crime could be investigated and, if found necessary, punished appropriately. Punishments ranged from extra work and prayers for minor offences, through to expulsion from the abbey for the most serious breaches.

The only place in the abbey where any fire was allowed, apart from the kitchen or the infirmary was the calefactory, or 'warming house'. In winter, the weather could be bitterly cold and if there was no fire, some of the older brothers who had become quite infirm would certainly not have survived. They could easily have died from exposure or frostbite. The warming house was often seen by most of us as a welcome place of refuge from the terrible cold of wet winds and winters.

At about two hundred and fifty paces distance from the abbey, on the western side, was the burial ground for the brothers who had died while members of our commune. Some travellers who had passed away were also interred there. In all, there were about four hundred graves when I joined the abbey. This number included the fifty or so paupers' graves at the far southern edge of the cemetery. Most of the graves were well over fifty years old, although some had been filled as recently as six months before I joined the abbey. Too many more were added during my stay there.

The last of the sections of the abbey I will describe here is the scriptorium. This was close to being my favourite area of the abbey. Here, all the writing was done. Copying of Bibles, wills and other legal papers and documents was carried out within this room. Those who would choose to be copyists were tested on rough sheets of flax or imported papyrus, on which it was rather difficult to write. The theory was that if you could make an acceptable copy on flax, it was more than likely that you would do a good job on vellum. Once the new scribes had proven their capabilities after many weeks of long practise, they were allowed to graduate to the use of the precious vellum – which took quite some time to prepare.

Brothers would be seated at desks with the document to be copied on one side and a piece of vellum on the other. Although every desk had at least two candles, those who were the finest copyists were given desks nearest the windows so that the best light could be had. Some windows had a sheet of green vellum, which had been oiled, covering the opening, so that the light would be more conducive to the comfort of the eyes. Some desks had a strange, spherical bottle, which was filled with water and focussed the sunlight onto one small spot, usually for illuminating capitals – the initial letter of a chapter of text. A penknife, used for cutting new quills and for scraping away small errors, was kept near each scribe. As well as these items, each brother would have a piece of pumice stone for cleaning and smoothing the sheets of vellum, after having scraped away the errors. Once the vellum was scraped and flattened, a boar's tusk or a large, smooth stone would be utilised to burnish the parchment, so that the ink would not soak too readily into it and blur itself into strange, unrecognisable shapes, ruining the work already done.

For those who were not so steady with their writing, a ruler and a small, thin lump of lead lay to hand, so that faint lines may be drawn to guide their quills. There would also be an inkwell and several prepared quills to hand, so that if the copyist's quill broke or split, another would be there, ready to take its place. All in all, the desks had to be fairly large to hold the bulk of equipment that a brother scribe would need for the writing or copying of documents.

At one end of the room, some brothers would be engaged in making or repairing quills, while others prepared the flax sheets. At the other end, another brother was responsible for ensuring that a pot of red lead was also available, for the drawing of the initials. Still others would be making more inks – reds, blacks, blues, greens and many other colours besides. There was always a small pot or two bubbling away, boiling the oak galls to make the inks, which made the scriptorium smell horrendous. Despite the smell, it was still a pleasant place to work. Those who worked there soon became used to it and were not as affected by the smell as those who visited irregularly.

Occasionally, gold leaf was used for illuminating the scriptures, although it was used as sparingly as possible. This precious material was kept in a special box with only a few brothers having access to the key. Only the best knew the secret of mixing gold ink. Manuscripts with gold ink were a wonder to behold.

The vellum was prepared in a completely different area of the abbey, because the excessive noise of the lamb's skin being beaten thinner and thinner while being stretched on a wooden frame was intolerable when trying to concentrate on the delicate task of copying. Sometimes vellum would be re-used, as it was so valuable. If a particular document was no longer needed or had been spoilt by a spelling error or a small ink spill, it could be scraped clean for use in another document. Of course, if it was scraped too thin and a hole appeared in it, or if the old ink could not be completely removed, it could still be used as scrap for testing new copyists or repaired quills.

Very little was wasted.

CHAPTER TWENTY

For the most part, I enjoyed myself at the abbey, occupied in learning to read, write and sing, memorising prayers and chants and, after some time, copying Bible passages and other documents. I was not quite so cheerful about some of the other chores that I had to perform at all hours of the day, although I completed them with as much good will as I could muster. I balanced the less pleasant tasks against the knowledge that I was reasonably well-fed, adequately clothed and given a place that was safe and relatively warm and comfortable to sleep. I had to admit that it was far more than a fair exchange. I was especially gladdened to be learning about Our Lord's work and His sacrifice for us – I embraced the Christian faith strongly and tried most enthusiastically to emulate Christ's way of life.

I was taught Latin, German, Italian and the Norman language, as well as courtly manners, in order that I might one day, if I applied myself diligently, be able to speak with foreign nobles and conduct business with them. Apparently, most noblemen had some healthy respect for the candid Cistercian monks and their honest dealings between peoples who cannot speak each other's tongue. Especially pleasing for me was learning about herbal and mineral remedies for various diseases and how to treat common injuries for the travellers and those who lived in the area who came to us for healing. The infirmary was the only place within the abbey that I enjoyed working in more than the scriptorium.

Ironically, I learnt that treating deep cuts from farm implements was a relatively simple affair, no matter how severe, as long as the treatment was started very soon after it happened. I wished that I had possessed this knowledge much earlier, as then my mother might still be alive. All of these different things were quite easy for me to learn, and I acquired a large amount of knowledge in a very short period of time.

One of the older brothers, by the name of Cedric, told us that we were living in luxury compared with some other abbeys and monasteries that he had visited in his travels around the country as a mendicant monk. At sixty-one, Brother Cedric was quite old. He said that the food and drink we enjoyed was far superior to that of some of the other abbeys to which he had been. Occasionally, watery thin porridge gruel, mouldy old vegetables and brackish water comprised the entire diet for weeks on end in a few unfortunate places. Brother Cedric had spent many thousands of days, since becoming a young postulant, working at near backbreaking labour from early dawn until late at night. His only respite was the two or three mealtimes each day and the set times of prayer. At the end of the day, he would collapse onto a bed which was often barely more than a hard bench and thin straw mattress, sometimes without a blanket. He soon learned that he had to make his body do the work required of him, regardless of the pain, weariness and hunger, or he knew that he would feel the wrath of some of the older men. We were, then, to be thankful for our 'easy' life here.

He had also seen young lads who started out with normal playful minds beaten into humble submission by spiteful, older monks. In some abbeys, he informed us, beatings were commonplace, even for such trivial offences as breaking wind, speaking, or even yawning or sneezing at the wrong moment. In other establishments, he told us, there were wicked sodomites who sometimes preyed on the young boys. We considered ourselves blessed that there were none of these immoral individuals here in Buckfast. However, had there been any, I always prayed that I would have the strength and courage to defend myself against such demonstrations of the devil's influence.

There were brothers in our Abbey who had ashamedly admitted that they had had thoughts of such things, but I did not hear that anyone acted upon these thoughts, although it was not a subject that was much discussed. These feelings were strongly discouraged and those who had them were shriven at our weekly Confession. The brothers' penance for such thoughts was, I thought, rather harsh. They were told that they would have to take an icy cold bath for two hours every morning and night for seven days. That treatment certainly took such thoughts out of their minds quickly enough and tended to dissuade further occurrences.

Every member of our community here at the abbey had another brother who was older, most of the time, or at least had been here for far longer, as his personal confessor. We took confession at least once every week, more often if we thought we needed it. The abbot's confessor was the oldest brother in the abbey, Johann, who had been there for forty-three years. Johann was now sixty-eight.

Because our Abbey was on the main route from Exeter to Plymouth, many travellers called in, either to the chapel to pray for the moral or physical strength to continue their journey, or, occasionally, to our infirmary, to replenish their medicaments or to have their many and various ailments treated by our infirmarians, one of which I was rapidly learning to become. This part of my duties was what held most interest for me. I suppose that this was due to what I saw as the unnecessary death of my mother. It also gave me a chance to do something that I considered special in Our Lord's work – healing the sick. I learnt much about the uses and applications of many herbs and ointments, as well as how to treat deep cuts and set broken bones.

A short time after arriving at the abbey, I met Brother John, who was seventeen years older than me. He had a very large nose and a hairy wart growing over his right eye. He had also become prematurely bald. He had a small gathering of hair on each temple and at the back, but very little anywhere else on his head. I never liked him and the enmity was mutual. He would tell tales on the young postulants to the senior brothers, sometimes earning the youngsters' severe punishments. It did not matter whether or not the stories were true – he simply enjoyed telling tales. Because of this, he had hardly any real friends. I was, most definitely, not one of them.

It was in my thoughts that he seemed to delight in telling lies about me more than about anyone else. I believed that he was jealous of me, especially of my quick mind. He was envious of any person who showed the slightest modicum of intelligence. The only use to which he would put his lazy brain was inventing lies. Possibly he was worried that I, as well as many others who were able to learn faster than he did, should surpass him in the abbey hierarchy while he remained merely a simple brother.

There were several times when I thought that the world would have been a better place without Brother John. I would never have done anything to harm the man, nor wish any harm to come to him, but I could quite happily have lived without him. Of course, these thoughts were contrary to the way of life we had in the abbey and they were confessed each time I had them. I was told that Brother John was a close relative of the abbot and rumour had it that he had some sort of hold over him. It was said that is why his tales carried such weight, even though most knew that the tales were untrue. What sort of influence he actually had, no one knew for certain.

There was one brother, Nigel, who seemed to be able to do nothing right. While his intentions were always pure, his misdeeds forever frustrated several of the senior brothers in the community. The only reason he was allowed to stay was that the abbot always held out hope that he might one day improve. As things turned out, he did eventually become a well-co-ordinated young man, although it took a long time and much patience. To give an example, Brother Nigel, who had learnt to be a healer, found an injured badger while out in the fields tending the sheep. The badger was quite a distance from its sett, which he had discovered some time previously and would occasionally take scraps to leave near the entrance for the animals.

The badger's hind leg was broken and the poor beast was found unconscious. Nigel decided that the best thing would be to bring the unfortunate creature back to the infirmary to be healed by Brother

Michael, so he picked it up and started running, carrying it toward the abbey. Nigel did not count upon the animal's waking from its stupor to discover that it was not only in pain, but also being bounced around by a clumsy human. The badger growled several times, then suddenly started wriggling and attacking Brother Nigel with the claws of all three of its good legs. Nigel fell to the ground in agony and let go of the animal. The badger landed on him and continued its attack for quite a few minutes. Nigel suffered scratching on his face, head, chest, back, arms and hands. As the badger clambered over the cowering, fallen man, presumably on its way back to its sett, it urinated over him, as if to display its disgust at being so badly treated. In the end, it was a very sorry, extremely smelly, empty-handed Nigel who was treated in the infirmary by Brother Michael. Nigel spent the whole of the next two days bathing, in a plainly unsuccessful attempt to rid himself of the smell. The odour lasted for several days. I believe that that was the last time Brother Nigel ever attempted to rescue a badger.

However, he was still very fond of all other sorts of animals. He loved puppies, kittens, squirrels and rabbits – anything small and furry. Unfortunately, this was to be his undoing. Playing with so many animals had given him a strange gait, as though he had a prickle lodged between the cheeks of his buttocks. This was due to having an extremely itchy posterior – the result of contracting intestinal worms from the many infested animals with which he played. He was quite often seen walking the village streets, bent backwards, scratching furiously at his backside. This peculiar gait was to become his trademark walk and was mimicked mercilessly and with great hilarity by the young children of the nearby village, until, that is, they too succumbed to the same worms from their own furry playmates and had to present themselves at the infirmary for their cure.

Brother Michael was aware that the children mocked Nigel and was sympathetic to the plight of his fellow brother, so he made sure that the children were treated by the most suitable person. As the bible says, "Revenge is mine, sayeth the Lord." Therefore, Nigel took care not to show his pleasure at having the naughty children at his mercy. And although he treated them to the best of his skill, he made sure they remembered all the times they had mocked him. He always confessed these feelings of vengeful pleasure later.

Another brother I might mention was Aubrey – as officious a man as ever walked God's green earth. He was tall, over six feet and as slender as an arrow. His elbows and knees looked as if someone had tied a knot in each limb in place of joints. His nose was long and thin, almost as if someone had attached a knife blade to the centre of his face. He had the thinnest grey hair I have ever seen. It was so thin that it was made almost invisible when caught by a breeze. He was not balding, but his scalp was clearly visible despite his hair covering his whole head.

Aubrey was the sort of man who, when once a set of rules has been learned, would stick to them with the entire force of his being. Not only that, but he would also attempt to make sure that anyone in his sight was to follow the rules in the same manner. He firmly believed in the letter of the law, rather than the spirit of the law. To give an example, in the Fourth Chapter of the Rule, we are exhorted to "keep a constant watch over the actions of our life." Brother Aubrey took this to heart and had become a self-appointed 'keeper of morals' for the entire Abbey. He reported every single breach of the Cistercian Rule that he saw, no matter how trivial it might have been. He did not talk to the 'sinner' first, as the Bible tells us we should, but he went straight to the prior with his tales. This meant that every brother, including the abbot and especially the prior, tried to avoid Aubrey at all times, and rather disliked having him around, in case they made any tiny slip up, which he believed he would be duty-bound to report to the prior. Aubrey must have had very thick skin, not to feel the hostility that came from almost all of us. He seemed not to notice the resentment that many people held towards him. Or if he ever did notice, he did not seem to care.

As if to redress the balance, we also had in our Abbey the kindest, most loving man I had ever met. He was six months my junior, and the day he arrived, Brother Vivien put him in my care. We soon became very good friends. His name was Durant and he was the type of man who would likely go unnoticed, except for his stutter. He would take almost forever to say the simplest of sentences, even his own name. His stutter was so bad that when he went to confession, he took all morning to pronounce anything but the preparatory sentences. However, he was blessed with large, liquid eyes, which could speak far more eloquently than his stumbling tongue.

When he prayed or read from the Bible, there was absolutely no trace of his impediment. Moreover, when he sang, there was no hint at all of any stutter. His voice would make the angels jealous. Also, text from any book he laid eyes on, once he had learnt to read, was forever embedded in his mind, to be recalled at a moment's notice, word perfect, without stumbling even once. I have never, before or since, met anyone with a talent such as this. Truly, God had been good to Durant, despite his speech impediment.

Brother Durant was sent to the abbey by his parents, who were embarrassed by the way he spoke. They supposed that no woman would ever fall in love with a man who could not quickly tell her how he felt. Because he was excused from being a confessor, due to his stutter, Brother Aubrey was forever at odds with him, as Aubrey firmly believed that every brother should take his allotted turn in the role.

Most men in the abbey, once they had given up their worldly profession for a godly one, rarely returned to their families or reverted to their previous life. One man who did choose this path was Simon. Before he joined the abbey, he was a soldier for the King, serving him in the Holy Land and in Outremer. He told us that while on his travels, he saw far too much death and destruction to continue in that lifestyle, so, when he returned to his home in England, he decided to enter one of God's houses and become a monk to atone for the many times he had killed while he was a soldier. He told us that during the time he was in Outremer, he met up with a young Welshman, another soldier, whose name he could not remember, but who had also decided to go into one of the orders, near Shrewsbury. This young Welshman had a very quick brain and was very good at solving puzzles. Simon often wondered how this man had fared.

It was after he had been in Buckfast Abbey for a period of nearly three years that Simon discovered that a monk's life was not entirely the right choice for him, so he left the abbey and moved to the nearby village of Essebreton, now known as Ashburton, to marry a woman he had previously known there and to raise a family. Due to his fighting skills, he eventually became the local sheriff's right-hand man. However, he never took up a sword again, preferring to capture wanted felons without undue violence.

CHAPTER TWENTY-ONE

After being in the abbey for a whole year, I took my temporary vows, those of obedience, poverty and chastity and became a novice, no longer a postulant, though not yet a full brother in the community.

There was a time, just over two years after I entered the abbey, when we were all called upon to evacuate the buildings completely and move to higher ground. The nearby River Dart had burst its banks and threatened to wash us away. The rain had been falling quite heavily for three weeks and there was so much moisture in the air that, no matter how we tried, nothing we had would stay dry. Travellers told us that people in the small towns of Widdicombe-in-the-Moor and Ponsworthy had only three days ago escaped from the flooding and had moved their possessions up into caves in the tors, to wait until the floods receded. They had told us of the loss of a few lives to the water and we prayed for their poor, departed souls. It seemed we were likely to be flooded out next.

Abbot Samuel ordered that all the valuable books, relics and other important items were to be placed into a travelling trunk, loaded onto a cart. and taken to a cave in the hills nearby. Those brothers who took the valuables were instructed to set up a small campsite outside the cave to accommodate the rest of us, should it be deemed necessary to leave the abbey for a short time. Those of us left were to continue in our normal routine for as long as we were able. We were told that, as soon as we had any news of the river rising from the next village upstream, we were to gather as many of our common possessions as we could and follow the valuables into the hills. We did not have long to wait.

Early one morning, thankfully just after we finished breakfast, the alarm was raised and we hurriedly gathered up our things and moved into the hills. Thank the Lord, we had a few asses left behind to carry some of the heavier boxes. We stayed up there for eight long, dreary days, sheltering from the incessant rain under trees, in makeshift tents and beneath lean-tos. Because we were getting next to no sleep, we engaged ourselves in praying that the rain would soon stop and the waters would quickly recede without causing too much damage to our home. The abbot had granted us a special allowance for a fire to keep us warm, but while we were in our outdoor accommodation, we had to make do with cold meals, as the wood we had brought with us was too scarce to cook with. There was barely enough to keep us warm. Besides, what new wood we could find and collect was far too wet to light.

When the river had returned to close to its normal levels and the floods receded sufficiently to leave the abbey above the water line, we moved back in, only to find that a layer of smelly mud, about as thick as a man's wrist, had settled everywhere. We spent the next month or so removing the awful stuff. God be praised, our cobbled and paved floors meant that it was relatively easy to remove the mess. Were the floors made of beaten earth, we would never have been able to clean out the muck. Eventually, we were able to return to a normal round of daily life, once the majority of the mud was gone, although every now and again, for six months or so, small pockets of mud would be found in the small rooms and corners that were rarely visited.

The Abbey had survived quite well during the flood, as the foundations were sound and the walls were thick. Several old books that were copies of records of transactions made decades ago and which we did not manage to take with us, had become soaked and destroyed. Some small amount of grain, also left behind, had to be thrown out as it had become sodden and rotted – some of it had sprouted. That which had sprouted we planted in an attempt to prevent waste, but it did not grow well. A few half-full barrels of wine had floated away and been smashed against rocks or trees.

Some slight structural defects had appeared in an old disused outbuilding, as the ground under it had shifted slightly with the water. The old shed had been nothing more than a small lean-to with two brick and stone walls, two wattle and daub walls and a wooden tile roof. The door was barely tall enough for a man to get through. The small building was destined to be pulled down and replaced soon anyway, so we were not overly troubled with the damage to it. Having seen the damage to the shed, we carefully demolished it, so that the remaining bricks and stone could be kept as intact as possible. They would be re-used for the new building that would be put up in its place. We needed a new, larger storeroom for the tools and barrows which we used for our work in the fields.

Apart from these few minor concerns, there was no real damage to the abbey. We all gave thanks to God that our home and our work were safe. We also gave thanks that we could once again sleep comfortably, eat hot meals and be dry and warm.

For the first three or four years I was at the abbey, my father occasionally sent donations and also wrote to me at least three or four times a year. One of the village scribes actually did the writing, as Ranulf had never had the opportunity to learn his letters, although he did know how to recognise and even sign his name. Then one day, when I had just turned eleven, he wrote and told me that life had become difficult in the town. Dry spells, raiding marauders and poor crops meant that the donations were going to have to cease. My father was forced to concentrate on feeding himself and my brother, as well as paying his dues to the earl and the King, rather than giving gifts to the abbey. I could not blame him. I wondered what life would have been like had I stayed in the village, rather than being sent away.

I then realised that I had quite a good life here. I wasn't just doing hard farm work, which could easily be undone by weather. I was working toward lasting results for the Lord. I continued to receive letters from my father, though far less often than before – maybe once or twice a year, if I was lucky.

There were many days for which I was extremely grateful to be alive, but some few days were barely to be tolerated. I looked forward to the day when I turned eighteen and could, at long last, take my final vows and become a full brother in the order. Once that happened, Brother John would – I hoped – finally stop his attacks on my honour.

For the next four or five years I found that I was becoming more and more content with my life amongst the brothers at the abbey. There was very little variety in our day-to-day activities overall, but we never – or very rarely – became bored with our situation. If we ever found ourselves discontented with our lives, we knew that we had forgotten the blessings that our Lord God had given us; the sunshine, the rain, life, doing His work and the ability to laugh at ourselves.

Although I missed my family and friends back home less and less as the years passed, there were times I felt so homesick that I almost ran away to try to find my way back to Portsmouth. Any day that I had those feelings, I went to find Durant and spoke to him about it. He was always able to help me overcome my anxieties with his friendship and prayer. Durant always seemed to me to be a tranquil centre in a mad, whirling world. His calmness was infectious. If you were to spend any amount of time in his presence, he could soon convince you of the truth that the peace of God was readily available to all.

During my time at the abbey, I had indeed grown into a tall man, as I had expected. My strength had increased, but I was more what one would call wiry, rather than brawny. While I would never be able to lift great loads unassisted like my father and my brother, I was no longer a skinny boy. I now had brown hair, my blond locks having gradually darkened, until my head was eventually wreathed in chestnut curls, about the same time that my voice changed from its childhood timbre to a more adult tone.

I was pleased, though not overly proud, of the man that had grown out of the boy I used to be.

CHAPTER TWENTY-TWO

In the May of 1223, about six months before the time of taking my final vows, my tasks began to include regular writing and copying of important wills and other legal documents, as well as the Scriptures. The Scripture pages I copied were to go with other pages, copied by other brothers, to make new Gospels, Psalters and Bibles. I had already learnt to read and write well and had a fairly good hand, although it suffered slightly in neatness, which meant I would only copy Scriptures for smaller projects, such as for our own use or for less important nobles. It was, however, certainly good enough for the legal and official documents, such as wills, contracts and the like. I would never be called upon to copy Scriptures for important people, as my handwriting was simply not good enough for that.

Writing the Scriptures was a new pleasure for me, spreading God's Word to other people who could share it with yet others. This task made me feel as if I was personally writing the Word of God for the very first time – just like the original biblical authors.

During the times when I was engaged in my copying duties, I noticed that there was one particular Book of Psalms – a Psalter – that was always kept under lock and key when not being used. All the other books were left on open shelves. I asked why this one book was kept so and was told that this very special and priceless Psalter had been brought from the Holy Land. The book was a little under a hand span's width, about a span and a half tall and half a span thick. It belonged in its own special locked box. Only a trusted few of the most senior brothers had a key to the box.

This Psalter had jewelled and gilded wooden covers of the

finest lamb-skin vellum. The twelve jewels set into the front cover were the most dazzling emeralds, pearls, amber and sapphires any of us had ever seen. Each chapter was headed with the most breathtakingly colourful and intricate initials, these magnificent illuminations having been created by an ancient order of monks, over two hundred years ago. The pictures of the mythical beasts within the initials were drawn with the most marvellously brilliant blues, reds and greens, along with copious amounts of gold leaf. All the text, in Latin of course, was written in a wonderfully regular and neat cursive hand.

A nobleman who had wished to remain anonymous to those not of our order had travelled to the Holy Land during one of the Crusades, and had brought the Psalter back with him and donated it to the abbey when he died, more than seventy years ago. As he was without family to whom he could leave it, he had promised it to the abbey in exchange for prayers for his soul after he passed away. The Psalter was removed, under the direct care of abbot Samuel and Mannus the prior, from the scriptorium and taken to the chapel four times every year, so that the lay people had the opportunity to pray with this Holy book in their sight. It had been proven to be a very holy item, as so far sixteen people, praying in its presence, had received cures for their deformities and diseases.

Of the three hundred and seventy-eight books in our library, this one book was worth many times more than all the others combined. This worth was not only the monetary value, which was great, but also, more importantly, the religious value. No wonder, then, that such extreme care was taken to ensure its safekeeping.

I asked if I could be allowed to examine the Psalter a little more closely and Brother Daffydd, a Welshman, told me that I could look but I had to keep my hands behind my back. Not many of the brothers were entrusted with handling this Book of Psalms and, as he was one of the very few, he was not about to be responsible for my damaging any of the pages. The beauty and craftsmanship astounded me. I immediately fell in love with this stunning work of art. I so admired it that I was foolish enough to say out loud, in the hearing of Brother John, that I wished that the Psalter belonged to me. I instantly regretted blurting out these words, as I knew that this was covetousness, a deadly sin, but I could not help myself.

I asked pardon from Brother Daffydd, who merely grinned broadly and assured me that, "Almost every postulant who had ever seen the Psalter has reacted similarly." He smiled gently as he instructed me, "Go to work in the pigsty for an hour each day for seven days as penance." I told him that I would. Then, as I looked at Brother John, I noticed that he had a strange gleam in his eye and an oddly satisfied look on his face.

For some reason I could not fathom at that time, over the next few weeks his slandering campaign seemed to increasingly concentrate on me, rather than on anyone else. These things were mostly small. Sometimes, contemptible lies were told to the abbot regarding me. Lies such as the way I was shamelessly flouting some of the order's rules and encouraging others to do the same. It seemed that, no matter how I tried, I could find no defence against these untruths. Then one afternoon, it was discovered that the precious Psalter had gone missing from its locked box! The abbot questioned all the brothers in possession of the keys, but all of their movements and keys could be accounted for. The brothers looked high and low in the scriptorium for the treasured book, but to no avail.

The quest spread to the rest of the abbey, which was turned upside down in the search. Refectory, infirmary, kitchen, chapel, no room was spared. All of the brothers and novices were instructed that every other duty was to be put aside, in order to enable the whole population of the abbey to assist in the hunt for this most precious and Holy book. When this too proved to be fruitless, the abbot had no other choice but to order a search of our dormitories and cells. Some of the brothers sullenly objected, muttering under their breath. These were the only small spaces within the abbey walls where we could go if we wished to be alone and, as such, they felt intensely private. The abbot ordered that the search go on regardless. We started looking through the cells.

Suddenly a cry went up! Fifty gold pieces, in a purse, were found in a cell. My cell. This was more gold coin than most of us could reasonably expect to see in any one place in our lifetimes. I had never seen as much as five gold pieces in a single purse. I could not begin to understand how this great amount of money came to be in my cell.

As soon as the abbot heard about the find, he had me summoned directly to his small office. Once there he questioned me vigorously about the money and I told him again and again that I had no idea how it came to be there. I insisted most strongly upon my innocence. I gave my strongest oath to the abbot that, as a firm believer in Christ and His teachings, I could not – would not – do such a thing. It was all I could do to keep from going mad with fear and anguish. I knew that the abbot had previously heard from Brother John about my foolish wish in the scriptorium. I was unsure as to whether he really believed the story. I fervently hoped he would not.

Brother John had, uninvited and unabashed, followed us into the abbot's office. He rudely interrupted the questioning and proceeded to remind the abbot of how I had coveted the Psalter. He then brazenly accused me of stealing it and selling it to a merchant outside the abbey that morning. He bore witness to the fact that I had done so and, further, said that he himself had actually seen me doing it. He explained to the abbot that due to the abbot's busy schedule, this was the first chance he'd had to tell him about it.

The abbot was shocked, as was I. The outrageousness of the lie stunned me into silence. I could find no voice with which to reply to these outrageous statements. I was struck dumb, as mute as Zachary, the father of John the Baptist, until he had agreed to call his son by that name. In light of my lack of reply, the abbot presumed that I was guilty, as I did not refute the accusations. He told me that he deplored my actions. He further told me that he was deeply disappointed that I, whom he considered an outstanding pupil, should turn out to be so terribly evil.

As it could not be found, the Book of Psalms would have to be considered lost, but the order would use the money found in my cell to help feed the poor, purchase a breeding pair of cattle, buy a new cart and some medicines and rebuild the old grain store. All of which would help the local mission of the abbey. He said that, regardless of the severity of the crime and as this was an Abbey matter, he did not have the inclination to inform the local shire reeve of this appalling act, which would surely bring disgrace upon the House of God and on my father.

By not informing the authorities, the abbot could avoid the scandal of a theft within the abbey walls and the need for a trial and I would not, God be praised, be spending time in gaol, or worse. Besides, the Church took pride in being able to punish its own criminals without perceiving the need to involve the civil authorities.

The abbot also ordered that the scriptorium would have a book made up to look like the Psalter, so that the people would still have an object of veneration. This would not be considered to be lying, as the substitute could be regarded by the brothers as accepting the prayers on behalf of the real Psalter. The abbot had often said, "It is the faith of the people that is the key factor in God's miracles, not merely the object being worshipped. If the people believe strongly enough, the miracles will happen."

What he told me next was to be one of the biggest shocks of my life. While he could forgive me my most grievous sin, I could no longer stay – not merely in Buckfast Abbey, but in any abbey. Not only that, but I would no longer be allowed to take my final vows. I would never be a brother in the order! This final blow to my dreams was too much. I fainted. When I recovered from my swoon, I was escorted to my cell and, at Brother John's insistence, put under guard, lest I should be tempted, in his words, "to try to steal some other priceless treasure."

The next morning, after a sleepless night, I packed what few items I would come to call my own, which were given to me to speed me on my way. They comprised a reasonably new set of clothes to wear, a pair of comfortably fitting boots, a scrip containing a few very small coins, a water bottle, a staff, a second-hand nef, an etui containing a few needles and some linen thread and, of course, my mother's satchel and headband, with some essential items, such as a few days' food and one other change of clothing.

As I prepared to leave, the abbot told me that my father would be told, if he or anyone else ever asked after me, that I had chosen to leave the abbey of my own free will and that the abbey had no idea of my whereabouts. He had ordered that no one outside the walls of this Abbey would be informed that a crime had been committed, not even the Mother Chapter. The method of my reconciliation with my father would be of my own devising. I then proceeded to leave life in the Church forever. I was stricken with grief, but I bravely held back the tears. My faith, while strained, remained strong. I believed that God would surely find a way for me, somehow.

As I was escorted from the inner door to the outer gate, I heard murmuring from the brothers. Almost every one of them openly glared at me – the only one of them who could bring himself to look me in the eye was my young friend Durant. He looked disappointed, as if he had been betrayed. I hoped he did not truly believe the lies about me. As soon as I looked at the faces of any of the others, they turned their heads away and pretended to carry on with their work. Nobody was fooled. Everyone knew what was happening. Gossip in a small community such as this was always rife. They were all thoroughly ashamed of the crime of which I had been accused. I noticed that Brother John was standing, with his arms folded, by the inner door, with an arrogant, self-satisfied grin on his face. He would be finally rid of what he probably thought of as yet one more rival for some of the higher positions in the abbey.

The abbot laid a hand on my shoulder, bade me farewell and spoke a short prayer for my wellbeing. He then watched me walk out of the gate and ordered it shut. It was the last thing I heard him say and the words made my stomach turn to stone. As the gate slammed shut behind me and I walked down the path to the main road, I wondered how in the world John could possibly be content with this horrible outcome – one less brother in the order to do God's work and my good name besmirched forever. How could he have done this? Why did he do this? What could he have gained from this?

What could God's plan possibly be for me that He would allow people like John to deal with me in this way?

CHAPTER TWENTY-THREE

My first thought at the time was to return home to my father and brother. But as I trudged along the road east towards home and the farm, I considered what I would tell them and how they would receive the news. My father would ask, "Why are you coming home instead of staying at the abbey?"

"Because I was expelled for theft," would have to be my sad reply.

I did not relish giving my father that news, nor could I lie to him, though I dreaded that eventually someone from the abbey might one day send word to my father about what had happened. The shame would be unbearable for both my family and I. My father's son, a thief! The thought would quite likely kill him. Home would certainly not be a pleasant place for me to be when and if they ever found out. Not only that, but I could not imagine myself trying unsuccessfully to work the farm with my brother, who would without doubt, resent my being there. I was still, despite my growth and experience, barely able to do the work he would require. He would despise me for taking a part of his share of the farm from him, not to mention the shame of my expulsion from the abbey.

My brother would surely hate me and wish me gone from the place. As I came to that thought, I also came to the conclusion that I could never go home. What an utter shock it was for me to hear myself thinking those words. I knew with a certainty that I had to follow a different path. I would not and could not return home in shame. I decided that as the matter of my supposed crime was not known outside the abbey, why should I soil my character by telling anyone? No one need know. I would not be lying – I just would not mention the matter. Besides which, I knew in my heart that I was falsely accused.

Having decided this, I turned my mind to what I might do. I thought I could become a travelling singer, as I could carry a fair tune. Of course, I would have to learn new tunes and songs, as not many people would pay to hear chant or hymns sung for them. I then thought that I could become a scribe, writing and reading letters for others, or making translations for nobles. I could even teach others to read or write. I had some skill in healing, too. All in all, I knew that I could quite easily make my way in the world, wherever God would take me. So it was that I just started going down the road, not particularly caring where it took me.

After I had been walking for about two hours or so, I chanced upon a small roadside shrine. I had often been taught that time spent in prayer is never wasted; I decided to unburden myself to God. As I knelt, I suddenly began to cry, and so I prayed long and hard for God's guidance and comfort.

Some short time later, while I was still in prayer, I heard a polite cough behind me. I slowly rose, making certain that I had wiped my eyes and nose before I turned around to see a tall, richly dressed man wearing a yellow hat. He had a little bundle in his arms. It looked like a small box wrapped in soft, thin deer leather. I knew him as a merchant in the nearby town. I remembered that his name was Nathaniel and that he was a Jew. There were many Jews in the cities and towns and a small number in a few villages. I remembered that there was one in Portsmouth, whose name I recalled was Benjamin. He had been a money lender, but he was also an excellent fisherman. He had been well-liked by most people in the village. If he noticed my red eyes at all, I hoped he mistook it for fervency in prayer.

Nathaniel lived near Buckfast and was known to have bought and sold all sorts of trinkets, books and, occasionally, some precious items. He also lent money to people who needed it. As I greeted him in God's name, I heard an ass bray gently. I looked over and noticed that there was another man, obviously his servant, holding four asses, each one loaded with many chests and parcels of various sizes.

Nathaniel spoke, "I feel guilty about what has happened, and I would make amends as soon as possible."

I was uncertain what he was speaking of, so I asked of him, "Could you please explain? I am not sure what you mean."

He replied, "You may know that I have connections all over this country, as well as in France and Spain. Brother John contacted me with a proposal to sell a precious item. He regularly made offers of this kind, whether it would be a silver crucifix, a jewelled knife, or some other valuable item. I took Brother John up on this latest offer, as I had done so many times before."

I urged him to continue, and he said, "Brother John had told me that people would die and leave these items to the abbey for the brothers to sell, in order to pay for prayers for the dead."

I did not tell Nathaniel my thoughts, but I did not recall that so many people had passed away leaving these things to us. I wondered if perhaps Brother John may have robbed these people, who were so badly injured that they could not protect their assets. How it was explained that their possessions had disappeared, I could not guess.

The merchant continued, "I had been certain that someone, somewhere, would buy the Book of Psalms – for such is the item – with no questions asked and that I would make a handsome profit over and above the fifty gold pieces I had paid Brother John. In fact, I wondered why he wanted to sell the Psalter for such a low price, given its history and obvious value. On the other hand, who am I to balk at such a bargain? So, once I had acquired this most beautiful Psalter, I very quickly started looking around for prospective buyers for the book, before John changed his mind and wanted more money."

I nearly jumped on Nathaniel to beat him within an inch of his life for being a part of my downfall, but restrained myself and listened to the rest of his story. Besides, I began to wonder about the fifty gold pieces that Brother John had obviously planted in my cell to be discovered. Why was he willing to forego such a large sum, just to have me expelled from the abbey? I again wondered what he had gained by my expulsion and what was his purpose in amassing his fortune – as the brothers in our order are sworn to poverty.

Where was he hiding the money? And where exactly did he acquire the items he sold? These questions arose unbidden in my mind, but I forced my thoughts back to what the merchant was saying.

"I started looking for someone to buy the Psalter," the merchant said, "but I felt strange, as if some strong force, or perhaps my conscience, was preventing me from making such an exchange. I began to suspect that the purchase might not have been as I had originally been told by Brother John. I was on my way to the abbey to return it, when I saw that you were praying by the side of the road and recognised you as one of the brothers from the abbey, even though you were not wearing your habit. I decided to approach you and ask you to return it for me, to save me a half day's journey."

We often went into town dressed in clothing other than our habits, when we did not wish to draw attention to ourselves. I was glad he did not ask me why I was not dressed in my habit. It was too soon for me to formulate a plausible excuse. He then told me that, "In order that I compensate God for what might be some great sin, I would consider the money I had used to buy the Psalter from Brother John as a contribution to the abbey. I realise that fifty gold pieces is a great deal of what you call penance, but I believe that the feeling of relief the donation will bring me would be well worth it."

He went on, "Please inform Brother John that I will no longer require any further items from him, as I believe I have already accepted too much to keep my conscience clear. Besides, I am now going on a pilgrimage to Jerusalem, as every good Jew should, where I will sell everything I have. There are many pilgrims who will pay handsomely for what I have to sell but, once everything is sold, I intend to give half my assets to the poor in order to make my peace with God."

I accepted the Book of Psalms, in its leathern wrappings, expressing my warmest gratitude. After Nathaniel and his man hurried on their way, I started back toward the abbey to return the Psalter, thinking of how I would use the book and the information given to me by Nathaniel to expose Brother John and his wicked schemes. I knew that my faith in God had been rewarded. Hugging the Psalter to my breast as I walked gave me a feeling of comfort, knowing that I would soon be back in the place where I and my father believed I belonged. After I had walked but a short distance, praising God all the while for this unexpected great fortune, I suddenly realised that I would not be able to go back to the abbey with the book, as it would be seen to be proof that I had undeniably stolen it. After all, it was obviously now in my possession.

Surely, if Brother John had his say, as he certainly would, the abbot would not question the idea that I was pretending to be repentant and attempting to gloss over my heinous crime. The fact that I was innocent would never be considered for even a single moment. I therefore made the decision to keep the Book of Psalms to myself, for the time being, and to continue on my way in the wide world. It had, after all, been given to me for safekeeping. While I could prevent it, I would definitely not allow any harm to come to the Psalter. I could read it at my leisure, copy from it and sell the pages I wrote, or simply admire its beauty. It would, I hoped, be well hidden and protected.

I sat down and started to sew the folded leathers in which I had received the book, to the bottom of the inside of my satchel to create a secret compartment. I replaced the wooden board in the bottom of the satchel with the Psalter. Considering the bag's age and the number of repairs to it, the leather was a close enough match for the colour and texture of the old patches not to be commented upon. The book fitted perfectly – almost as if the satchel were deliberately made to house it. I hoped that if things became desperate, God would forgive me if I prised off one of the smaller of the jewels to sell for food or medicines. I earnestly prayed that things would never become so bleak.

Once I had completed the alterations to the satchel, I stood up, slung the bag over my shoulders and started walking. Although I was completely and utterly alone in the world, I felt much happier than I had done since leaving the abbey. Having no clear idea regarding where I should go, I picked a direction at random at the next crossroads and therefore found myself headed towards Salisbury.

CHAPTER TWENTY-FOUR

About a week later, when the sun was starting to drop towards the horizon, I heard the sound of music and singing, the clip-clop of hooves and a jingling of bells behind me. I stopped walking and turned to see what was coming along the road. As the cause of the noise neared, I stepped to one side and watched the approach. I saw that it was a train of three brightly painted wagons, one drawn by two oxen and each of the others by a pair of asses.

I hailed them and when they stopped, I asked as to who they were and where they were heading. I was told by one of the men, "My name is Fynch and we are a troupe of wandering performers who have had enough of the hard times and the cold winters in the north of England and we are moving south to warmer, more pleasant climes. We had heard that there were many good times and abundant riches to be had in the southern towns and cities for such superbly talented players as we are, and therefore, we have come to this part of the country to partake of these bountiful treasures."

Once Fynch had finished speaking, the others with him quickly introduced themselves all at once and began telling me what each of them did within the group. I could not distinguish one speaker from the next, save for the one girl in the group, but I tried to extract as much information as I could from what they said.

It took me a few seconds to accustom my ears to their unusual speech patterns and strange accents, but after listening for a short while I understood them perfectly. They were from England's northern areas, except for the girl, who was Irish.

I thought that their lifestyle might be worth trying for a while, so I asked to be allowed to join them. I told them some of my own journey, leaving out the story of the Psalter, and they were willing to provisionally accept me into their ranks. They introduced themselves again, each in turn this time, and I, in my turn, gave my own name. There were eight of them – four actors, who also had some talent in singing, Fynch, Louth, Thirn and Watt; Hude, a strongman; Aislinn, a dancer and two musicians, brothers, who gloried in the names of Leofric and Leofard. They were all jongleurs, playing music and entertaining in many other ways. As we rode along, Aislinn began to sing and I thought that she had the best voice I had ever heard, rivalling even that of Durant.

As a group of free thinkers, they had no leader, as such. They made decisions by consensus, on which way they should go, where they should stop and what they should do when they got there, although Fynch seemed to hold some fair amount of sway in most discussions. If there was an issue on which they could not readily come to a mutually agreed decision, they drew lots for an answer.

After spending but a few days with them, I ascertained that they were a fairly gruff group of people, given to wrestling and grappling playfully but roughly amongst themselves at any time. However, they were very kind and likeable in their own way. They accepted me for the person I was and treated me well. Not being at all much of a fighter and therefore not well able to defend myself, I tried to keep out of the way of the rowdiest of their bickering.

Over the next few months, I became a little infatuated with the pretty Aislinn. She was two years older than I was, with thick, reddish-blonde hair reaching halfway down her back. Her figure was exquisite and her face quite beautiful. Her bright blue eyes were captivating. While I realised that I was becoming besotted, I knew that I could never consummate any relationship with her. My faith and religious training were far too strong. I was soon able, however, to come to terms with my infatuation and we became firm friends.

Aislinn had a lively brain and was well able to use it to her advantage. She told me that she came from the south of Ireland. She had been captured in a raid as a very young child, taken to York and sold to be a slave to a Danish thegn. He would beat her many times because she would not obey him or submit to his many whims. Two summers ago, he took her with him while he went hunting. Aislinn ran away and travelled on her own until she eventually joined this group. The fact that she had avoided recapture for more than 'one year and one day' meant that, by law, she could remain free – though whether the thegn would observe this law was another matter.

On several occasions since hearing this story, I asked Aislinn the name of this thegn, but she would never tell me. I guessed that she was concerned that someone might find out who he was and then go and tell him in case there was a reward. I did not believe that she had cause to be worried, as the thegn was likely to be a very long way from here. I thought that even if he were told where she was, by the time he reached the place, she would have been long gone. Still, she was extremely wary about revealing the name of this monstrous person.

Aislinn was aware of her appeal, as an attractive and clever young woman, but she did not let this knowledge give her airs. She merely knew her assets. Most men upon whom she set her sights had no chance of escaping her charms, as she quietly and sweetly robbed them blind. It seemed that even after they were stripped of their purses they did not complain. They had got their money's worth, or so she let them believe. Fynch told me that she had an almost magical way of making men believe they were bedding her, though they were not actually doing so, yet having it appear excitingly real.

I made up my mind never to succumb to Aislinn's charms, should she try to seduce me. I knew that as a friend she respected my faith in Our Lord and although she would not admit to it, I believe she shared my faith, or at least had the desire to do so. I came to this conclusion because she constantly questioned my beliefs. She would ask who Jesus was, why He should have died for our sins, why I had faith in God and many other similar enquiries. She had been to church on occasion but had received no formal education regarding what happened there. She seemed to believe there was something grandly mysterious about the Christian faith. I judged that this gave me some defence against her allure. Thanks be to God, she never once tried to get me into her bed, nor did I ever try to get her into mine. Perhaps we both understood that it would be an unsuccessful venture – either that or she honoured my earlier life in the abbey.

Fynch was not a tall man. In fact, I was taller than he. But he was well-built. I would not fancy a wrestling match with him. Not only was he far stronger than me, but he had much experience in the art of wrestling. He was brown haired, with hazel eyes and a personable character.

Although they were slightly different in looks, Leofric and Leofard always dressed the same as one another. If one wore blue or red, so did his brother. While Leofric had dark brown hair with green eyes, Leofard had red hair and blue eyes. They would often finish each other's sentences when they talked, which was somewhat disconcerting at times. They had been born within a year of each other, with Leofric being the elder. There was no noticeable domination of one over the other; they seemed merely to come to a mutual agreement on any choice they made.

Louth, Thirn and Watt were rather quiet, self-contained men. They originally hailed from near Turuoldesfeld – what we now call Thursfield – in Staffordshire. They were older than the rest of the troupe by several years. They only came out of their shells when they performed. Apparently, they had been part of another, larger troupe which had suffered a tragic accident some years ago. It was while coming back across the Irish Sea that their boat had sunk in a storm, close to England, losing all their equipment, as well as all the people on board but these three. After they had swum to shore, they tried to start again with just the three of them but were unsuccessful. They eventually met up with Fynch and his small band and had been with them ever since. I was never able to get a proper description from them of the make-up of their old group. They refused to discuss them. They told me, "Those people are dead. Why disturb their ghosts with unnecessary chatter?" When I told Fynch what they said, he shrugged and told me that these men had had some bad experiences while in Ireland and preferred not to discuss it. There we let the matter lie.

Sitting around the campfire at night, after our shows or between towns, was the best time to find out more about my new-found companions. They would weave their various tales, some were humorous, some were wild, most were highly embellished fictions. These stories kept us all entertained and laughing long into the night. While I inwardly disapproved of their actions in some of these stories, I was wise enough to keep my mouth closed. It was not for me to be seen to judge these people. I kept my thoughts to myself, as it seemed a good idea not to offend my companions.

Hude, the strongman, was a huge mountain of a man. His arms were as large as most men's legs. His hair was blond, but he had a red beard and moustache. For the shows, he often dressed only in a pair of wolf skins, sewn together and hung over one shoulder, with a wide belt around his waist keeping the pelt in place to preserve his dignity. The rest of the time he wore green hose and a variety of tunics of diverse colours and materials, all made in different countries. He kept all of us laughing with stories of his dealings with women acquaintances in many towns all over the country and abroad. He was the only member of our troupe who had travelled overseas, if you do not count Ireland. Hude had been born in Germany and moved all over France, Austria, Spain, Flanders and many other countries besides. Due to his height and magnificent physique, women considered that he was far and away the most handsome man of our troupe and he seemed to attract a bevy of lovely young women in just about every village we visited. He spoke a nearly undecipherable mixture of German and English and would relate tales of his exploits with the beauties he had met on his travels and the children some of these women claimed he had sired.

Over the next year or so, the group toured the country, playing in towns such as Gloucester, Bath, Dover, Colchester, Winchester and even London. We were casually naming glorious townships and cities, of which I had previously only heard from travellers, as though they were nothing more than the local tavern we were visiting. It was very seldom that we were not welcomed in any town to which we went. Most places were quite happy to have us bring them entertainment. Travelling minstrels were often the only amusement towns and villages ever saw. They were also the main source of news from other regions of the land.

Some of our plays were religious – which I often recognised from my time reading in the abbey, some humorous, quite a few were rather bawdy. Nearly all were new to most of our audiences. Nonetheless, there were always one or two plays or songs that were familiar to somebody in any town we entered. Sometimes we would learn new songs from resident bards in villages or make them up ourselves along the way from one place to another. In this way our repertoire was expanded. Almost every town or village had their own local songs for us to learn.

I had taught the group the monastic method of writing music using numes – a system devised about a hundred years ago by a monk named Guido to enable his students to learn and write new music, making the learning of the chants we used easier. When I had been at the abbey, I had soon learnt that each space and line on the music page represented a different note and that the shape of the notes on this page meant different timings and voice techniques. This made our writing of new songs, as well as some of the older ones in our range, more convenient.

There was one tiny village we passed through, which I shall not name as I do not wish to add unwarranted fame to such a narrow-minded place, where we were chased away. The fields surrounding this hamlet looked extremely poorly husbanded, so we didn't think we would get much of in the way of donations here as there were only a few ramshackle buildings erected around a small chapel. I mentioned in passing that most of them desperately needed re-thatching, although Hude expressed the opinion that burning them down would be a better way to go.

However, we decided to treat these people to a small demonstration of our talents, as we considered that they might need some cheering up. As usual, we entered the town singing and playing our instruments, with Aislinn following behind, dancing to the tunes played by the group.

A small crowd had soon gathered – mostly men, thanks mostly to the barely hidden charms of Aislinn – and they watched us intently as we moved seamlessly from singing and dancing to juggling and acrobatics to presenting our chosen play for the day, while one or two who were unoccupied in entertaining unhitched the oxen and asses.

The local priest had come along too, to see what sort of show we were putting on for his small flock. He was a scrawny creature; his hair was in a mess and long overdue for a trim. He looked as if he had not had a decent meal for far too long. His robes, if that was what they were, appeared to be made of a rough sacking material and must have been very uncomfortable. He obviously wanted to show that he was an extremely pious person. We decided to keep an eye on him. We thought he might be trouble later.

We had been entertaining for the best part of an hour and a half in total and were about halfway through the show. The play we had decided upon for that day concerned a lover and his lass and her mother and father. I confess it was somewhat bawdy. We had reached the part of the play where the young lad 'mistakenly' gets into bed with the father. Suddenly, the priest took offence to what the actors were doing on the stage.

He jumped up from his seat on a small log, berated us all loudly, calling 'spawns of the devil!' and telling us to take our 'filthy, heathen exhibition elsewhere'. He assured us that they neither want nor need that sort of disgusting display in their village and told us in no uncertain terms that we should be ashamed of ourselves. Then, by the simple expedient of swinging his staff wildly at the village men, he exhorted them to leave, which they did very quickly. He continued swinging his staff, all the while shouting, "Get back to work, you lazy, idle good-for-nothings!" until there was not a single villager left in sight. He then commenced to attack each of us in our turn with his rod, as we hurriedly packed our equipment back onto our wagons.

"Get out of here!" he cried, "Get out! God forbid we should ever see your like here again."

We tried, with some small measure of success, to defend ourselves from him, but continued to gather our goods and chattels. We found that it was rather difficult to pack efficiently when someone was pounding on your back with a heavy stick. Hude became increasingly incensed at our treatment by this thin man. He growled and started angrily towards the priest, obviously with a view to engaging him in a one-sided fight. We all shouted frantically at him. "Stop, Hude! No! Do not attack him, we will leave peacefully." Had we not stopped him, I am sure that Hude would have picked up the little man and snapped him in half, in much the same way that he broke thick wooden planks in our shows.

Disappointed that he could not hurt the nasty little man, he satisfied himself with snatching the priest's stick from his hand and breaking it into several short pieces, whereupon the priest staggered back some distance in dismay. He would not approach us any closer than he thought safe, but stayed within shouting range and continued to harass us vocally. We hurriedly hitched up the animals, boarded our wagons and left as rapidly as we could, the priest quoting scripture after scripture at us the whole time. He even followed us as we went along the road, screaming at us, calling us all kinds of horrible names, throwing any stones he could wield, invoking from God the damnation of our souls, until we were well clear of the place.

As we left the village far behind us, we suddenly realised that we had not yet taken our collection, as we usually conducted that little piece of business at the very end of our performances. We laughed uproariously at ourselves for this oversight and knew well that we should give it up as a lost cause. We would make no profit from this village.

We made certain that we never called into that particular place ever again.

CHAPTER TWENTY-FIVE

As many months passed and we travelled the road, visiting countless towns and villages, I shared my gift of reading and writing with the troupe, in exchange for learning some of their talents. I was able to learn lots of new songs – some that were not even slightly religious in nature – several dances, and how to play different musical instruments. Alongside these skills, I had need to learn to fight, for the sake of our plays. Thus it was that I again became able to use a bow. It had been a long time since I'd had one in my hands. Abbeys have no great need for archers. Thankfully, for the plays, appearance – not accuracy – was the issue. Besides, we used blunted arrows and very light powered bows.

I could wield a sword too, after a fashion. Likewise, swordplay was required in some scenes of our plays. I also learned a little of the art of the pugilistic encounter, at least well enough for our scripted performances, though I knew I would never become well able to defend myself in any real violent encounter. All of our stage fights were very carefully choreographed and rehearsed. I soon knew to a nicety when each stroke or blow was to come and from which direction, so that I could place my sword or shield into the path of the weapon or fist or dodge myself away from it.

I also acquired the ability to juggle three items at once and practiced a little sleight-of-hand. I found that juggling small balls was the easiest for me, while the others used clubs, axes and other items. I could recite, from memory, the lines of many characters from at least fifteen different plays. My mental training at the abbey came in handy for this. While there, I'd had to learn many prayers and Bible verses by heart, before I learned to read. Over time, my knowledge of the world of the theatre began to expand.

I came to the realisation that not everything bad that happens had to remain bad. Brother John was the cause of my leaving the abbey, which I had thought of as most terrible at the time. But, had he not done what he had, I would never have met these wonderful people and learned all the things I now know. I realised that I had to forgive Brother John for his actions, even if I could never tell him so. I found it easy to do. I constantly included him in my prayers each night from the day that I came to this realisation. Without intending to do so he had done me a great favour, inadvertently ensuring that my education had broadened.

In order to help pay my way with the troupe, as well as teaching them their letters and music, I assisted with the erecting of tents, the gathering of wood and water, tending their wounds and injuries, carrying all sorts of loads and collecting donations from the crowds that came to see our shows. Occasionally, I appeared in some few of these performances in various guises, often wearing a mask that showed which character I played. I particularly enjoyed acting out these masked parts. They gave me a freedom I had never known before. I could say and do things while wearing a mask that I would never have dared to do outside of the playacting. I soon lost some of my inhibitions through this role-play.

One day, while we were in Canterbury, I was involved in a mock swordfight as part of the play we were performing. Suddenly, our swordplay was interrupted by a drunken thug, who obviously decided that the acting was not real enough for him. He drew his own short sword, jumped onto the stage and started roaring with laughter and swinging his weapon at me and anyone else within reach. As I was not a very skilled swordsman, while I was vainly attempting to parry his hefty strokes, the brute struck me hard with the flat of his sword, breaking my fingers. I fell to the floor in pain, clutching my hand.

The remainder of the troupe, once they recovered from the shock of this intrusion, were able to subdue the man and remove him from the stage. I learned, long afterwards, that Hude and a couple of the others had subsequently sought out the thug later that night in the village, beaten him senseless and left him outside an inn to be found by his friends. The next morning, I guided Aislinn's and Leofric's hands in the treatment of my injuries, but it took several weeks for my fingers to heal.

Once my hand had healed, I discovered that, while I could still do most of the things as well as I could previously, my writing ability had suffered greatly and my script now looked like a drunken hen had wandered through the ink. However, I knew that I was still able to teach people to write. I also discovered that I could no longer lift heavy objects with this hand. After this incident, I thought that perhaps it was high time I left the troupe. I began to long for the fellowship of people who were more refined than these rough troubadours. Please do not misunderstand me! I am not haughty. I was well aware of the worst of the seven deadly sins – pride.

I knew that my own situation did not allow pride to take much of a role in my life. Besides, my faith required that I love my fellow man as myself and I did. I loved these people as I would my own family. They did, after all is said and done, save me from a lonely, uninteresting and, quite likely, very short life after I left the abbey. However, my travelling companions had rather a rough and tumble manner, liable to become involved in tavern brawls at the slightest provocation. I had decided that, after the sword fight episode, I could not risk remaining with them for much longer, in fear of becoming embroiled in some more dangerous situation from which I might not be able to extricate myself without serious injury. Worse still, I might have the precious Psalter discovered and taken from me. If there was any thought that I might have stolen it, I could end up in gaol or, God forbid, murdered for the value of it.

It took several weeks for me to finally make up my mind to leave the troupe and to concoct a story to tell them when I did find the opportunity to leave. Once I had made this decision, I travelled for only a few more weeks with the company, taking great care to avoid trouble for both myself, and the troupe. I had no wish to have my secret exposed at this late stage.

In the latter half of June, just after we had entered Dorchester on our way towards London again, the company were sympathetic enough when I told them that I'd had enough of travelling. I told of my relatives here and desire to stay with my cousins until I could find a position of work and a place of my own to live in. As my hand was now as healed as it was likely to become, finding work should not take me too long. This story was a blatant falsehood. I had no family in Dorchester of which I was aware, but they seemed not to discern the lie. I was certainly not about to tell the troupe that I no longer desired their company. While this was somewhat nearer to the real reason I was leaving, I would not think of hurting their feelings in this way – or any other. For the many kindnesses they had shown me, they deserved much better than to be insulted in that way.

While they were disappointed that I would be leaving, they gave me a sharpened short sword in its scabbard as a parting gift. It was more like a very large knife; light. They laughingly warned me about slicing off bits of myself. They also gave me a short bow and some arrows in a small quiver. With these, they took the opportunity to have another gentle attack on my trifling skills. I was warned by Leofard and Leofric to aim carefully when shooting at rabbits, lest the arrows became stuck in the clouds. I laughed with them for the joy they took in their friendly mirth and prayed that their journey would continue to be safe and prosperous.

They allowed me to take some of the musical instruments we had made along our journeys and with which I had acquired a small amount of skill at playing. I was permitted a variety of sizes of fipple flute, a small tambour and a shaum. As well as these, they allowed me to keep some copies of the musical manuscripts I had made for them of the many tunes we had written and learnt along the roads. All these musical items were contained within a small wooden case, purposely designed to keep them safe from breakage.

Fynch presented me with a leather purse containing a small amount of money. He told me that I had earned it several times over and that this money was to help pay my way until I had earned enough to properly support myself. After he and everyone else had shaken my hand and bade me farewell, Aislinn hugged me firmly, kissed me for quite a few seconds on the lips and told me that she would miss me terribly. These actions and her comment drew forth a ribald cheer and many comments from the rest of the group and a red face from me. They wished me well, mounted their wagons and went laughingly on their merry way, calling, "God be with you!", "Take care!" and "Godspeed!" waving to me as they went off down the road. In all, it was nearly one and a half years that I had enjoyed travelling with the players.

I waited until after they were well out of sight, then I started travelling towards Wimborne Minster, in the private hope of being allowed to enter another monastery or abbey. I had not told the group that I decided to attempt to re-enter the priesthood. I would adopt a new identity with a new name and a new life history. After all, nobody in that part of the country knew who I was. I was not going to let my past keep me homeless for long.

As I made my way, it struck me that I had seen less of the country than I would have liked. I decided that I would spend some time wandering on my own while I had the chance, and somehow acquire more money so that I might attempt to buy my way into an order. I knew that I had skills that could earn me this money and I could – if necessary – beg for meals. I had no compunctions in this regard and had already done so while travelling with the Brothers from the abbey. I preferred not to sell or destroy the precious Psalter in order to pay my way into another order, if at all possible. I would continue to hide it in my satchel unless there were no other viable option.

I changed the direction of my footsteps and headed north. I wanted to see Wales. I had heard that there were many beautiful places there, and I was going to see them. I was also told that the Welsh had a different style of singing, which I wanted to hear and, possibly, to learn. Once I had seen Wales, I would then choose another direction for myself. I hoped that God would, as always, be good to me and keep me – and the Psalter – safe from harm and trouble.

CHAPTER TWENTY-SIX

One day, early in September in the year of our Lord 1226, not long after I had spent the anniversary of my birth alone for the very first time in all my twenty years, the sun was nearing the horizon. I had travelled widely and found myself walking along a narrow path which wound through a bushy, wooded area in the approach to a small town.

I had been travelling alone for a year or more. Occasionally, a kind person in a small village or hamlet had allowed me to sleep under cover, but for most of the time I had been sleeping under the sweet-smelling green trees and God's blue sky. I had acquired a large, oiled cloth and two woollen blankets which I used as cover and bedding for those inclement nights I could find no other shelter.

I had collected together nearly five pounds in coin from my singing and writing abilities. At this rate, I might be able to buy my way into a monastery by the time I was sixty, if by the grace of God I should live so long. But I still had hopes that better fortunes might one day come my way.

I had been to the Western Marches, through into Wales and to the shores of the sea between Britain and Ireland. That was a very rugged coast, with winds blowing strongly constantly. The countryside there, through which I had travelled, was quite wild but very beautiful. Thanks be to God, I had seen no sign of bandits or other marauders in that part of the country.

The Welsh language was wonderfully incomprehensible, though it sounded as if they were singing even when they were merely speaking. Their intonation – the lilting rising and falling of their voices – was a joy to the ear. There were charming vocal sounds that had no parallel in my mother tongue. Their singing style was indeed not far different from what I had learned in the abbey or with the troubadours. I was successful in learning some of it, but decided that I was more comfortable with what I already had.

Very few men in Wales had the skill of writing. I was able to learn very few written words of that language, however, and was equally unsuccessful in learning to speak many words. I did learn that any place name beginning with "Llan" means that a saint is venerated there, though which saint is any Englishman's guess – as they have their own versions of the names of the saints. To give one example, Mary, the blessed mother of God, is known in Wales as "Fair," and that is pronounced "vire." Therefore, Saint Mary is known as "Llan Fair" in Welsh. Is it any wonder then, for the most part, that the Welsh and the English do not get along peacefully, when one cannot understand the speech of the other?

I had also travelled north of that great wall built by the Roman emperor, Hadrian and had seen some of the highlands and lowlands of Caledonia, which is now called Scotland. That was a bleak place, beautiful in its way, but the weather was terrible. Every day I was there the rain fell continually. I barely saw the sun. I was glad to return to England.

At any rate, now that I had seen the lovely green country of Wales and the dark foreboding lands of the Scots, I returned to England and was back in Dorset, on the southern coast, taking my time in heading towards Kent. I had been told that holy marvels had occurred there, though of what sort no one could give me the least idea. I decided to find out for myself. As I walked, I enjoyed the odours and colours of the open countryside and the pleasant weather to be had in these summer months. I could hear a brook bubbling along, off to one side of the path, so I decided that I should refill my water flask as it was nearly empty. As I made my way through the prickly bushes, I thought I heard something – or someone – cry out, just to my right. It was not very loud – the noise was just barely audible. I stopped, drew my small sword and held it in front of me, more for show than for any real protection it would afford me. I called out to discover who or what was making the noise.

I said, "Is someone there? I have no money for you to steal. Hallo? Who calls?" I was wary of my safety, as bandits were known to be in the area. I had already heard of lone travellers being accosted by these rogues. Whoever it was called out again, this time a little louder, but raspingly as if in great pain. Well aware of my own fears and still brandishing my sword, I pushed my way through the thin shrubbery and discovered a youngish man, about my age, lying on the ground, covered in blood. What I presumed were his possessions were scattered around. His face was covered in bruises, with one eye completely closed due to swelling and his left leg at an odd angle. I could tell by his style of dress that he was a nobleman, or at least fairly rich.

He coughed painfully and I quickly sheathed my useless sword, knelt by his side and examined him. I said to him, "Pax tecum, my name is Rolf. I have some skill in healing, and I will do what I can for you."

As I looked him over, I told him everything I was doing, mostly to set his mind at ease, but also to assure myself that I missed nothing of importance in my examination. Once I had opened his shirt, I could see that he was bleeding from several knife wounds to his chest, arms and abdomen. He was thoroughly bruised and battered. I discovered that the wounds were only skin-deep, but two or three of his ribs had been broken. An ugly bruise was growing before my eyes over the breaks. I could do nothing about them for now, with what little resources I had with me at the time. The visible growth of the bruise told me that the attack on this man had been a very recent event.

One of the biggest and most urgent dangers was a stab wound to the inside of his left thigh. The cloth of his leggings was cut and I could see the gaping wound. The blade had obviously punctured a major blood vessel, as a large pool of blood had started collecting underneath his leg and was spreading fairly rapidly. I immediately leaned on the wound, which eventually stopped the gushing blood. While holding the wound closed, I examined the rest of his leg; God be praised, there was nothing that appeared broken and I smelled no infection.

I told him, "I am going to straighten your leg." He nodded his understanding and groaned a little as I gently did so, but when I had moved the leg, he told me that he felt a little more comfortable. I pulled out a tunic from my satchel, the cleanest I had and packed the wound with it, tying it on tightly so that, eventually, the bleeding stopped completely.

In order to try to keep him calm while I was doing this, I asked him to tell me a little about himself – his name and that of his father, for example. Amongst other things, he told me that his name was Geoffrey and, "I be on my way to Puddletown to be presented to the King's Chief Justiciar, Hubert Walter, to be elevated to the rank of knight."

I noticed that he omitted to tell me the name of his father. In order to reassure him, I said, "I know of Hubert Walter. He is a large man with the eyes of an eagle. He visited a place where I had been staying, several years ago. He had then been presiding over a court, in the name of the King, to deal with a crime of theft and one of destruction of a large amount of property. If my memory serves me correctly, he was at that time Archbishop of Canterbury. Now be silent and let me treat you."

"I do not doubt your skills," he replied. "However, I know how severe my leg and chest injuries are and I do doubt that I will live to see my father again, nor shall I see my knighthood ceremony come to pass."

I replied, "I am certain that, with proper treatment, you will soon be sturdy enough to continue your journey and you will yet become a knight and a good strong one, no doubt." I then chastised him gently, smiling as I said, "You should have no need to fear. I am quite certain that my meagre healing abilities will keep you alive, at least until we can get better help for you in the nearby town."

The young man laughed darkly, coughing up some bright, frothy blood. That sign immediately told me that he had quite likely punctured a lung with one or more of his broken ribs. Geoffrey probably knew as well as I did that he would soon die, and very painfully, if I could do nothing that would prevent it. I had to act extremely quickly. I told him to try to relax for a few moments while I made a quick search for some healing herbs. I assured him I would return as soon as I could. He nodded his understanding and I ran to the trees and swiftly began my search. I looked around for and quickly found some trillium, feverfew and evening primrose.

Once I had these few plants, I decided that I had spent more than enough time searching. I would make do with these, as they would stop the bleeding, ease his pain and prevent infection when made into a poultice and applied to his wounds. I quickly returned to him and treated him as best I could, using my knife to cut up strips from my spare clothing to use as bandages to tie the poultice and prevent his ribs from moving too much.

Once I had done this, I asked him, "How did you come to receive these injuries?"

He replied, "We were ambushed by several men not over an hour ago. My servant and I tried to fight them off, but I was cut on my leg and hit in the face with the edge of a shield and I fell under the attack. I have no recollection of anything that happened after that. I do not know where my man is or whether he lives or has died."

I spoke reassuringly, telling him, "Do not worry about your man just now. Your recovery is the most important thing. He might be uninjured and looking for you as we speak. We will search for him later. I am going to fetch water. Try to be at ease until I return. I shall be very quick." I ran to the nearby brook to bring a small amount of water for him to drink and to clean him. While on the way to the brook, I tripped over a dead man's body behind a bush. It was only by grabbing at a small tree that I prevented myself from falling flat on my face. I guessed that the man was either one of the attackers slain or the nobleman's servant. I would ask later. The living needed tending first.

By the time I had returned to Geoffrey, he had lost consciousness, but I continued my ministrations anyway. While doing so, I kept talking to him, telling him what I was doing as though he could hear me. I had been told, while working in the abbey infirmary, that people who were unconscious sometimes do hear the speech of those who minister to them.

Once I had finished treating him as best I could, I collected together what things I could find, whether they may have been his or not. Then, using my sword as an axe, I cut down four long saplings and constructed an 'A' frame – a trepalium – so as to be able to transport him to the nearest town. We had occasionally used these trepaliums in the abbey to carry heavy loads when a horse and cart were not to hand, or were not practical. Large loads are manageable even when only one person is available to do the carrying. A relatively weak person is able to transport much more weight on a trepalium than he could do by carrying it on his back. I had padded this one as much as I could with what cloth I could find, to prevent too much bumping as I carefully moved him along the track.

Dusk had fallen by the time I could see the houses of the town and I began calling loudly for help. I kept calling until some people came to see what the noise was about. We attracted considerable interest from the populace. A few people relieved me of the trepalium and pulled it the rest of the way into the town. I explained how and where I had found him, asked the location of the nearest inn to which I could take my patient and asked for the village physician to be sent for, if there was one. I found out that this village was known as Affpuddle, which I knew to be close to Puddletown.

Arriving at the inn, some of the town's folk gently lifted the man from the trepalium and, with the help of the innkeeper, the unconscious Geoffrey was put to bed and I was taken to the ale room and told to wait there for the physician and the bailiff.

Very shortly afterwards, the local bailiff arrived and asked me for details of where the nobleman was found and in what condition. The bailiff assured me that I was under no suspicion of causing this man's injuries. In fact, I was to be commended for treating him and bringing him here. Anything I could tell the bailiff would be helpful in finding out what happened to the young man.

I answered as best I could and the bailiff then rounded up some men, lit some torches and went to search the forest for any possible clues as to the identities of the attackers and to recover the body of the dead man. I told them, "All you have to do is follow the trail of scratch marks made by the trepalium and you will easily find the place."

Just as the bailiff and his party left the village, the physician arrived at the inn. His name was Ælfric and he was quite the oldest person I had ever seen. He beckoned for me to go with him to see the patient. I followed the physician into the bedroom and we saw that Geoffrey had awakened. The physician examined the young man thoroughly, asking many questions regarding what he felt here and there. He made a few notes in a small book, which he carried on a strap, hanging from his belt.

Ælfric then administered some sort of cordial from a phial he took from his bag, saying it would make the man sleep for some time and therefore aid in the healing process. When he had finished his inspection, we left the room and the physic commented favourably on the treatment I had given him, which he said had quite likely saved his life. He asked about the poultices I had placed on Geoffrey's wounds, as he had noticed a familiar smell. I told him which plants and herbs I used, whereupon the old man made notes of the things I had told him in his little book. It seemed to me that he may never have heard of using those herbs in that way. Or perhaps he was merely feigning ignorance and trying to determine my level of competence.

When the physic had finished with these questions, I was taken back downstairs and into the alehouse and shown to a seat where I could eat, drink and talk. We sat for a while, over a table of food and drink, exchanging information and discussing my medical treatments and training. Ælfric told me that he had been the only physician in this town since his old master died fifty-eight years ago. He had been training under him and travelling the country with him since he was six years of age. The old physician had been forty-six when he was first apprenticed to him and had died at the age of sixty-four.

When his old master had died, Ælfric returned to Affpuddle, as it had been his hometown. The old man was now eighty-two. I was amazed that a man could be so old. For all that I knew, none of the brothers back at the abbey had ever reached that age.

For my part, I told him about my life back in Portsmouth and in the abbey, leaving out the reasons that I had left and moving on to some of my merry adventures with the troupe of performers, as well as the not so happy times I had spent travelling alone. He appeared to have a few doubts about my story and then told me that he had some small powers of foreseeing. I, for my part, must have appeared rather sceptical, as he immediately sat bolt upright, made some odd, quick movements with both hands and stared at me with a strange look in his eyes. I felt as if someone had taken hold of my head and squeezed slightly. My eyes unfocused and for a moment I could not move a muscle. All I was able to do was breathe and stare. When the feeling had passed, the old man smiled and told me that I had a secret to keep hidden. He said there was something about a very important book which would play a significant role in my life.

Knowing within myself that he must have meant the Psalter, though not wishing to mention it, I asked him to elaborate, but he just smiled and advised me to keep my secret to myself. He told me that all would be revealed to whoever needed to know, at the appropriate time. I no longer had any doubts about his claimed ability.

I foolishly asked him to reveal some more of my future, as I was eager to find out what was likely to happen to me, but he refused any further demonstrations of this peculiar talent. As he said, "It tires me too much at my advanced age. Besides, if God had wanted you to know what was going to happen in your life, He would have ensured that you would already know what it was."

After which, he would say not one word more about this strange gift of his.

CHAPTER TWENTY-SEVEN

We talked well into the night and – I am embarrassed to say – I
fell asleep on the table in the middle of our conversation. I
had, after all, quite a day. The nobleman was my first major injury
patient since leaving the abbey. I had treated some small cuts, bruises
and the like while travelling with the troupe, as well as advising on
how to treat my own broken hand, but nothing until now had been
anywhere near as serious as Geoffrey's life-threatening wounds.

I supposed that Ælfric must have seen to it that the innkeeper
or one of the servants had helped put me to bed, because when I
awoke the next morning, I was in a room of my own. After rising
from my bed, my first thought was for my belongings – especially
my satchel and the Psalter. I need not have worried, as they were
safely placed on a chair beside the bed. I guessed that Ælfric placed
them there for me. While I appreciated having the instruments and
the pages of music in their little case, I was much more concerned,
naturally, for the Psalter. As closely as I could inspect it, I could not
determine that anybody had tried to open my satchel or interfere
with it in any way. The secret of the Book of Psalms was still safe.

Late last evening, after I had fallen asleep, the bailiff had brought
back the dead man and had him put in a safe place until Geoffrey
could say whether the body was that of his man. I supposed he
would be tossed into an unmarked grave if he proved to be part
of the bandit gang. The bailiff told us that three other bodies were
also found, but that they were familiar to the area. They had all been
found with various injuries suggesting a protracted sword fight.
The people of the village were not sorry to find that these men

were dead. They were known to be part of a gang of murderers and bandits. All who saw their bodies supposed that they had died fighting with or against the dead man the bailiff had brought back.

It was proposed by Ælfric and agreed to by the bailiff, that I should remain with Geoffrey to watch over him and the few belongings he had left, while a message was sent to nearby Puddletown, so that Geoffrey's people would know he was still alive and to give them the reason that he would be delayed in his arrival. This arrangement had the added benefit of giving me access to food and drink and somewhere dry and warm to sleep. I think that Ælfric had guessed that I might have needed the rest, as I had been on the road for many months, sleeping in fits and starts in all sorts of weather, on a mostly inadequate diet.

Two days later, I was at Geoffrey's bedside when he awoke, coughing. I told him that he should not try to speak too much for a few minutes. I told him where he was and reassured him that he would indeed recover and then moistened his lips with a small quantity of watered wine. I very slowly increased the small amount of liquid I gave him until he could comfortably drink from a cup on his own without choking. When he was finally able to speak without difficulty, he asked my name and we eventually became engaged in a lengthy discussion regarding my part in his rescue and recovery. He seemed not to remember the conversation we had while I was treating him when I found him.

I asked him about the dead man, describing his clothing and appearance. Geoffrey asked that I help him sit up and that we have the man brought in for identification. The body was put on a stretcher and carried in. It turned out that the man was indeed Geoffrey's servant. He also happened to be his cousin on his mother's side. The man had been in his employ for more than twelve years. They had grown up together, not just as master and servant, but also as playmates and friends.

As you would expect, Geoffrey was upset over the loss of his long-time companion. It was at this point that he asked for a messenger to be sent to take word to his family that he was still alive and on his way to Puddletown. He was informed that a boy had already been sent on this errand.

We continued talking together. Geoffrey thanked me for what I had done and asked about my life's journey. I told him just about everything. I felt that we could trust each other, although while I would not lie to him, I still did not tell him about the Psalter hidden in my pack. I was obviously not an accomplished liar, as I think he suspected that I was holding something back, but he did not press the issue for which I thanked God. I believe he was simply trying to discover what sort of character I had – whether I was helping him out of duty, self-interest or true pity. I hoped he understood that I would have done the same for any man, not just a rich one.

After a period of about ten days, Geoffrey told us that he felt that he should be able to continue his journey. He had met with one of his father's servants who had brought news from his family that they were sending a carriage to take him on to his appointment. The next day, the small carriage arrived. Several men helped Geoffrey out to it and loaded him on it. He asked me to stay at the inn – at his expense – and to await a message from him. I told him that I would obey his wishes. I had no idea what was in store for me at the hands of this young man, but I stayed in that village. There was nowhere else I needed to go, besides which, I was being fed and housed at someone else's cost. If there was to be a financial reward, this might help me get into some monastery or other. I might not even have to pay for the privilege – Geoffrey's family may ease the way for me by recommending me to whatever order ran an abbey near their demesne. I would wait and see. I stayed in Affpuddle for over two weeks before I next heard from Geoffrey.

After this time, a page arrived, announcing himself as one of Geoffrey's household. He brought good tidings of Geoffrey, saying that he had been doing well in his recovery. He explained, "I have business to conduct here and when that has been concluded, I am to wait with you until word comes from my master. In the meantime, I am to ensure that you are instructed in the basic etiquette of court."

Every afternoon for the next two weeks, he and I spent time

together, refreshing my memories of correct courtly manners and relearning who was who in courtly circles. We were both pleased to discover that I had not forgotten too much whilst in the company of the players, so my lessons were not tedious for either of us.

While I waited at the inn, Ælfric came to talk with me daily. We continued to exchange remedies, treatments and stories. I also helped him in his work as a healer. Regardless of how often I asked, he would not tell me anything further regarding my future. As he said, "If you knew too much about your future, you might change it and then it would be a waste of my time telling you about it in the first place." What he would tell me, however, was all he knew about many places to which I had never been. As he was well travelled, he knew about many towns and villages all over the country. He would regale me with tales of faraway places that I could only hope to see one day. While listening raptly to Ælfric, I also wondered what would happen to me when I met up again with Geoffrey. Would he reward me, and if so, how? Would it be in riches, lands, entry to an order, or in some other way? Oh, how I wished that I had Ælfric's gift of foreseeing.

One evening, fifteen days after the arrival of the page and nearly two months after I had first dragged Geoffrey into Affpuddle, another page came to me, wearing a tabard which I recognised as Geoffrey's livery. I was told that I was to accompany him to Puddletown. There, I would receive my reward for saving Geoffrey's life.

No matter how many times I asked, he would tell me no more until we reached our destination.

CHAPTER TWENTY-EIGHT

arly the next morning, we started travelling by coach. Although I had seen many before and had even glimpsed the inside of a few, this was my first time riding in such luxury. The seats were leather with soft padding and covered with the softest, deepest sheepskins I had ever seen. It was much more comfortable than riding a horse or being on a dray and far better than walking.

It took us all morning and some of the afternoon to get to Puddletown, and when we approached I was amazed – there were banners everywhere! From the variety of banners, including the royal banners, as well as baronial bannerettes and knights' banners, I could tell that this was an important event. Never had I seen such colourful cloth and in such abundance. There were quite a few banners and pennons that I recognised from my time in the abbey, including those of Hubert Walter, but very many more that I did not.

When I asked what the event was that so many banners had been flown, I was told that the village of Puddletown had recently been granted a charter by the King, to be a market town. The market was to be held every Thursday with a market and fair to be held on the Feast of the Assumption, on the fifteenth of August. These markets and fairs were to be held at the manor house of the local lord. This large gathering was called to present the charter to the people.

Once in the village, I was escorted to a large inn, where I was bathed, fed and given clean clothes that fitted reasonably well, in place of my dirty, patched clothing. I was still rather apprehensive, although completely unafraid. I knew that my good deed would be rewarded, not punished. I was, though, still concerned for my pack and its hidden treasure. I never once let it leave my side. When one of the servants picked it up from a chair while I was being bathed, I called out to him that I would prefer that it should stay where it was. He was surprised and somewhat disconcerted, because the bag was rather dirty, but nonetheless, he left it on the chair as I had asked.

Once I was clean, shaved and fed, I was taken by a liveried manservant to the largest pavilion with the grandest red and blue banners on the top and told to wait outside until I was called for. The manservant lifted a flap and went inside. I did not get even the slightest glimpse of who or what was within. I could hear several men talking and, now and again, laughing loudly. I stood outside, nervously waiting, not daring to move from where I was placed. I smiled at the guards either side of the pavilion entrance, but they would not even acknowledge my existence. I had no doubt, however, that if I was to make a nuisance of myself, they would have no hesitation about running me through with their huge swords which they held in readiness for action.

Finally, a well-dressed man, who looked to be about my age, poked his head out of the tent flap. He looked around, saw where I was standing and came out to me, his hand held out to greet me. I straightened my tunic, wiping my sweaty palms on it as I did so. I shook his hand as he introduced himself as Joseph, eldest son of Franklin, the Baron of Stone and told me that it was time for me to come inside. He held open the tent flap for me as I straightened my tunic once more and stepped inside.

I could not believe my eyes. Hubert Walter sat on the High Chair, his device hanging on the tent wall behind him. I recognised him, obviously older than when I had last seen him, but there was almost no difference in his appearance. I hardly knew what to expect, but to see the King's Chief Justiciar holding court in Puddletown?

Standing around him were the knights and other members of the Knights' Guild of Wessex and Mercia. All the knights were wearing their white mantles. There were quite a few of them, engaged in their various conversations, all of which quietened as I entered the pavilion. They all turned and watched me as I was led to the centre by Joseph and introduced to the Justiciar. I had very little chance to take a look around and I could not see Geoffrey anywhere.

Hubert looked up at me and instructed me to come before him. I showed my courtesy and complied. As I moved forward, though I could not see them as my eyes were fixed on Hubert, I sensed that the Guild members were separating and moving to line up on each side. I was told to kneel on the cushion at his feet. Once I had done so, he asked my name and I nervously replied.

He then asked me, "Do you know why you are here?"

I replied timorously, "I am not quite sure, but I believe it may have something to do with Geoffrey."

Hubert laughed and told me I was correct. "I happened to be holding an assizes court in this town and heard tell of your good deed," he said, "I asked the Baron of Stone, the Master of the Knights' Guild, to allow me to preside over this Guild court as his representative. The Master would have you rewarded for saving Geoffrey's life, as would I. So therefore, in the Baron's name, I ask you, are you bond or free?" I replied that I was free. His next question was, "Are you in law or out law?" I answered that I was in law, as no one had any crime to hold against me to the best of my knowledge – though I did not say this latter part aloud. He then asked me, "Is there any hue and cry after you?" I hesitated a moment, thinking about the Psalter, before answering, "No, my lord, there is not."

This was true, as far as I knew, because no one who had wanted it actually knew that I had the precious book. Therefore, nobody was actively pursuing me. I hoped that my hesitation would be taken for simple nervousness. Hubert then told me, "You have been recommended by young Geoffrey and by myself for entry into the Knights' Guild of Wessex and Mercia as a sergeant, from which you could, with the proper training and attitude, eventually rise to become a knight. Lord Franklin, here on my right, the Master of the Guild, has agreed to accept you as a member, should you choose to do so." I looked where he indicated, to see a man about the same age as my father, but smaller. I was in the company of some important people indeed.

I was then informed by Hubert that, "In the event that you do indeed wish to become a member of the Knights' Guild, and I would strongly counsel you that you so choose, the fine for your doing so would be willingly and happily paid by Geoffrey, recently raised to knighthood, whose life you were instrumental in saving." He asked me if this was what I wanted. My heart was pounding with joy at such a wonderful prospect. I did not need his prompting to be able to make this decision. I nodded vigorously as, when I tried to give voice to my affirmative reply, all that escaped my throat was a choked gurgle which elicited a murmur of politely stifled laughs from the knights who were standing nearest to me. I gave a small cough to clear my throat, then said proudly, "Yes, my lord, that is indeed what I would wish."

I knew that if I could become a knight, I might quite conceivably be given, or at least earn, my own lands, possibly with servants. I might perhaps even be married and able to settle down with a family of my own. While these thoughts raced through my brain, I felt something being laid around my shoulders. I looked down to see that it was a Guild mantle, snow-white, reaching to the ground in my kneeling position, with the Guild badges already on it over my left shoulder. It felt, to me, as if the most fabulously rich cloak had suddenly become mine and I was in a transport of delight.

I was instructed by Hubert to stand and turn, which I did, to see, just as I had suspected, the ranks of the Knights' Guild standing in their lines. They were applauding, smiling, cheering and calling, "Was hael!" and "Drinc hael!" These were the traditional toasts, to wish each other good health.

Geoffrey, the nobleman whose life I had saved, had been standing behind me. He now came round to stand in front of me, grinning broadly and extended his hand to welcome me into the Guild. He later told me that he had claimed the privilege of laying the mantle over my shoulders. He must have entered the pavilion after me, which was why I did not see him earlier. As I took his hand to shake it, he pulled me into a hug, to which I responded heartily. Too heartily, it seemed, as he gave a small wince of pain, so I quickly eased the pressure and gave an apology which he dismissed with a wave of his hand, a wry grin, and a shake of his head.

When he stepped back, I noticed that he looked in rather good condition, so I quickly asked after his health. Geoffrey replied that his leg still gave him a little pain now and again, but he was happy with the speed with which it was improving. His chest wound too was rapidly becoming more completely healed. He also said that the price he had paid to enable me to become a member of the Guild and the pain he had just now suffered at my hands, was very small when compared to the gift of renewed life I had given him. He then said that we could spend as much time as I wanted talking later, after the court. He then looked towards Hubert Walter, bowed and asked to be excused as he had business elsewhere. Hubert gave him leave to go and when he had done so I was suddenly mobbed by many strangers, heartily welcoming me into the Knights' Guild of Wessex and Mercia.

As I thought about what had happened here, I suddenly knew that this was where my life had been leading – to a time when I could be free and happy, as my mother had wanted for me. I would again be travelling the countryside, this time serving the King, not merely wandering aimlessly. This was something about which I could write to my father and finally make him proud. I would not have to tell him the real reason I had to leave the abbey, which would have disappointed him terribly. With this latest turn of events, if I ever found that the time had come when I could see him face to face and tell him the whole truth, at least the burden of it would be mitigated by the good news of my joining the Knights' Guild, which, by all accounts, was a very prestigious group indeed.

CHAPTER TWENTY-NINE

I was placed in Geoffrey's household until it was determined that I was able to conduct myself in the manner appropriate of a member of the Guild. He was to be my forespeak, taking responsibility for me, ensuring that I was properly trained and had learned everything necessary to behave properly as one of this group.

During my time at the abbey, I had acquired some knowledge of how to conduct myself in the great courts of the high nobles, and with Geoffrey's servant in Affpuddle, that awareness was rekindled. However, I still had much to learn to acquit myself with due decorum in this company. As service in the Guild was not a full-time commitment, it took me some time to become familiar with everyone who belonged to the group. People joined us for their service and left to go home again on a regular basis. However, I soon discovered that there were many high-ranking men who were members of the Knights' Guild. Spending time with them and learning from them would enhance my possibilities for advancement immensely.

The Guild travelled all over the country in the King's service and when Geoffrey and his household – which now included me – were not with the Guild, we went to his father's home in West Dereham, in Norfolk. Living and working so closely with Geoffrey enabled me to finally discover the name of his father. I was rather surprised when I found out who he was. Geoffrey's father was no less than Hubert Walter himself.

No wonder Geoffrey had been so eager to become a knight! He

had his father's reputation to live up to and so what better place for Geoffrey than within the Guild. Anywhere the Guild was, there the King's work was done and done well.

Whenever and wherever the Guild travelled, we carried with us our portable altar. The King had successfully applied for special Papal license for the Knights' Guild to build this altar and it fell to the chaplain of the Guild to ensure it was maintained to the high standard expected. This portable altar enabled us to hold our own church services anywhere we were, regardless of whether or not there was a religious building in the vicinity. The altar was a rectangular slab of wood, about six hand spans long, by three wide and a single span thick. It was made of oak, with a finger bone of St Edward the Confessor set into the centre of the top. About one third of the length in from each end, there were holes inset into the slab in which candles were placed.

The time I spent with the Guild was, up until then, the best period of my life. We visited places in a way which travelling with the troupe could never compare. We did not merely get to a town and set up our tents and wagons, hoping for a warm welcome. When the Guild came to a town, we were housed in manors, castles and abbeys. We were always assured of a warm welcome – whether the townsfolk were sincere or not – and good food, fine drink and comfort were never in short supply. We were, after all, the King's people. We enforced his laws and agreements with the various local powers, whether they were barons, bishops, shire reeves, or whoever. If anyone thought he could get away with disobeying the King, he would ultimately have to deal with us or other agents of the King. This meant that every man in the Guild had to be well trained in the many and various forms of the art of warfare – and that included me.

I spent many long days in training with a sword. In keeping with the traditional training methods, I started with a wooden sword, then progressed on to metal ones. This was nothing like the swordplay I was used to while travelling with the players. With the troupe, the sword was swung to a specific place and parried. This was vastly different. This was training for real battles.

Even under instruction I saw men sustain injuries when struck with blunted metal swords. Sometimes these injuries were rather severe, with tips of fingers being lopped off, bones broken, and deep gashes sustained which needed stitching. Thanks be to God, these accidents did not occur very frequently at all, nor did I ever receive any such misfortune.

At first, I found the training rather difficult, but it soon became much easier. Allowance was made for my injured right hand, but with the constant use of the correct techniques, the strength in my hand soon recovered and became almost as good as it was before it had been broken. I still suffered occasional twinges of pain from the old injury, but they were few and far between.

The training I received was usually given to young children. Despite my late start and much to my surprise, my strength and co-ordination grew with the training, until I eventually learned to use my sword well. I also learned to use it in combination with a shield, as well as a sword and buckler, sword and dagger, two swords, a sword and axe, two axes and many other variations. Furthermore, I learned to use a variety of other weapons, such as the pole arm, axe, mace, glaive, flail, staff and many more besides. My father would now have someone in the family who could come close to matching his weaponry training, although I had no wish to test what skill I claimed to have against his. I would have been thoroughly overpowered, I am sure. Alongside these new skills, I again took up the bow and arrow. With some further instruction, I became a far better shot.

Other subjects of which I gained knowledge during my training included art, poetry, the rules of courtly love and several dances – including a number of estampies and a few farandoles. I was being given a very broad education, most of which, though very serious, was also quite entertaining. I was becoming not only educated but cultured as well. I learned that the Knights' Guild of Wessex and Mercia had a long and distinguished history. Although no one knows the exact dates of their origins, what is known is that there certainly was a Wessex Guild and a Mercian Guild by the time of the mid-Eighth Century.

They had had a troubled history with regards to feelings towards each other. The Mercian Guild fought and beat the Wessex men in 779 and the Wessex Guild, in 974, trounced what was left of the Mercians when they arrived at the Wessex court of Alfred the Great.

Burhred, the King of Mercia, had fled from the battlefield after they were defeated by the invading Vikings, leaving his men to be slaughtered. Burhred subsequently abdicated his throne and left for Rome, where he died a few days later from his wounds. Eventually, the two Guilds learned to get along, even if they did not completely trust each other. As time went by and as new blood was introduced by each branch of the combined Guild, the feuds lessened – though never stopped entirely. There were always, and still are, some niggling insults passed from one side to the other.

It was the responsibility of the Guild to keep the King's peace in the land. One of the ways this was accomplished was by ensuring that all his nobles were of one mind – the King's mind. There were about three hundred knights within the Guild. They were knights for and of the King, loyal to him – directly answerable to the King and to him alone.

There was a tale which stated that after William the Bastard had defeated Harold Godwinsson at the Battle of Hastings nearly two hundred years ago, he then travelled to London and was crowned King by the Archbishop of Canterbury some months later. Almost as soon as the crown had settled on his head, the Marshall of the Wessex Guild, followed by all that remained of the two separate Knights' Guilds, had burst into the cathedral, all still wearing their swords. The Marshall had demanded of a very surprised William, "By what right do you call yourself King?"

William was reported as calmly replying, "I claim the right by conquest. I also have the promise of Harold Godwinsson and that of Edward the Confessor." None of the Guild knights were overly impressed by this, but William continued, "And finally, I have been elected by the Witan and here I have been anointed and crowned the rightful king."

It is said that it was only at this last that the entire Guild took to their knees and swore allegiance to William, saying, "It is the anointed King whom we serve."

After the battle at Hastings, the separate Guilds' numbers had been depleted to such an extent that both were in danger of dissolving. The two groups decided to become one, although each of the Guilds still tried to outdo each other in the service of the King. Occasionally, a hot-blooded young man from one side would demand a show of strength from one of his counterparts on the other side. Then swords would fly and blood would flow until they rid their system of whatever humours were raging through them. Thankfully, these displays of strength were rare.

CHAPTER THIRTY

The day I became a knight has always been what I consider to be the high point of my life. No longer would I be known as merely the younger son of a peasant farmer. I would have a title of my own. 'Sir Rolf' was the name to which I would be entitled, from that moment onward. The reason I was raised to the rank of knight was because I quite possibly saved the entire Knights' Guild from complete extinction. How that happened is related hereunder.

The Guild had been sent by the King to encourage Peter de Montford, the Baron of Henley–in–Arden and Beaudesert, to publicly show support for the King's overall policies. This Baron had been wavering between support and opposition for many months and had finally rebelled completely.

In response to this, we gathered seven hundred men who owed service to the knights in the Guild and had taken them with us to help enforce the sovereign's will upon the Baron and his followers. When we arrived, we discovered that he had gathered all his followers inside the castle and had lowered the portcullis in front of the main gate, denying access to the Guild knights and our troops. They were protected from attack by the curtain walls of the building. We had not much hope of sapping these walls by digging under them, as they were built atop a hill, over some of the hardest stone we had seen, so we had decided to encircle his castle and wait him out.

We therefore surrounded the Baron's castle, cutting off everyone inside from the supply of fresh food and trade. We had no firm idea how long their food supply could last and with a deep well inside the castle we knew they had water in plentiful supply.

As well as laying siege to the castle itself, we decided to send a small company of men to guard every road approach to the village to ensure that no one could either get in with supplies to relieve those inside or escape to enlist reinforcements. The rest of our troops had gathered along the road leading to the front gate of the castle, on the western side, just out of bowshot. We camped at this position, which was in the middle of a broad gully, to wait for the Baron's next move. We did not have to wait very long to find out what that move would be.

Two days after we camped ourselves in front of the main gateway, we were alerted by our watchers to the fact that the huge grill of the portcullis was being raised. It stayed up just long enough to allow the Baron's troops to march out across the bridge and form up to face us. There were several hundred men at arms formed up in front, with a hundred or so archers lined up behind.

We were immediately called to arms, whereupon we quickly dressed in our armour and grabbed our swords, bows, or whatever weapons we used and the knights and other Guild members took up their individual responsibilities. I had been given control of a small squad of about fifteen archers, to be positioned on the far-left flank, beyond a thin stand of trees, as a test of my leadership. We expected to see very little action, being so far over to one side. Most of the battle, we hoped, would take place towards the centre of the gully, which was where the vast majority of our troops stood in their formations waiting for their chance at glory.

Suddenly, there came a single long trumpet blast from within the castle, followed by a loud shout from the ranks of men lined up in front of it. Those men who had just roared started beating their shields with their swords, axes and spears. They started moving forward, one step at a time, keeping themselves in their shield wall formation.

Every man in our army had his eye on this advancing wall of men. Suddenly, just as the two lines of fighters met and started their battle, I smelled smoke coming down the wind from my left. I knew we had no one further to that side than I was with my men, so I quickly turned to try to find out where the smoke came from. Taking great care to avoid detection, my men and I moved in that direction. I stopped them as soon as I spied what I supposed were the Baron's men, at which point I moved forward alone. I peered around a large tree and discovered that there was a small group of six or seven men, struggling to finish arming a small trebouchet, which had a fireball sitting in its sling, ready to be sent flying into the middle of our army.

There was also a pile of missiles, which looked to be soaked in some flammable mixture, sitting next to the machine. I guessed that the men and the trebouchet had emerged from the next field, where the machine had probably been hidden under a haystack. They had tried to outflank us with their war machine. I could not allow them to attack our troops.

As they continued winding the trebouchet, I moved back to my men. I noiselessly tapped on the shoulder of the leader of my archers and, motioning to him to keep quiet, we crept forward and I pointed out what I had seen. He nodded his understanding, then turned to the other archers and quietly ordered all of them to move forward and shoot at those operating the machine. As I joined in the volleys, I saw two or three of the men under my command pull string cutters from their quivers, take careful aim and loose their arrows. It would have been a startling sight for the enemy to see volley after volley of unexpected arrows landing amongst them, when they had believed they had the element of surprise on their side.

I was gratified to see that a few of our arrows cut through the ropes used to tie the arm of the trebouchet to its frame. This caused the whole thing to collapse in an explosion of flame, setting fire to the pile of waiting missiles and, when it splashed, to one of the men standing beside it. The burning man fell to the ground, screaming in agony. Whatever fuel they were using stuck to his skin like tar and burned horribly. There was nothing anyone could do to put out the flames licking at his body.

The whole group of would-be missile throwers ran away in

terror, with the stench of burning flesh in their nostrils. No fireballs would land on our troops from this machine. My men picked the fleeing men off with their well-aimed arrows.

As my men and I carefully advanced on the burning trebouchet, wary of any enemies who might have remained hidden, I maintained my watch on the progress of the main battle in front of the gate. We encountered no one as we approached the wreck. My men made certain that the machine would never be used again.

I could see many of my friends fighting in the battle. It was a battle they were about to lose. I knew I had to do something to help and quickly. I then had the idea of fighting fire with fire. If the Baron could attempt to outflank us, we could outflank his troops. I ordered my men to collect what arrows they could find and wrap them with strips of cloth ripped from the dead who lay around. The archers quickly caught on to my idea. They dipped the cloth-wrapped arrows in the burning pile of fireballs and while half the archers shot towards the men in the back rows of the Baron's troops, the other half shot the flaming arrows over the castle walls. We soon had a result from our improvisation.

Very shortly after the first arrows fell over the other side of the wall, there was a series of short trumpet blasts from inside and, as I turned to look at the main part of the battle, I saw all of the Baron's surviving men turn and run back inside the castle, abandoning the fight.

We were surprised that the whole army had run as they did. We had been expecting some kind of strategy, such as one section pretending to retreat while the rest moved in on any who followed. There were many dead and injured men from inside the castle left on the battlefield.

What happened after the last of the enemy had re-entered the castle was a surprise to everyone outside. The gate was not lowered. Instead, shortly after the last of his troops had gone back inside the castle, de Montford himself came out of the castle, walking alone, without any armour, holding his sword in its scabbard above his head.

He called out, "Quarter! I ask for quarter! I yield!" He then walked towards our troops, knelt on the ground, placed his sword on the grass in front of him and remained kneeling, his head bowed forward in surrender.

I found out afterwards that Baron de Montford's troops had been making ground during the fight against our men, until my archers had started shooting at their backs. Also, as our flaming arrows hit random targets inside the castle, some of the fire from these arrows splattered and hit men and buildings, which also caught fire. The Baron's youngest son was one of those who had been thus injured and de Montford was desperate for him to receive treatment for these injuries, which he could not get while the battle was raging. The Baron had then decided that he should cut his losses and ordered his troops to retreat.

Franklin, the Baron of Stone, the Master of the Knights' Guild, had sustained a minor wound in his right shoulder during the battle from one of the enemy's arrows. Although injured, he was strong enough to formally accept the surrender of de Montford. A garrison of men was posted inside the castle to ensure that the new-found loyalty of the rebel Baron continued. The Guild sent in their best physician to treat his boy and after having performed our allotted tasks we travelled back to the Master's manor in Stafford.

He retired to his chambers to receive treatment while the rest of the Guild, led by William de la Colline, the Captain of the Guard, gathered together in the large main hall of the manor house to discuss what had happened on the field of battle and to detail any losses we had suffered as well as any gains made. Thankfully, like the Master's, most of the wounds suffered by our men were very light. We had lost one knight, Colin, a long serving member of the Guild, who had been unfortunate enough to have been surrounded by four opponents. He was so skilful with the sword that three of the men had been killed by him before the fourth stabbed him in the back. Three archers who had moved in too close to the castle walls also died and four men at arms. We also lost several conscripted peasants.

William then asked of us, "Where did those fire arrows come from? I was unaware that we had been employing such weapons. Who was responsible for shooting the Baron's men that way?"

I stood and gave my account of why the enemy was shot at in such a manner. I explained, "While waiting for my signal from you or your lieutenants, I had smelled some smoke. I gave charge of my men to the largest of them and went to investigate. I discovered where the smoke was coming from – there was a trebouchet setting up to send fiery missiles at our troops from our left. The Baron's men must have thought they could not be seen, hidden behind the trees. I doubted I had the time to send a runner to warn you, so I crept up to and destroyed the trebouchet, with the assistance of my archers and had then attacked the Baron's men from behind and sent some fire arrows over the wall, using their own resources against them. We suffered no losses or injuries in doing so."

As I detailed the exploits of the men under my command, William's smile grew into a wide grin. When I told how I had ordered the fire arrows shot over the castle wall, he laughed and said, "A taste of their own medicine, eh? Brilliant, my boy, well done! You may just have saved our whole company from disaster. The Master shall hear of this, I shall see to it personally."

I bowed, acknowledging his kind remarks and then resumed my seat. There was quite a lot of other business to discuss, which meant that the meeting went far into the night. For most of the meeting, I wished I could leave and get to bed, but every man was expected to stay and offer his thoughts on what plans were to be made for the future of this place. By the time I did get to my bed, due to the excitement brought on by surviving my very first battle I was completely unable to get any sleep at all.

Considering what happened the next day, I fervently wish that I had slept like a baby.

CHAPTER THIRTY-ONE

When I arose from my bed the next morning, bleary eyed and weary from lack of sleep, I was summoned to appear in the small hall, before Franklin, the Baron of Stone. I was not entirely certain of what he wanted, but I did not intend to keep him waiting longer than necessary. I quickly washed my face, dressed and presented myself at the appointed place.

I was announced almost as soon as I arrived and was immediately instructed to enter. The bulk of the Guild members were already there in their places, which surprised me, as I had presumed that this was to be a private audience. The Master called me forward, so I showed my courtesy and came before him, kneeling at his feet as I had done with Hubert Walter when I was inducted into the Guild as a sergeant.

Lord Franklin announced, "Be it known by all present that through this man's actions on the battlefield, certain defeat had been averted. Many lives had been saved because of what he has done. Not only that, but a quicker victory had been won." He then surprised me by what he uttered next. "This man has been with us for slightly more than one year. He has, during that time, frequently displayed many qualities justifying his membership of the Guild. Does any knight here have any objection whatsoever to this man being raised to the rank of knight at the first available opportunity?"

I was stunned by this turn of events. I had thought that many more years would pass before I could ever begin to aspire to the warranting of a knighthood. There was no negative reply to his question – quite the opposite, in fact. It seemed that all present were agreed to my becoming a knight of the Guild.

Lord Franklin looked me in the eye and quietly said, "When you are sent away, I want you to go with Joseph, my son. He will tell you what to do. Obey his every command and all will be well. I shall see you again tomorrow." Then, out loud, he said, "As there is no objection, I command that there will be a vigil held tonight and a knighting on the morrow. I require knights to stand with Rolf. There will be two needed every hour for the vigil. Rolf, you are dismissed, go with Joseph." As I left with him, I noticed that several of the knights were already moving forward and volunteering for the position of who would stand vigil with me.

Joseph took me to his room. Once there he held out his hand to congratulate me, followed by the offer of a hearty breakfast. He then instructed me, "After you have finished eating – and I advise you to eat plenty – you must be shriven by confession. When that has been done, you will fast for the rest of this day, which is why I had all this food brought here. You will spend the rest of the day and all night in prayer in the chapel. Now that we have returned to my father's residence, I would advise you to call on our resident friar for your confession. The friar is a good man, and besides," at this point Joseph smiled gleefully, "his penances are not odious."

I told him, "I thank you for the meal. I had not slept at all last night with all the exhilaration of my first battle. Now, though, I wish I had done. I hope I do not fall asleep during my vigil."

Joseph laughed aloud. "Ensure that you do not, for if you do," he said, "you will have to do it over again at a later date. And besides, the knights who stand vigil with you will not thank you for a second opportunity to lose sleep. This is one of the reasons you will have two knights to stand vigil with you – to keep you awake. I will now help you get ready for your night and then, once you see the friar for your confession, I will leave you and you must go straight to the chapel and stay there until you are called for in the morning."

After saying this, he sent to my room for a clean under tunic and some braies and hose for me to wear during my vigil. Once I had dressed in these, he took me to the friar for shriving. I did not see Joseph again until he joined me for some short time during my vigil. I spent the best part of an hour with the friar and then, after completing my penance, went to the chapel to begin my vigil. I was instructed to kneel on a small cushion in front of the altar, in an attitude of prayer. My sole task was to maintain this attitude, awake, until morning. I was to remain silent for the entire period.

There were two knights, one either side of me, for the whole time I was performing my vigil. They entered the chapel and silently tapped those who were already there on the shoulder. Those men then rose, nodded to the men relieving them and left, while the new men knelt in their place. Apart from the gentle footsteps, there was complete silence throughout the whole procedure.

I was glad of the time I had spent in the abbey, as it had given me the training to maintain my silent prayer for the whole night. There were many times I felt like going to sleep, but at each instance I willed myself to stay awake and keep praying. I prayed for strength to continue, for the power to concentrate on the task at hand, for the time to pass more quickly and, most importantly, for the courage to maintain a chivalrous attitude for the future.

The next morning, Geoffrey came into the chapel, placed his hand on my shoulder and bade me rise and follow him. Geoffrey had also been one of the knights who had come to pray with me earlier in the night. He took me back towards the main hall of the manor house and instructed me to stand outside the door and wait with him until I was called for.

He told me, "Ready yourself by putting your hands together, as if in prayer and keep them in front of your chest, like this." He demonstrated the pose. Then he continued, "Stand next to me and as we walk, keep pace with me, but do not get ahead of me."

I prepared myself as I had been instructed and had to wait only a very short while before I heard the herald call from the other side of the closed door, "Bring forth the supplicant!" The door was opened by servants on the inside, and as we moved forwards

Geoffrey whispered in my ear, "Have courage, my friend, do not waver in your resolve. All will be well."

As I processed slowly forward, I saw almost every knight from the battlefield standing in their lines, wearing their best tunics, their snow-white mantles over their shoulders. I also noticed that a young woman, whom I knew by the name of Ælicia, was sitting, ready to take notes of the ceremony. Apparently, she had done this often, as she was reported to have had a working knowledge of the required procedures and quite a neat hand. She therefore filled the clerk's position whenever he was required to be elsewhere.

Ælicia was the ward of Joseph's father, placed under his protection by the King after her husband had died. She was a pretty woman, with hazel eyes and auburn hair. Ælicia travelled with the Guild for most of the year, returning to her lands for a few weeks at a time to ensure that the estate was being run properly by her steward.

As we walked between the lines, a group of people sang an entry hymn, a *Conductus*, accompanied by several musicians playing a variety of instruments. I was stopped at various points on my journey down the aisle, to be dressed in a tunic, boots, spurs, jewellery, a maille coat and coif and, finally, a sword belt with an empty scabbard, all gifts from the knights of the Guild.

As they were put on me, the names of the donors of these items were told to me, although the scabbard was put on without telling me who gave it. No doubt I would soon discover the name of my mysterious benefactor. I was instructed to kneel before the Baron of Stone, who asked me, "What is it you wish?" To which I replied, "I wish to become a knight, my lord." I was then prompted by Geoffrey, as I gave my oath of fealty. This was followed by a reading of my achievements, those deeds of note that I had performed which led to my being in this place, deeds such as the saving of Geoffrey's life, being the cause of the Guild winning of the battle, and some other less remarkable acts. As the list was read out, I was surprised. I had not realised that I had done so much that was considered to be of importance, or that it had been noted.

The Master of the Guild then turned to William, the Captain of the Guard, received a naked sword from him, held it up above his head so that all could see it. He said, "This sword was recovered from the slain body of Colin, whom you all knew, a knight who died on the field of battle against de Montford the day before yesterday. He bravely gave his life in the service of the King." He then turned to me and said, "I pray God that you carry this sword with pride and that you possess the courage to use it, as Colin would have had you do. To defend the Church, to assail infidelity, guard the truth, do what is right, to venerate the priesthood, to protect the weak and the poor from injuries, to pacify the province, to pour out your blood for your brothers, face your enemy without fear and, if need be, to lay down your life. Will you promise to do this, to the best of your ability, as God allows you to do?"

I answered, without a trace of a tremor in my voice, "Yes, my lord, I promise that I shall do so, as God will give me strength." The Master then held the sword in front of my face, point down, to form the cross, so that I could kiss it as a symbol of my vow, then, once I had done so, placed the sword in its scabbard on my belt. He then hung a plain, unadorned, chain link necklace around my neck, kissed me on both cheeks and loudly declared to all who had gathered in the hall, "This man is henceforth to be known throughout the kingdom as Sir Rolf of Portsmouth, a knight of the kingdom. He has sworn his oath of fealty and made his knight's vow. And this is to ensure that he always remembers his promise." At this, he struck me, not very softly, with his open right hand behind my left ear. I swayed but did not fall. As spots of colour exploded inside my eyes, the room resounded with cheers of "Hurrah!" from all gathered within. I was glad he had used his right hand, as that was his injured side. Had he used his left hand, I doubt I would have remained erect after the blow.

When I had gathered my wits, I heard the Master instruct me to stand and turn to face the rest of the knights who had come to watch me inducted into their ranks. They were all cheering, fists waving in the air in celebration. That was a day I would never forget. It would not have taken a blow from the Master to enable me to remember it. Every single detail of that day has been burnt indelibly into my mind. It was as if that was the first day of my life, as though all that went before was not to be counted.

After the ceremony, as I was being congratulated by all the knights there present, I discovered that a feast had been organised. The feast was not only in celebration of my having become a knight, but also to celebrate the victory over Peter de Montford.

The Master advised me to go to bed for a few hours, but I told him, "Thank you, my lord, but I doubt I would be able to sleep today, even though it has been two days since I last slept. I am far too excited to do so just yet. Besides, this feast is partly in my honour, I could not leave now anyway." At that, he laughed, told me to enjoy myself while I lasted and then went about his business elsewhere. As he left, I was surprised to see Ælicia coming straight towards me. I turned to face her and the men between us parted when they saw at whom I was looking. When she came within arm's reach, she smiled sweetly and said, "Congratulations, Sir Rolf of Portsmouth. I am certain you will make a fine knight." Whereupon she placed her hands on my shoulders and kissed me on both cheeks. I noticed that she did not have to stretch up to do so, as she was reasonably tall for a woman. She then turned and went on her way. I felt suddenly hot and bothered, as if the room temperature had abruptly increased. I guessed that, somehow, I would never be completely at ease in the presence of Ælicia again. As it turned out, I was right. I was never the same when she was with me, especially when we were alone together.

I changed into more casual clothing, placing my knighting outfit and sword into a box given to me by Geoffrey specifically for that purpose. I asked Geoffrey to wake me after an hour, as I had to have some sleep before attending the feast. I had never realised that simply lying down could feel so good. He let me sleep for two hours.

The feast went far into the afternoon and the high spirits continued long after sunset. I eventually made my excuses and shuffled off to my chamber. I removed my outer garments and almost fell onto my bed. I took almost no time at all to fall asleep. I slept the dreamless sleep of the contented.

When I awoke the following day, there was a young man sitting on the wooden bench just inside the door to my room. He was practising a game of Nine Men's Morris by himself. I recognised him as one of the servants belonging to the Guild. He looked up from the board as I greeted him. As I sat up in bed, the young man stood, bowed and introduced himself, "Good morning, Sir Knight." He smiled at this, knowing I was not yet used to being greeted in this fashion. "My name is Dagbert and I have been appointed to be your personal servant. I look forward to working for you. Here are your clothes for today." He indicated a set of clothing, lying on top of my trunk, which stood at the end of my bed.

The clothes consisted of a full-length over tunic made of russet linen, with a trim of green and yellow leaves embroidered on a linen strip, along with an under tunic of white linen, also full-length. Sitting on top of these was a white leather belt with roundels riveted at regular intervals, interspersed with oak leaves embossed into the leather. On the floor next to the trunk was a new pair of boots made of dark brown leather.

I was surprised and I asked Dagbert, "Where did they come from? I have never these clothes seen before. Are you sure they are mine?" He replied, "Yes, my lord, they are indeed yours. They are gifts from the Master of the Guild. It is the custom within the Guild for a newly knighted member to be presented with a new set of clothes. The belt was made yesterday using the oak leaves in your headband as a pattern."

As I took off my old underclothes and washed myself and dressed in the new, Dagbert informed me that his duties were to clean my clothes, my sword and any armour I would acquire and to ensure I had everything I needed for each day, as long as I was with the Guild. He would also be my personal messenger, or at least assign men to be messengers for me, if I ever needed one.

Dagbert was to become a good friend, as well as being very useful to me, as he seemed to know everybody within the Guild and was able to give me helpful information about each member. He was also very knowledgeable regarding almost all the nobility. There was hardly a time that he did not know every earl, baron, thegn, or minor noble when councils met or when we attended other large gatherings under the instruction of the King. Thanks to Dagbert, I always knew the names of people before I was introduced to them.

Dagbert was also instrumental in helping me design my personal device. As a newly raised knight, I had to have one to offer to the King of Arms for his approval. Dagbert had received some training in the art of heraldry and we put it to good use. He had often seen the headband I wore and, having been told when he asked about it that I had received it from my mother, he suggested that I use the oak leaf as the central part of the device's design. I decided to enclose the oak leaf within a lozenge, also to honour my dead mother. I had always enjoyed the open grasslands through which I had travelled, both with the Guild and with the troupe, so the field – the background of the device – was to be green. As I had been in an abbey for quite some period of my life, we added some crosses – two in the top corners and two in the bottom corners. These four crosses, Dagbert said, could symbolise the four periods of my life – the few years I spent with my family, the years in the abbey, the time spent with the troupe and my latest episode with the Guild. The crosses and the lozenge, following the rule of tincture, had to be of a metallic colour, so we chose gold, or "*Or*" as it is described in heraldry.

My shield was therefore blazoned thus: "*Vert*, on a lozenge, *Or*, between four crosses, crosslet fitchée *Or*, an oak leaf, *vert*." To put it in simple English terms, I had a green shield, with a gold lozenge in the centre and a green oak leaf in the middle of the lozenge, the whole being surrounded by four gold crosses with cross pieces on each arm and a pointed bottom end. This style of cross was carried when travelling on pilgrimage or to the Crusades. The pointed end meant that if the company stopped for the night where there was no church or other shrine, they could hammer the cross into the ground to form their own temporary place of worship.

About three months after the battle with Peter de Montford, Baron of Henley–in–Arden and Beaudesert, Joseph's father died from the small injury he had sustained. The wound, which was at first thought to be minor, had not healed properly and wept continually. He succumbed to a fever after the first month. Then, about two weeks later, his joints became very tense. The first sign we had that he was really in trouble was a stiffness in his neck and jaw which prevented him from eating properly. He then started to convulse in his bed where the physicians had confined him. His breathing was daily ever more laboured, until finally, he could breathe no more and died.

Joseph, as the oldest son, was soon proclaimed as the new Baron of Stone and subsequently elected Master of the Knights' Guild of Wessex and Mercia at the next Guildmoot, as the gathering of all of the knights in the Guild was known.

CHAPTER THIRTY-TWO

Early one morning, some months after Joseph had inherited the title of Baron of Stone, the Guild were travelling along the road toward Gloucester when we passed a mendicant monk at a crossroads. As was customary, he was begging for his next meal. These begging monks were nothing unusual and were to be seen everywhere. Most of them were not attached to any particular monastery or abbey. They had usually either been thrown out or had left of their own accord.

This monk's clothing was the most ragged I had ever seen. I urged my horse slightly forward, to get a better look at this man. He was vaguely familiar. There was something strange about his face. His features resembled that of the lions I had seen illustrated in a book in the scriptorium at the abbey – his large nose was flattened somewhat, his eyes stood out proud of his face and when he called out for alms, I noticed that his upper front teeth were missing.

As he faced my direction, I received the worst shock I had ever suffered since leaving the abbey. I had to look a second time to make certain I was not seeing things. It was Brother John – the man who caused my expulsion from the abbey! I very nearly jumped off my horse to run at him and attack him for what he had done. I restrained myself, however, remembering that I had long ago forgiven him for what he had done to me and had concluded that he was part of the intricate design that God had planned for my life.

I quickly turned my face away, moving so as to keep another knight between me and him and, so far as I could tell from his lack of reaction, he had not seen me. If he had, then at least he did not recognise me. I shook with nervousness as I turned my horse away before Brother John had the chance to see me, and I immediately went to seek out Geoffrey. Once I found my former forespeak and had taken him aside so that I could speak confidentially with him, I told him who it was sitting by the side of the road. When I had finished explaining why I was concerned about this man, he asked me, "Are you really sure it is him? If it is, why would he be here, so far from the abbey? How can you be sure it is him?"

I am ashamed to admit that I raised my voice when I answered him, "Yes, of course, I am absolutely sure! I lived in the same Abbey with him for over ten years. How could it be anyone else? I recognised him, even with the changes to his face. He has a wart over his eye that no one could ever forget. I am not entirely sure, but I believe that he may have succumbed to leprosy. He has the signs. I am on familiar terms with lepers from my days in the abbey. As to why he is here and how he caught that dread sickness, if he has, I have no idea. I am not sure what I should do. Although I cannot actually prove it, I know that he was the direct cause of my being thrown out of the abbey because he accused me of stealing the Psalter."

As soon as I had said these last few words, I wished that I could have taken them back. Even after all this time with the Guild, I had still not told anyone the real reason why I had to leave the abbey. Nor had I told anyone, not even Geoffrey, about the Psalter in my satchel.

Naturally, Geoffrey was surprised. As far as he, or anyone else, knew, I had left the abbey of my own volition and to find out that I had been expelled was news to him. He demanded that I truthfully explain the whole situation. Seeing no other alternative now, I told him about the missing Psalter, the money that was found in my cell, that I had been taken before the abbot and forced to leave the abbey in disgrace. I gave Geoffrey my word that I had not stolen the book. I explained how it had come into my possession and how I had carried it everywhere I had travelled and protected it through all these years.

Thanks be to God, Geoffrey said that he believed me. He said, "We should take your tale to the Master of the Guild, Lord Joseph. I will vouch for your honesty. He will believe you, as do I. We will see what he has to say regarding what we should do about this Brother John. Perhaps we will also be enlightened as to how he comes to be so far from his home."

We waited the two or three hours until we reached Gloucester and had seen to the set-up of our pavilions and the other tents for the servants to sleep in while we moved into the monastery. With great trepidation, I accompanied Geoffrey to the Master. We requested an audience with him in private, to which he readily agreed. We gained permission from the prior of the monastery to be able to use a small, closed room for our discussion.

Once there, I explained that I had seen the begging monk on the roadside and knew him as Brother John. I told him what this man's wrongdoings had meant for me and then related the tale of the missing Psalter, along with the discussion with Nathaniel the Jew. When I had told him everything I had to tell, including my suspicions that he might have been suffering from leprosy, I brought out the Psalter and showed it to Lord Joseph. He took it and examined it with great reverence.

Geoffrey told the Master, "Rolf told me this tale earlier today and I believe him. I have never heard Rolf utter even the smallest lie and, as you well know, he has been scrupulously honest in all our Guild dealings. So much so, that I have no reason whatsoever to doubt the truth of what he has told you."

Master Joseph thought silently for several minutes, then apparently having come to a decision, told me, "I want you to write down everything you have just told me. Make sure you miss nothing! Not even the slightest detail. When you have produced your statement, I will make a submission to the Justiciar to have your case heard. Although it may take a few days, I want this matter cleared up as soon as possible."

He thought for a moment longer and said, "Be prepared to swear an oath, twelve handed if necessary, as the Justiciar will most likely require it. I can make no guarantees that your case will be successful, whether you are telling the truth or not, as you were indeed expelled from the abbey and it is a monk you are accusing."

I replied, "Yes, my Lord, though I do not know where I shall find eleven witnesses to stand with me. As I vowed when you made me a knight, I will obey you in all things, even if my case is lost and I suffer punishment for keeping all of this from you for so long."

As he returned the Psalter to me, Master Joseph said, "As you have obviously taken great care of it for so long, you should keep the Psalter with you, but be sure that it is always readily available, should it be necessary to remove it from your care. I shall not say that this will indeed happen, merely that you should be prepared for it."

Master Joseph then dismissed us and sent for his Captain of the Guard. As we were leaving the small office and moving to our own room, we passed William de la Colline answering the Master's summons.

Geoffrey came with me to the scriptorium to help me acquire some parchment so that I could write down the whole account. I thanked God that I was able to write for myself, so that no one else need know the story until it was made public at the trial. I was still somewhat ashamed of the whole thing and preferred that as few people as possible knew about it for as long as possible. I spent all the next day writing down, in the neatest hand I could manage, the events that led up to my eviction from the abbey. I wrote that I was innocent and that Brother John had made false accusations against me, how I came to be in possession of the Psalter, why I had not previously returned it to the abbey and what I had done with it since then. I also related the conversation I'd had with Nathaniel.

When I had finished, I folded the parchment, sealed it and sent Dagbert to take it to the Master of the Guild for his perusal. I then decided that I should not worry about it anymore until I had to and that I would try not to think about the consequences that might follow. I had to wait for five days before I was told what was to happen to me. I still had no idea where I might find eleven oath helpers to stand with me. I would have to hope that God would find a way through this. I should have trusted Him more, as He had already made His plans for me.

In the afternoon, I was taken by Geoffrey and Master Joseph to the courtyard of the monastery, to face a court. As we approached, I was quite surprised to see Brother John there, in a wooden tumbrel. He was tied by rope so that he could not approach the sides of the wagon. He looked, as one would expect, extremely downhearted and sullen. The man was not wearing his habit but was instead dressed in the ordinary clothing of a villager. He looked as if he had been beaten, as one eye was swollen and closed. I turned to William de la Colline and demanded, "What is the meaning of this? How did he come to be here? Why is he injured so?"

He told me, "Those injuries are none of our doing. The same night you told your story to the Master , he sent me and ten of the Guild's menservants out to capture Brother John with as little harm as could be done. We approached him and told him that he was to accompany us here. He refused to obey, then started to run away. The men vainly attempted to catch him without touching him, because they were told that he might have been a leper and he nearly got away. He turned off the roadway and ran down a steep slope, which led down to a stream. It was while running down this embankment that he stumbled over a tree root, rolled down the hill, hit his head on a rock and lay still. When the menservants got near to him, they took out a long rope and tied it around his waist. Then, at spear point, keeping him as far as possible from them, they moved him here and had him placed and tied into the cart as you see him. The men swear that they caused his injuries only indirectly. The fall did it to him. I believe this to be true, as none of the men would have dared touch him, in case he indeed has leprosy, as you supposed. However, in order to preserve what dignity he has left, when he arrived here some clothing was thrown to him, so that he might replace his badly tattered habit, which had fallen apart in many places. The habit, of course, has since been burned."

I cautiously approached the cart containing Brother John. As I neared it, he looked up to see who this new tormentor was to be. When he saw my face, his jaw dropped in surprise. "You! You are the last person I expected to see. What have you to do with these people who harass and bedevil a poor, innocent beggar? Is it because of you that I have been tied in this manner? Was this your doing? I demand that you have them release me, immediately. I have done nothing to warrant being treated in this manner."

I was surprised that his voice was slurred and somewhat difficult to understand, though I should not have been, as leprosy does that to a person. I gruffly told him, "I am indeed responsible for your being brought here. I believe you have not been as honest and forthright in your dealings with several sick and injured travellers as you might have been. Besides, the Psalter has been recovered. You do remember the Psalter? It is in my possession and has been for quite a long time. Since just after I left the abbey, in fact. The merchant to whom you sold it gave it to me to return to the abbey and told me of your many other dealings with him. So, I think we do indeed have reason to hold you. I think you can guess why I did not go back with the book. You would have poisoned the abbot's mind against me and I would still not have been able to re-join the abbey." I softened my tone when I said, "Though you may not believe it, I assure you that I did not wish for you to be injured when you were brought here. I merely wanted to have the truth discovered. I meant not for you to be injured or badly treated."

He then looked at me with such scorn that I thought that if he could have broken the bonds which held him, he would have attacked me with his bare hands and possibly tried to kill me. Instead, he merely grunted his disbelief. I turned away from him and went to speak to Geoffrey. I was not happy to see how the disease had disfigured poor Brother John, despite my dislike of the man. I was, however, glad that he was still able to speak to argue his case, even if it meant I might lose, although Geoffrey had assured me that he and Joseph the Master doubted that this would happen.

CHAPTER THIRTY-THREE

s we approached the part of the yard where the court had been convened, and I was shown to the place where I was to stand, I was gratified to see that almost the whole Guild had gathered to stand by my side to watch this trial. Seeing them standing there was a great comfort, even if it was to be me alone that faced the court. Brother John was taken, in his tumbrel, to the other side of the court.

The Justiciar, whom I recognised instantly as Hubert Walter, was reading a parchment; the one I had written. He was acquainting himself with my side of the story. I also noticed Ælicia sitting in the place normally reserved for the clerk of the court. She had taken this man's place, as he had recently fallen from his horse and had broken his wrist.

Hubert cleared his throat and then spoke to Brother John. "I have read this submission from Rolf that he has brought against you, and I now require that you tell your side of this story. I am sure you are familiar with the man who accuses you and of what." At that, I saw Brother John looking at me and I could feel the hatred streaming from his eyes. Hubert continued, "Included in this document are details of some very serious charges indeed. You will have until tomorrow to find eleven oath helpers to plead your case."

Brother John spluttered, crying, "How can I find so many people to do this? I am far from home and no one here knows me; and even if they did, who would help me in this place. This is most unfair!" The Justiciar looked at him and replied, "You are, or were, a monk. This is Gloucester, go to the abbot of this monastery and ask for permission to gather some monks. Surely some of them would be willing to support you in this case, as you are one of their own. Bailiff, ensure that he arrives at the abbot's office safely and, when he has found his oath helpers, if he can, bring him and them back here tomorrow morning." Brother John did not look at all pleased with this solution, although it was as fair as any other judgement he could have received. He was taken from the wagon and led away by the bailiff and three other men, each keeping him at the end of a billhook, so as to keep his distance. I was also dismissed until the morrow.

As Geoffrey and I walked back to the pavilion, I asked him why the Guild members were standing next to me in the court, rather than waiting outside. I quickly added, "Do not be mistaken! I was glad to see them there, even though they will take no part in the proceedings." William, who had been walking with us out of the court, laughed and then answered, "We were all waiting in case Hubert called upon us to swear for you. Every single man there had been told what had happened to you and was standing ready to help you in this case. We will be there again tomorrow to stand for you. You truly are a highly respected man."

I was stunned. I had no idea the Guild held me in such regard. I also noticed that there seemed to be no such thing as privacy within the Guild. At least, I thought, when others know your business, they know what to expect when one of the group needs assistance. An idea suddenly sprang into my head and I decided to seek out Master Joseph. When I had found his clerk, I asked for an audience with him. Then, when it was granted, I knelt before him and asked, "My Lord, I would that you allow me to beg you to plead with Hubert Walter for clemency for Brother John. I have forgiven the man, regardless of his actions and his feelings toward me and had he not done what he did, I would not be here with the Guild, but would still be an unknown monk in Devonshire. He has done more good for me than he knows, or would have liked and I would reward him for this, even if he does not thank me for it. Is this at all possible?"

Master Joseph smiled and replied, "I make no promises, but I will convey to the Justiciar your desires. What he does with this man, if he finds him guilty, will be entirely up to him. That is all I can do. However, you surprise me by showing uncommon forgiveness and mercy for a man who has been so wronged, regardless of the good fortune you have received." At that I was dismissed and so I went to my bed, knowing that I had done all I could for Brother John.

The next morning, we went back to the court. Hubert was in his chair, with Ælicia and the minor clerks in theirs and the Guild members once again standing beside me. I looked at them differently today, with a considerable amount of pride, knowing that any or all of them would be prepared to stand witness for me.

Brother John stood on the other side of the room, alone, guarded by the bailiff and his men-at-arms, who held him in place by means of ropes, looped around a rail and tied to his arms and waist. He looked despondent, almost desperate. Hubert spoke to Brother John, "Well, have you your oath helpers? I do not see anyone. Where are they?" Brother John answered curtly, almost spitting, "Of course I have none! The monks here would not accept the word of a leper, even though I told them I had been a monk all my life. You knew very well that I would not find anyone to be an oath helper to a leper, even here, yet you allow this ridiculous farce to continue and have the temerity to call it God's justice!"

"Silence! Restrain that man! And do so carefully, he has just twice admitted to being a leper!" roared Hubert. Several men-at-arms tightened the ropes from what they hoped was a safe distance. Hubert continued, "I will not permit you to speak to this court in this fashion. You have had ample opportunity to convince your fellow monks to support you. If they choose not to do so, that is God's will and, as a monk, you should realise and accept that."

He then ordered that the reliquary, which contained the holy relics of King Oswald of Northumbria, be brought forward. Hubert turned to me and asked, "Have you your oath helpers?" Before I could even open my mouth to reply, the Master of the Guild stood and called out, "Here, my Lord! You have but to choose as many of us as you wish, and we will all gladly step forward to swear that what Rolf has to say is indeed the truth."

A lump rose in my throat, but as I stepped forward to speak my oath, I discovered that I had a new-found confidence and could give the oath easily. I stumbled in my speech not at all. After I had given my oath, with my hands on the reliquary, Hubert pointed at five of the Guild members at random. Each of the selected men, in his turn, placed his hands on the holy relics and gave his own oath in a loud, clear voice. Not once did any of them trip up or hesitate in his speech in the slightest.

When all had given their oaths, Hubert turned to Brother John and asked, "Do you wish to give your oath?"

Brother John sneered, pointed his jaw towards me and replied, "I would rather hang now than give this man the satisfaction of hearing me say any single thing that I know full well would be disbelieved in this travesty of a court." He then glared at me with a poisonous look in his eyes, as if he hoped I would fall down dead in agony on the spot.

Hubert sat in silence for a short while and then looked towards me and declared, "This is my judgment. Rolf is to be set free from this court with no fines or costs set against him. He is to return the Psalter to Buckfast Abbey at the first opportunity. His duty to the Church in this matter is then to be considered discharged."

He turned to Brother John and continued, "As for you, Brother John, there would be no point in fining you, as you obviously would not be able to pay it. Therefore, I decree that you are to reside in the leper hospice of St Mary Magdalene, here in Gloucester, for the rest of your life. You will be treating and comforting the other poor souls who inhabit the place, for as long as you are able, as you will be so treated and comforted once you are come to meet your own end. May God have mercy on you and your soul."

Brother John looked disgusted, but murmured, "Yes, my Lord," as he hung his head in defeat.

Then, rather than dismissing the court, Hubert picked up another document, briefly read it, and made a surprise announcement.

Brother John had been found guilty in Buckfast, in absentia, of the theft of many items of significant value. When he heard this, Brother John went mad with rage and had to be restrained by the many men-at-arms who held the ropes tying him to the rail. He was surrounded by spearmen, at the furthest possible extent of their spears and was made to listen as Hubert read out the details of his crimes.

Apparently, several family members of the travellers who had passed through our Abbey had lost track of their relatives and, having made lengthy enquiries, found that the last place that any of them were reliably seen was at Buckfast Abbey. Their travelling companions had told the family members that their missing loved ones had been stricken with various ailments and had called in to the infirmary for treatment while they, the companions, continued on their journey. The sick and injured travellers were never to be seen again.

After enquiries at the abbey, it had transpired that every time someone disappeared, Brother John was the bursar on duty. The bursar was the one who held the valuables owned by the sick while they were being treated. Each item was listed in a book, so that the patients could collect their property when they were well enough to be on their way. Brother Aubrey had kept meticulous records of who had been in charge of each department of the abbey at any time. Everyone at the abbey, at that time, had supposed that Brother John had listed the valuables and placed them in a safe place to wait until the patients were healed. It seems, though, that the list was incomplete. The sick or injured had simply gone from the abbey and had, as far as anyone knew, continued their journey to wherever they were headed with their goods.

Brother John, when he heard of these inquiries, had absconded from the abbey and was nowhere to be found. Once it was found that Brother John had been the last to see these people, his cell was searched. It was while rummaging around in the cell of Brother John that one of the brothers had dislodged a loose stone in the floor. The stone was pulled out of the floor and in the cavity underneath was found a box with hundreds of gold pieces and a small bag containing many gems and small items of great worth. Several of the items found in Brother John's cell were recognised by Brother Aubrey as belonging to people who had supposedly left after being healed of what was thought to be an innocuous malady.

The abbot immediately declared that Brother John was no longer to be considered a brother in Buckfast or any other abbey. He would send word to the Mother House to that effect and there should be a hue and cry set for him as soon as possible. I know not if anyone else in the abbey had noticed, but to hear what the abbot was reported to have said meant, to me, that whatever hold Brother John had on him, it was now broken forever. I guessed that the abbot realised that he was finally free of concern that Brother John could blackmail him for any reason. He had his own power over Brother John that was stronger than whatever he had held over him.

The search, meanwhile, was widened to include the whole of the grounds of the abbey. In a copse by a bend in the nearby River Dart, quite a few bodies were discovered, in various stages of decomposition. They were not buried, merely thrown into the hidden hollow. The smell of the bodies had not been previously noticed because the abbey dumped its rubbish just a few score paces away from where the bodies were found. Many of the bodies were identified by their clothing. There was not much else remaining of them by which they could have been identified.

Hubert related that the abbot had also written, "Since Brother John has been so dishonest in this matter, it is very likely that he was dishonest about many things. I intend to send notices to every abbey and monastery in the land that Rolf is to be found and informed that he may return to us, so that we may hear his story and, if he is found to be innocent of the crime of which he was presumed guilty, we will beg his pardon for evicting him. Also, if he so desires, he may be reinstated into the order and be immediately eligible to take his final vows."

Hubert then spoke directly to me, "Now you know that you are no longer an outcast from the abbey and you may return there whenever you wish, you must now choose. Will you continue with the Knights' Guild or will you return to the life of a monk? I will not ask for your answer now; it is not for me to rule on this matter. It is for you to decide which path you elect to follow. You are, after all, a free man and a knight and may make up your mind as you wish.

He then turned to Brother John. "As for you, John, I pass judgement that you will indeed spend the rest of your life in the hospice. The lepers here have no belongings for you to steal and because they know that they will soon die, as will you, they will have no fear of you and your previous ways. They need not even be made aware of your earlier crimes, unless you so choose to tell them. It would serve no purpose to have you hanged. Your death would be of no use to anyone. I can do no worse to you than you have done to yourself by contracting this illness. You will never leave the hospice. The bailiff of this area has the responsibility to ensure that you stay within the place. If any man finds you putting foot outside of the hospice grounds at any time, however, you will be taken to a distant place outside the town and put to death. Do I make myself perfectly clear to you?"

Brother John could do nothing except to bow his head again and reply, "Yes, my Lord," and accept his fate. Hubert then declared that this case was now finally closed and dismissed all of us.

CHAPTER THIRTY-FOUR

Jwas free! I need no longer have any fear that the marvellous Psalter would be taken from me by thieves. It would now be guarded by the Guild until I was able to return it to its rightful place and once it was restored to the abbey at Buckfast, my conscience would be totally clear for the first time in many years. I could hardly wait to get there to present the book to the abbot and the rest of the abbey community.

I was glad that God had allowed me to keep the Psalter in its original condition, as I had never found myself in such dire straits that I'd had to remove even a single gem from the cover. To be sure, the pages were a little less clean than when I had first picked it up, but that was to be expected, as I had taken every possible opportunity to read the precious book, for the best part of five years.

I was given leave to attempt to visit Brother John in his cell within the hospice every morning and evening for the next few days, in order to find out how he had contracted leprosy and to tell him that I had forgiven him for what he had done to me. At first, he refused to even see me, let alone talk to me, but my persistent calling upon him must have changed his mind, so that he consented to listen to what I had to say. I sat several paces from him, with prison bars between us. After I convinced him that I bore no grudge against him, he reluctantly told me his sorry tale.

He began, "Some time after you were expelled there was an investigation into several missing travellers who had last been seen at the abbey and also of their possessions. This investigation revealed that several bodies had been placed in a ditch, which, to my unending shame, was my doing. I swear to you, brother to brother, that I did not kill them – they had died of their own accord. Rather than enter their valuables into the register, I stole their possessions and hid the bodies, in an attempt to make it seem as if they had left of their own accord after being healed. I should have made a better attempt to hide the bodies. This was my undoing. I could not even go to my cell and collect the money I had gathered together and had to leave just as I was; empty handed, poor as a church mouse.

"I left the abbey late at night so that, for a short while at least, no one would realise I had gone. I travelled in secret, hiding from everyone who might have recognised me. I knew well what would have happened to me had I been caught. I skirted several towns and villages, stealing or begging for what food and drink I could get.

"One afternoon, I came across a small hamlet that at first sight seemed deserted. I decided to search the cottages on the chance that there may be some food or valuables I could use. As I walked along the main thoroughfare into the hamlet, I heard a crash and a cry of pain in one of the nearby cottages.

"Although I was absent from the abbey without permission, I still considered myself one of God's workers, so I knocked on the door of the cottage where the noise came from. Having heard nothing from within, I called out two or three times the usual greeting, 'Peace be to this house,' and entered. In the building, I found a man who had fallen from a ladder. He was lying unconscious on the floor with a beam of wood across his chest and his arm at an angle which suggested that it was broken.

"It seems that he had been engaged in repairing a roof beam. I went to his aid, moving the beam off him and discovering that he had broken his ribs as well as his arm. As I bent over him, the man coughed, his blood going all over my face and clothes. I concerned myself with treating this man's injuries rather than cleaning myself and by the time I had done what I could for the man, it was too late for me to save myself, for I discovered not long after that this village was a community of lepers. The place had been deserted as everyone who lived there was occupied in attending a funeral; burying one of their number who had died two days before I had arrived. The blood that had splattered over my face was from a man who had only recently discovered that he had contracted leprosy. He had lost part of his right foot to the disease, but I had not noticed this, as he was wearing boots. Had he remained conscious after his accident, he would most likely have warned me not to touch him. I was shocked to discover what had befallen me. I could not even speak.

"I knew what was in store for me. If I showed even the least sign at all of the disease over the next few weeks, I knew that no matter what happened afterwards I could never be in company with ordinary folk ever again. So, I stayed in isolation within the hamlet for a short while, in one of the empty houses, until I discovered that I had indeed contracted the disease. I had no desire to die within that foetid village, so I left. I moved far away from Buckfast and became an itinerant beggar. And that is how you found me."

I asked him, "Since Nathaniel told me of your dealings with him, I have always wondered what need you had of money? To what end were you amassing such a fortune? How could you reconcile that with our vow of poverty?"

He replied, "My father was a wealthy man. As his only son, he had promised to leave his estate to me. I would have become someone of high social standing. But as I was already in the abbey when my father died, my cousin contested my father's will, stating that as I had chosen to take the vow of poverty, he should inherit the land. He stole my land from me and ruined my plan to become a person of note. I had no wish to stay at the abbey, where I was constantly overlooked in favour of people like you, the pious souls who were always getting in my way and being given higher responsibilities that should have been given to me.

"My one great desire was to become someone important; someone who could make vital decisions for the church, someone who would be properly respected and remembered. I was saving the money so that I could travel to a large city – such as London,

Winchester, or Chichester – and purchase my own bishopric. Then people would know who I really was, that I was a significant person within the Church. Now, it seems, I must remain an insignificant nobody for the rest of my days. All my grand plans have failed. God has sent His punishment on me for my pride, my vanity and my greed. I shall never achieve my ambition. All my efforts have been for nothing."

I waited for him to continue. He took a few deep breaths in silence, then looked at me and concluded, "So now you know. It does not matter what that man Hubert has ordered for me, I shall not live long enough to be much trouble to anyone. You may go on your way, smug in the knowledge that you will have a far better life than I am ever likely to enjoy again. Now, please, leave me alone to die in peace and obscurity."

I told him, "You will be remembered. I shall never forget you, Brother John. You have been the instigator of my downfall, it is true, but because of you I can now rise far higher than I ever dreamed and for that I would give you my thanks, even if you will not accept them. I know that you were disliked by many of the brothers. Even so, many in the abbey respected you."

I continued, "You may never rise any higher than one who eases the pain of others while you stay here, but to them you will be a great blessing. They will praise you and thank God for your work, I am certain. This is surely higher than insignificance – to be praised, respected and thanked. The poor unfortunate people here may indeed be the outcasts of society, but God still loves each one of them and you too, as much as He loves the King himself, if not more so.

"If greed was your driving force in the abbey, let love be what compels you here. I beg of you, allow God to be your guiding light for the rest of your days. You will then have all the riches you desire, stored for you in Heaven."

I then asked him to tell me if the rumour within the abbey was true – that he had some sort of influence over the abbot. He replied, "I did have some small measure of sway over the abbot. Soon after he joined the order, during the time when I was his confessor, I discovered that he had been a murderous outlaw, hiding from the sheriff of Rye before running away to Danmonia and entering the order. The hue and cry for him had long been called off, so he was no longer a wanted man, but he knew that I knew of his crimes and he feared exposure. There were other things he told me, which I refuse to relate, that strengthened my hold over him. At least they did, before he rose to become abbot.

"Once he had reached this position, my influence was weakened, but I was still able to have my way in most things. No one, now, would believe me if I dared tell of his past."

As he began to turn away from me, I told him, "Brother John, please believe me when I say that I sincerely wish you well. I will pray daily for a miracle that you are cured of this illness. Though your desire was to do me mischief, I thank God daily that what you did has done more to help me than anything that anyone else has ever done. I tell you again that I forgive you everything and feel truly sorry for you.

"Both of us have, through Christian charity, helped a stranger in dire need after leaving the abbey, but the consequences of our actions could not have been more different. I shall pray for you always. God's ways are indeed strange to us mortals whom He loves. His miracles are still possible." I then left him to his fate and never saw him again.

The next day, I talked with Geoffrey only to discover that plans had been made for me and the Psalter to go to Buckfast Abbey. As things turned out, I was not to go alone. The Guild had some business thereabouts, so we travelled together, about a week after my trial had concluded.

Some seven years later I was told by a member of the Knights' Guild, who had spent some time near the Gloucester monastery and who was now passing through where we were, that Brother John had indeed mended his ways. He had served Our Lord very well for a little over six years in the hospice before he himself had totally succumbed and eventually died from the terrible disease.

Although he was a leper, he was not, as they usually were, thrown into a mass grave with no recognition. He was given a Christian burial in honour of his years of hard work and I sincerely prayed that God would forgive him, as I had done.

CHAPTER THIRTY-FIVE

The Guild travelled to Buckfast Abbey en masse. As usual, we sent runners ahead to give notice that we were coming and would require food and lodging. As we approached the abbey, I felt a little homesick, remembering the good times I had spent there. I also felt somewhat nervous, wondering how the brothers who had known me would treat me as I returned. I was not sure whether to feel happy at coming back or to turn my horse around and flee. I decided that I should show no qualms until events proved them necessary.

When we arrived at the abbey, Abbot Samuel and Prior Mannus were waiting outside, their arms folded inside their sleeves, a smile on each of their faces. Many of the abbey's brothers were lined up behind them, in front of the main gate. Before the rest of the Guild dismounted, I turned to Master Joseph , who waved me forward. I jumped down from my horse and walked to the abbot and prior, bowed to them and knelt as I moved my satchel around to the front of my body. As I did this, I heard the rest of the company dismount.

With a smile on my face, I reached into the satchel and produced the Psalter, slightly worn, but still in good condition, wrapped in the original leather in which I had received it. I had removed the leather from the bottom of my satchel and replaced the book with a new thin board. I had also attempted to clean the somewhat dirty cover in an effort to restore it to something near its original state.

With trembling hands, I opened the leather and presented the Psalter to the abbot. Tears started to gather in his eyes at the return of this precious book to his care. He bowed over me to kiss me on both cheeks, hugged me and then knelt to receive the prized Psalter with both hands, cautiously, so as not to drop it. He slowly stood and carefully rewrapped the book and passed it to the prior, then bade me rise and asked forgiveness for his lack of trust in me. I readily hugged him again and told him and all gathered that I heartily forgave him and all the brothers who thought I had stolen the valuable book. I was then invited into the abbey for a thanksgiving meal to celebrate the Psalter's return.

I easily recognised many of the brothers who had gathered to meet us, including Durant, Daffydd, Aubrey and Nigel, although there were many new faces who clearly wondered who I was. The abbot then said aloud, "I invite the whole Guild to come inside. I encourage you to stay here for the night and to join the brothers for a celebratory evening meal."

Master Joseph replied, "We would consider it an honour to enter the house of God, especially one in which one of our number had spent so much of his life and in which he was so well respected." I could not be sure at the time but, from the tone of his voice, I thought that Master Joseph was making a reference to the way I was expelled from the abbey. If that was indeed his intention, the abbot either missed or ignored the suggestion. The Master continued, "With your permission, I have a notion to contribute a side of beef toward the meal." The abbot smiled and bowed, then waved us forward to enter the abbey.

I noticed that the faces of the brothers who had assembled to see us had lit up upon hearing what Master Joseph had said, as this meant more than a slice or two of meat would be on the tables tonight. This Abbey strayed from the Cistercian Rule in this one respect. Normally, meats were forbidden, except to be given to the ill to enhance their recuperative abilities. At this Abbey, the abbot usually allowed small slices of meats to be served to one and all whenever important guests stayed for the evening meal. However, on this occasion, due to the large amount of meat donated, each brother would have his fill of it.

Once we were inside the main gate and our horses and asses

stabled, we were shown to our quarters for the night and acquainted with the whereabouts of the necessary offices – the lavatorium, the garderobe and so on – so that we could be comfortable and wash ourselves, prior to partaking of the meal.

When we had all gathered for the evening meal, with the Master of the Guild seated on the High Table, the abbot at his left, several announcements were made, for once breaking the rule of silence at meals. He justified this by not having the meal brought forward until after the speeches had finished. After a time, abbot Samuel stood, called for attention, and said, "As the prodigal son returned home to find his loving father running towards him with outstretched arms, so our beloved Psalter has returned to us." He raised the book to show the brothers. He continued, "What you have seen in the chapel and in the scriptorium for the last five years and more has been but a substitute copy of this book, placed there after the original went missing. Unfortunately, one of our number was, at that time, falsely accused of its theft. The real culprit has since been discovered and we most humbly beg the pardon of the man so unjustly maligned." He bowed in my direction. I blushed with embarrassment and smiled and bowed my head back at him. "But the man who was once wrongly cast out is the same one who has brought the Psalter back to us. We heartily thank him, and we undertake that we will henceforth pray for him each and every Sunday at the public service, so that his name will be remembered from this day forward within this Abbey as that of an honest man."

I was somewhat abashed at this, but I was introduced and called on to say a few words. I believed the Abbot Samuel was hoping I would declare that I would re-join the abbey. Unhappily, he was to be disappointed. I stood, cleared my throat nervously and said, "My lord abbot, brother prior, brothers, novices and postulants, greetings. It has been over five years since I was last inside this Abbey and a great deal has happened to me since then. I have been a beggar, a cook, a minstrel, an actor, a healer and a scribe – the talents for which I had learned while living and working within the precincts of this community. Through all that has happened to me in the years since I last took a meal in this hall, my faith in God has kept me strong. If I had not learned to love God so, nor learned so many skills here, my time away from the abbey could certainly have been tragically different. The Psalter might have been lost forever. God be praised, all has turned out for the good."

I continued, "I wish to thank the abbot for his kind words and his even kinder, though unspoken, invitation to re-join the order, but I do not believe that I would belong here any longer. I believe that God took me from this place for a purpose. There must be some work He has for me to do outside these walls. It is with that belief, therefore, that I must decline my lord abbot's very generous invitation and request that he give me permission to leave this Abbey, formally and completely. I will remember all of you, my friends, in my heart and in my own prayers. I thank you."

I resumed my seat to a small amount of applause, with Geoffrey grinning and patting my back. I looked at the abbot. He smiled wryly and nodded to me. He obviously agreed, albeit reluctantly, with my reasoning. I had severed my ties with the abbey and would never go back to that part of my life. From here onward I would follow a different path from the one my father thought he had laid out for me. This brought to mind the next thing I knew that I had to do. I must go and see my father and explain to him all the things that had happened to his son. Once I had settled back in my seat again, the abbot called for the meal to begin.

Once the meal was over, we were shown to our beds. Master Joseph was taken to the abbot's quarters, as was the custom, while the rest of us were shown to individual cells or to the dormitories. The next morning, we gathered together for a silent breakfast, after which the Guild met to discuss our plans for the near future.

It had been previously planned that the Knights' Guild was to call upon Hugh de Portcestre on our way to London, as he was wavering somewhat in his support of the King, who at this time was Henry, the third of that name. Several barons had shown themselves to be disloyal to the King. As mentioned earlier, it was the work of the Knights' Guild to ensure that all the earls and barons kept to the bargain they had made with King John at Runnymede in the year of our Lord 1215, as well as other such subsequent agreements and that they continued in those agreements with the present King Henry, who was the dead King's lawful successor.

Once our meeting had finished, we had a quick audience with the abbey to formally take our leave and be on our way. The abbot wished us well and, as we all went to mount our horses, he approached me and told me, "I am saddened by your choice, but it is evidently God's will that you not return to us. I thank you again, most heartily, for the return of the Psalter. We will ensure that such thefts do not happen again. John was a blight on this establishment and one of which we are well rid. I hope he serves the Lord well in his new position, though I pity the man for what has happened to him. God bless you, my son, in all you do. May He watch over you until we meet again in life or in Glory. If ever you pass this way, please be assured that you will have a warm welcome here for as long as you wish to stay."

At that I knelt and asked to receive his blessing. Once he had given it, I mounted my steed and found my place within the Guild ranks, then we rode away. When we stopped for the night, I sought out Master Joseph and asked for and received permission to take leave, for a day or so, to visit my father and brother. This was granted, so long as I made certain that I re-joined the Guild at Portchester in time to leave for the next mission.

CHAPTER THIRTY-SIX

Two days later, I rode near the front of the Guild, just behind the Master of the Guild. I had argued against this, as I knew it was a clear breach of protocol, but I was ordered to accept it by both the Captain of the Guard and by Master Joseph. Why I was given this honour was never explained to me, so I just accepted it and did as I was told. My new pennon, carried by Dagbert, flew proudly, flapping wildly in the wind as we rode.

As we neared Portchester Castle, I could restrain myself no longer. I called to the Master and said, "My lord, I crave your pardon, I must go and see my father, we are so close," and without waiting for a reply, moved to ride away from the Guild. The Master laughed and shouted, "Go, young man, enjoy your day. We will meet you back here at Portchester when you have done visiting your father."

I waved my reply and whipped my horse to as fast a gallop as he would go, so that the amount of time it took to get to Portsmouth was not much more than it would take to say but a score of *Paternosters*. Yet I still wished the horse could have run much faster. My servant was left to keep up as best he could.

As I arrived at the outskirts of the town, I slowed my horse to a fast walk, so as not to have the citizens overly concerned. All the children came running to see this strange knight riding through their town. Although I knew none of the children, as I looked at them, I had the notion that some of them resembled the sons and daughters or perhaps younger brothers and sisters of the friends I had known when I had last been here, so very long ago. I momentarily considered the strange fantasy that it was almost as if the children of this place had never grown up and that I was the only one who had reached adulthood.

I rode to the area where I guessed my father would be toiling. I searched the sweaty faces of the workers in the fields and eventually found what I was seeking. Once I spied my father, my heart leapt in my chest and I immediately jumped off my horse, running at full tilt into the field where he was working with my brother. My brother had grown to resemble our father in build and appearance, although his beard was somewhat lighter and his hair every bit as red as was my mother's.

I called out my father's name and raced up to him. He turned to see a grown man, dressed as a knight, running towards him and he naturally looked puzzled. In my delight, I had momentarily forgotten that he had not seen me since I was a skinny little child, barefoot, in a small brown tunic, over twenty years ago.

Here was I now, a well-built man, dressed in fine linen, with a surcoat displaying my personal device over my expensive clothes, with leggings, leather shoes and spurs, as well as a Knights' Guild mantle fixed around my shoulders. It was no wonder that he did not immediately recognise me, even though I made certain that I had put on my mother's headband and carried her satchel over my shoulder before I took this trip to see him.

As I reached him, I knelt before him. He looked down in wonder at this knight kneeling in the dirt before him. I looked up into his eyes and, with a choking, sob-filled voice, I took his hand and said simply, "Father, I have come home." He staggered a little with this possibility; that his young son, whom he had sent to an Abbey all those years ago, should now be kneeling at his feet.

He quickly recovered his composure, grasped both of my hands and lifted me to my full height, still a head and shoulders less than his own. He stared into my watery eyes, as if in an attempt to determine whether I was an impostor playing some cruel joke on him. My father must have either recognised something within my eyes, or perhaps Switha's headband and satchel had convinced him, because he suddenly pulled me into his breast and cried out, "Rolf, my boy! It is so good to see you again." He hugged me unmercifully until I gasped and complained for lack of breath. He then held me at arm's length in order to examine me from top to toe.

He roared with laughter and called to my brother, "Ralf! Ralf, see who it is! God be praised! Your brother has come home. Ralf! Come, greet him." Ralf had stopped working and stood, gripping his hoe with both hands, watching to see what business this stranger would have with his father.

The rest of the workers had also ceased their labours, wondering why a knight would act in such a strange manner, kneeling before a villager. Once called, however, Ralf immediately dropped his hoe and came over to us, slowly, perhaps thinking that our father may have been jesting, but when he came within arm's reach, he recognised something in the way I looked and he too threw his arms around me with great joy. Those of the workers who had known me before I left the village also came to welcome me home. It had been quite some time since any of them had last seen me riding away, a small boy on a borrowed ass. Now I had returned on a large horse.

My brother and father hugged me between the both of them. They instructed the rest of the workers that they could take the remainder of the day at home, then gathered up their tools, laid them on a barrow and bade me come home with them and tell everything that had happened since I left. The barrow was left near the door of the cottage as we made to enter it.

Dagbert arrived, his small horse sweating, just before we were entered the house. I introduced him to my father and then he took the horses out the back and looked after their needs. He stayed with them and set to cleaning our equipment and talking to the horses.

Once we were inside and seated, our hands full of mugs of ale, questions fell from their lips like rain. No matter how much I told them, they asked more and more questions. "Who is Brother John? Who is this Geoffrey? How is it that you are a member of the Knights' Guild? When and how did you become a knight? Do you have any land yet? Have you met a girl that you could take for a wife?"

At this question, I abruptly stopped talking, suddenly remembering Aislinn. I had not thought of her since I was made a sergeant in the

Guild. I wondered where she was now. Would she be a suitable wife for me? Was she still with the troupe? Had the Danish thegn caught up with her? Was the troupe still together? Where were they now? I had too many questions of my own running through my head to hear those of my father and brother. I also thought of Ælicia, the ward of the Baron of Stone. I had been visiting her on and off for a few months, but I had as yet entertained no thoughts of love. I was from humble beginnings and she was high born. But now that I thought of it, why should I not? I was now a knight of the realm. I had as much right to the happiness she could no doubt bring me as any other man of my rank.

I swiftly realised that I was indeed at my happiest when in her company. I decided that next time I saw her, I would tell her that I believed that I was falling in love with her and observe her reaction. I doubted that she would laugh at me. At least, I hoped that she would not. When I realised that I was daydreaming, I shook my head to return to the present and apologised to my father for doing so. I told him that I had not yet found a wife, but that there was a woman with whom I had been spending time, when I had no other pressing business. I started to describe Ælicia to my father.

"She is a person of exceptional beauty, with a kind heart, which is shown every time she has to deal with difficult people. She will always remain composed and collected, let the complainers run their course, then show them how to resolve their difficulties whatever they might be, with logic and with dignity. She will let nothing disturb the air of calm she exudes. Ælicia is very intelligent and often solves a problem well before many men could even understand that the situation even exists. Her artistic skills are unparalleled. Her needlework is precise, her writing is the neatest I have seen for a long time, even rivalling that of many of the brothers in the abbey and when she sings, ah, her voice is as sweet as a nightingale's." The more I spoke about her, the more I was determined to tell her of my feelings.

Then, to change the subject before I became overly romantic, I told them of the time I spent in the abbey, and about the brothers who stood out in my memory, for better or worse. I described the talents that I had acquired while there; my writing and reading, musical knowledge and so on. I also nervously related to them that I had been falsely accused of stealing a precious book and had been expelled from the abbey. At this, my father looked shocked. I quickly reassured him that the real culprit had been caught and punished, not only by the King's justice, but by God as well. I told him of the misdeeds of Brother John and the dreaded disease he had caught and what happened to him during his trial and sentencing.

I explained that I had spent many months with a troupe of minstrels and that I had gained a wider range of skills during the time I was with them. I described how and where I had left them, where I went afterwards, my return to the south of England, how I had saved the life of Geoffrey and whose son he was. When they heard this, my father and brother were most amazed. They were stunned to think that I was directly connected to one of the most powerful and influential people in all of the country.

I told my father and Ralf that it was thanks to Geoffrey that I was introduced to the Knights' Guild, that I had served with them for a few years and had been raised to the rank of a knight. I then related the events of the return of the Psalter to the abbey and the fact that, in order to better serve the King, I had been formally discharged from the abbey and now served with the Guild.

We talked long into the night, until my throat was sore from so much talking. I eventually told my father and brother that I should go back to Portchester Castle to be with the Master and the rest of the Guild, but they would not hear of me leaving so late. They insisted that I stay in the cottage with them, break my fast in the morning and move on afterwards, if indeed I must.

"If your Master complains," said my brother, "let him deal with your father and me. I will not spend one moment less with my brother than is necessary, now that, thanks be to God, he has been returned to us."

I had no need to think for a second time before accepting their offer. I excused myself and went outside to tell Dagbert that I intended to stay the night with my family. I brought him inside and told him that my father would allow him to sleep within the house also and we would both return to the company of the Guild on the morrow.

I pitied the prodigal son in the Bible story. His brother had not wanted anything to do with him when he returned home from his philandering. I, on the other hand, knew that I was warmly welcomed by my brother, as well as by my father.

When the time came for us to extinguish the candles and retire to our beds, Ralf insisted that I use his and he would sleep in the larger bed with our father. I heartily thanked him and went to settle down in his bed. As I made my way to his bed, I was surprised to see that my old cot was still in its little nook. Had I thought about it beforehand, I would have guessed that Ranulf might have disposed of it long ago. He had no need to keep it, as it was not likely to be used again.

When I asked him, father told me, with a smile on his face and a tear starting to well up in his eyes, "You will think me a foolish old man. Every time I tried to get rid of it, I found that I could not. I had not the heart. I knew that you would most likely not be coming back and even if you did, the cot would have very soon been too small for you. I also reasoned that, if I threw it out, or even took it apart to re-use the wood, it would be as if I was cutting you out of our family completely. That is why I still have it." I hugged him again and went to bed, where I passed the night in the most relaxed sleep I had had for many a year.

The following day, after breaking our fast, my father convinced me to stay another day. I sent Dagbert on his way with my apologies to the Master. While Dagbert went back to Portchester to continue his work there, I spent the next day touring the land owned by my father. It seemed to me to have shrunk. I realised that this was merely because my perceptions had changed, as I was so much bigger now than when I left.

There was not much difference on the land, when compared to what I remembered of it the last time I saw it. The crops were the same, the animals had increased slightly in number and the tools were the same ones they had when I left, just with new heads and hafts. It seemed to me that for Ranulf and Ralf time had stood still.

Although I was glad to be with my family and to see that they were well and happy, I discovered, to my surprise, that what I really wanted was to be back with my new family – the Guild. I was shocked to come to the realisation that I had outgrown my father and brother.

Regardless, I happily spent the rest of that day helping where I could around the house and with the crops and animals, but my heart was not really in it. I believe my father saw something in me, perhaps in the way I moved around the place. Over the table during the evening meal, my father asked if I would be happier staying with the Guild or returning home. I thought long and hard before giving him the answer that I really did not want to give, but knew I should. I told him, "Being with the Guild makes me very happy indeed and while spending time with you and Ralf is just what I needed, I believe that my true calling is to serve the King with my duties in the Guild."

He replied, "I am glad that is your choice. Much as we would wish to have you stay here, there would be no great future for you in doing so. Had you chosen to stay, we would have tried to help make a living for you. We truly wish we could make a place for you, but this land is not very productive. The produce we get from it is reducing each year. It supports us, but barely.

"Serving the King is the highest honour anyone in the kingdom could wish for and I am very proud of you for achieving what you have done. It is true, I would have preferred that you had stayed within the walls of the abbey, but it appears that God had other plans for you. He has led you away from the Church and into the service of the King, though no doubt serving one means serving the other. So long as you fulfil your duties with honour and wisdom, I could ask for no more. You have done some great things and brought honour to the family. Though I would have you stay, I give you my blessing to leave whenever you wish. My heart will go with you always, my son."

Ralf nodded his agreement, "What our father says, I say also. I wish you well in your life, brother. May God be good to you." With tears in our eyes, we shook hands and hugged each other. The next morning, while I was breaking my fast, Dagbert returned to remind me that I was due at Portchester by midday. I asked that he pack what few belongings I had brought with me so we could be ready to leave at a moment's notice. Soon after the morning meal, I mounted my horse and, waving goodbye to Ralf and Ranulf, set out for Portchester Castle at a canter, Dagbert following on behind.

We rode in silence, because I was sad to leave. Although the distance from father's house to the castle was not very large, it seemed to take a very long time to get there. By the time I arrived, Master Joseph was on his horse, giving instructions to the footmen to break camp and to prepare to travel to London.

He caught sight of me as I rode into camp, rode towards me and called out to me, "Welcome back, we have more of the King's work to do. Dagbert already knows where we are going. He will tell you what you need to know, if he has not done so already. Come and find me tonight and we will discuss your next task." He rode off to see to his next responsibility. I was just in time to travel with the Guild to our next assignment, whatever that would be.

As it happened, I was to be extremely glad that I had visited with my family when I did. I was very happy that I had the opportunity to speak at such great length with my father and Ralf and to tell them all that had happened to me in the years that I had been gone from the household. It filled my heart with joy to know that my father and my brother were proud of me and of what I had accomplished. I treasured the time that I had spent with them. I looked forward to being able to visit them again sometime soon. I knew that every detail of their faces would be forever in my memory.

I thought of sending them some things now and again from my travels with the Guild that they could use. I began making a list of things they needed. Money, cloth, good quality grains, spices, sugar, high-class platters and many other things were written on my list so that I would remember what to send. Sadly, I was soon to discover that I would never have need of that list because, as events unfolded, that was to be the last time I would ever see either of them alive.

CHAPTER THIRTY-SEVEN

Ælicia had been married once before, but her husband, Franklin, had left for the Crusades before the marriage could be consummated. He had been killed by the Saracens and so she was widowed. While she retained possession of the properties that she had inherited from her father, they were being administered by Master Joseph, as she had been appointed as his ward by the King after the death of Franklin. Her lands were to be found in the areas around the town of Henlistone.

Ælicia and I had become good friends almost as soon as we laid eyes on each other. The first time I saw her, I thought that she was the most beautiful woman I had ever seen. I knew immediately that we could never be anything more than friends, due to my social standing. I could not have been more wrong. I had not considered the rights and privileges to which a knight was entitled. The very first moment I could see her on her own after visiting my family, I told her that I loved her and, thanks be to God, she replied that she was extremely fond of me indeed. This was no infatuation on my part, like that between Aislinn and me. This, I told myself, was real love and I hoped it was returned. Over the next few months, we spent countless hours walking through the many gardens of the castles and abbeys we visited, admiring the flowers or merely sitting and talking to each other about nothing and everything. We had very similar tastes and soon realised that we were fast becoming much more than friends.

She confided to me later that when we first met, she thought that I could never love a woman in such a manner as she wanted to be loved, especially since I had once been in an abbey. She thought that I was unattainable. Our love grew by the day and sometimes we talked of marriage, but not with any seriousness, although I dared hope for the possibility of such a fortuitous union.

One day, without telling Ælicia that I planned to do so, I nervously approached Master Joseph and asked him to intercede with the King, in order to gain his permission to marry her. I guessed that I had not many prospects, but I had to know what possibility there was. Master Joseph laughed gently when I asked him this. I asked as to why he laughed, and he replied, "I have been noticing you two together. I wonder that it took you so long to come to me. You would make a great match. She would be just the woman to bring you properly to manhood. Do not look so shocked, I mean no disrespect. You are a fine man, but you are incomplete. I think Ælicia would do you some great deal of good. She would complete you. Besides, she has also told me about her feelings towards you." I was somewhat surprised and embarrassed by his candid comments, but I thanked him sincerely and took my leave of him. As I walked away, not noticing the feel of the ground under my feet, it seems that I did indeed have a chance at happiness with Ælicia.

It was about two months later that Joseph sought me out to tell me that he'd had a reply from the King. What he told me made me the happiest man alive. He said that the King had decided to allow us to marry, provided Ælicia agreed to accept me as her husband. The marriage fine was set at fifteen pounds should it go ahead. An extremely small price, we thought, for a lifetime of happiness. He then handed me the writ from the King, which stated that I had permission to marry Ælicia.

The Guild was due to visit the village of Gaven in the first week of May to settle some affairs there. The village folk were holding a market and fair, which was a bonus for the Guild. We have fun at times like these – with no battles to fight, we merely enjoy the fun of the fair once business has been completed.

I decided that I would surprise the Guild members – and Ælicia as well – by proposing to her publicly at that fair and take my chances of rejection in front of the whole group. Surely I considered myself the bravest man in the world for tackling the matter in this way. If she were to say no, I would be thoroughly and publicly humiliated. I would suffer the jibes from my fellow knights for many months, were I to be rejected by her. I sincerely hoped – and had to believe – that she could not, would not, do so. I was sure of the woman I loved.

As soon as we had finished setting up our pavilion, a court was held by the Marshall, as Master Joseph was engaged elsewhere. The court is our usual practise whenever we arrive at a village or town and, once all other business had been concluded, the time had come for our members to press any further suits. As the youngest knight present, I waited until all the other knights had had their say and then stood in order to make known my intention to have my petition heard.

When I was called upon to speak, I bowed to the Marshall. I told him, "I have a petition to plead and ask you to accept this writ which I had received from the King, by the hand of Master Joseph, the Master." The Marshall read the writ, with a surprised look growing on his face. Then he smiled, looked at me and said, "I see the King has granted your application to make your petition. Have you asked the person in question whether your request will be granted?"

I replied, "No, my Lord, not as yet. I had planned to do so here and now, with your permission, of course."

The Marshall smiled again and nodded to show that I would be allowed to proceed. I bowed once more, turned and bowed to Ælicia, then dropped to one knee and, with an ecstatic but trembling voice, asked, "My lady Ælicia, I love you deeply. Would you please do me the great honour of becoming my wife? I pledge my heart to love you, my arms to keep you warm and my sword to keep you safe." I was so nervous while making this speech that the only thing I could see was Ælicia's face. All else was invisible to me.

For a few seconds I thought that the look on her face meant that she would indeed reject me but, as she told me afterwards, she was simply attempting to speak without bursting into tears. At last she stood, looked down to me, straight into my eyes, smiled broadly at me and said, "How could I refuse such a gracious request? Of course I will marry you."

As I stood to embrace my beloved Ælicia, grinning like a madman, my ears were filled with the sound of cheers from the whole of the gathered men and women of the Guild, who, it seemed, had been caught totally unawares by my speech. The Marshall then stood, walked over to us, shook our hands in congratulations and offered us the services of the Guild and its assets for our wedding ceremony, whenever and wherever we chose to hold it.

Arrangements were made for the nuptials to be celebrated in three months' time, on the first Saturday after the feast of the Assumption in mid-August. As my new wife's lands were near Henlistone, she wanted to take me there to show them to me after the wedding, before the Guild had to return to London and the King's Court.

We obtained permission to take two weeks' leave from the Guild after the wedding, in order to view the estates. We were told that we would be expected back in London by the second day of September to assist with more of the King's business.

The wedding was a grand affair, with many different items of entertainment and far too much food. Almost every member of the Knights' Guild was there to offer their support and friendship. We received many gifts from many people, and we offered the Guild twenty-five pewter trencher plates and a further twenty-five linen napkins, which was deemed by Master Joseph to more than cover the cost of the fine for the marriage.

The only unfortunate thing I regretted at the wedding, was that my father and brother were unable to leave the farm due to the harvest having to be taken in at that time. We would have to make a visit, as husband and wife, to their house as soon as we could get there.

We set out for Ælicia's lands the morning following the wedding celebration. We were attended by Dagbert, as well as three of Ælicia's women servants and several other people, including three men at arms, a scribe and a herald. These others came at the insistence of the Master of the Guild as being essential for two people of the Guild who wish to put forth a proper display of wealth and dignity.

It took us a day and a half to ride over the whole area of

Henlistone. I was amazed to realise that I was now the co-owner of all this land. The land in total consisted of eight hides. The Master of the Guild, while Ælicia was his ward, had control of her lands. Now that she was married, the lands were returned to her control and, through her, to me. Admittedly, the land would always legally belong to my wife, but as her husband, it was now my responsibility to administer the land in a financially sound manner. Ælicia and I both knew that we had to see the lands and the accounts for ourselves, to get some idea of how we should look after them to our best advantage.

There was a small village within Ælicia's manor, with about fifty people living there. Sheep herding and fruit growing were the main occupations in the area. Thankfully, the estate had been handled by the Master of the Guild in an honest and fair manner, with very little on the property needing our immediate attention. There were some minor repairs needed to the manor house, but generally all was well.

The first person we met when we arrived was the Steward of the House. He had been expecting us and the first thing we did after bathing to rid ourselves of the dust of the road, was to inspect the house accounts. They were all in perfect order, with nothing missing. Ælicia expected nothing less from her steward, as he was well known for being very pedantic when it came to the house rolls. Every single item, no matter how minor, was entered on these rolls, so that he had a perfect account of who was using how much of the precious stores. I thought, rather mischievously, that he would probably get on quite well with old Brother Aubrey from the abbey.

We had a very agreeable time touring over the land, enjoying each other's company in what was very pleasant weather. We spent the first few days riding over the area, hunting, practicing our archery, chasing and racing each other over hill and down dale. All in all, I found that this was a very satisfying time to be alive. I fervently, but in vain, wished that we did not have to go back to the Guild.

I would much rather have spent every day here with my new wife.

CHAPTER THIRTY-EIGHT

Six days after arriving at Henlistone, while out hunting on Ælicia's manor grounds, a rider approached us at full gallop. All three of our guardsmen, were, as you would expect, a little apprehensive and made ready to draw their swords. After seeing the diminutive size of the man I stopped them, saying, "Stand down, he is only one man and rather small at that. We should be able to defend my wife if necessary, should he wish to attack us at close quarters."

He rapidly brought his horse to a halt when he saw our men reach for their weapons. He then made his horse walk slowly towards us and when he was within speaking range, dismounted, bowed and called out, "Are you Rolf, son of Ranulf and brother to Ralf?"

I naturally answered in the affirmative. The rider then slowly approached, leading his mount, with his hands held well away from his weapons, bowed again and said, "My lord, I have bad tidings. May we talk in private? The news I have is not for the ears of common guards." I guessed that he wanted to deprive them of the pleasure of knowing his tidings, in return for the menacing manner they showed as he arrived.

I thought I recognised him and asked, "Have I not met you before, in Portsmouth? You are the son of Henry, son of Roger the miller, is this not so?" At which he smiled and answered, "Yes, my Lord, I have been sent by the sheriff, my grandfather, to bring you urgent news."

I then motioned for my guards – more for their peace of mind than for any worry for my own safety or that of Ælicia – to remove the messenger's sword and dagger and to search him for any other weapons and for one of them to hold his horse. He allowed my men to take his weaponry, such as it was, then I motioned to him to rise and follow us as Ælicia and I walked away from our men. When we had moved about twenty paces from the guards, I asked him, "What is this news you bring that is so important you must ride across this land so fast, yet so terrible that you cannot speak of it in front of my men?"

He knelt, bowing his head yet again and replied, "My lord, I regret that I should be the one to bring this news to you, but I must inform you that your father is dead, as is your brother. I am so sorry. They were both killed as they were leaving church on Sunday last, four days ago. It has taken me this amount of time to discover your whereabouts and to reach you."

Naturally, I was shocked, but managed to compose myself enough to ask him how they were killed. He replied, "They were leaving the new church in Portsmouth by the west door, when part of the steeple collapsed and landed on them and a few other church goers, killing them all instantly. The rubble was quickly removed, but there was nothing anyone could do to save them.

"It is believed by the chirurgeon that, by God's grace, they died quickly, without suffering overmuch. Several other villagers were injured in varying degrees by parts of the falling steeple, but most of those have survived with treatment from the healers. Again, my lord, I am so sorry to have to bring you such sad tidings."

By the time he had finished, I had turned to my wife and covered my face, sobbing slightly. Ælicia put her arm around my shoulders in an attempt to comfort me. As I slowly regained my composure, she thanked the messenger for his trouble and asked him to convey to his grandfather the message that we would be there as soon as we could make arrangements to do so. She then instructed him to go to the kitchen to replenish his food supplies and to take some refreshment before dismissing him. He nodded, bowed again, slowly walked back to his horse, retrieved his weapons, took the reins of his horse and followed us as we returned to the manor house. Once we reached that building, I sent one of our pages with the messenger to arrange for a replacement horse for his return journey to Portsmouth after his meal.

The rest of our day was spent back at the manor house and it was a difficult time. Having decided to return to Portsmouth as soon as possible, we made an end to our happy break. Even so, it would be a day or two before we could leave, so that I could pay due respects to my father and brother and stake a claim for my father's lands which would now most likely become mine. Packing for this most terrible of journeys was indeed an odious task.

A day and a half later, we started out. The trip back to Portsmouth took less than two days, but throughout the entire journey my head was full of happy recent reminiscences about my father and brother, and the ride to my hometown seemed to take forever.

When we arrived in Portsmouth, eight days after the accident, Roger the sheriff had been expecting our arrival, as he was forewarned by the messenger and so was there to meet us. He shook our hands and offered his sympathies, for which we thanked him. He then took us to the church, with its fallen steeple, in which once stood the shrouds that contained the bodies of my relatives and the others who had died in the accident. They had all since been buried. The steeple was already undergoing repairs.

My father and brother had been very popular men in Portsmouth and as such, the sheriff told me, every person who could attend did go to their funeral. It was no grand affair, merely a simple service in the new church and the burials in the churchyard. Two small wooden crosses, with their names written on them, had been erected to mark their graves.

I spent some time in prayer for the souls of my family and those others who had perished. I then made arrangements to pay the priest for my family members' burials and for continuing prayers for their souls. This was the only time in my entire life that I had not wanted to come back to Portsmouth.

We stayed for a few days at what would soon be my house, to help settle my father's and brother's affairs and to make my claim for the land and their possessions. The sheriff knew that, as we belonged to the Knights' Guild, he would be required to send messages to us wherever we happened to be and we would return word as to how we wished to proceed, once our claim had been heard. In the end, the process was quite long, taking over ten months to settle, but eventually I became the proud owner of lands I could call my own. Now, my wife and I had lands in two places. I took leave from the Knights' Guild and moved into what was once my father's house and took stock of what we wanted to do with it.

Some time after we took possession of the land and all the rights attendant to it, the two-roomed cottage my father and brother had lived in was extended, with the help of several of the men in the village to increase the living room. It had been a reasonable size, in which two or three men could eat and sleep, but for a man with a wife and expectations of children, I considered it somewhat cramped. We added two rooms on to the back, the south side, with a covered area attached, underneath which we could sit comfortably on fine evenings.

Some years later, Roger took ill and died and I was appointed as sheriff. I was the only knight in the town, and as a trained man at arms, I faced no opposition apart from Henry. He was reluctant to put himself forward for the position, but his wife pushed him into it. However, as he had almost no skill with any weapon but bow and arrows, her lofty ambitions for her husband failed.

After having lived in my father's cottage for a few years, I decided that due to my new status as a knight and shire reeve, and as I had the resources and the funds to do so, I should have a new house built. This one was to be made of stone. I wanted to build my new house with stone quarried on the Isle of Wight. With that in mind, I contacted the master mason building the church and told him of my requirements. He was kind enough to look at my rough drawings and, when sufficient payment had been negotiated and made, he drew up proper plans and sent one of his men whom he considered competent to oversee the construction of my grand new house.

I hired fifty men to do the work and it took a little under a year to complete. The stone was a beautiful pale cream colour, with seams and patches of reds, blues and greens running through it. The new house was sixty paces across the front and twenty paces deep. It was a two-storey building with a garderobe on both levels. It had four bedrooms, a kitchen, a bathing room, a sitting room in which we could entertain guests and a special room set aside for any of my business as the shire reeve. As well, there was a laundry, a wardrobe for our clothing, one for our spices and plate and a feasting hall, which took half of the upstairs floor area and was big enough to seat over fifty people. There was one room downstairs where Ælicia practised her calligraphy, painted, read and embroidered.

Every single room had a window with clear glass in it. To purchase the fine glass cost me almost as much as the stone for our front wall, but it was worth it. The process for making the flat glass accounted for the high cost. We had two men in our village who had studied under master glass makers in Venice and they were happy to show off their skill. The ingredients for the clear glass had to be imported. The glass blowers first made a large hollow globe, then cut it open and laid it flat. Before it cooled too much, they cut it to size using shears.

The old cottage became our guesthouse, consisting of four good-sized sleeping rooms, to house our frequent guests. We also built a bigger stable for our four horses and made it large enough so that if Geoffrey or the Master of the Guild and his retainers visited, as they often did, there was sufficient room for them and their animals too.

After a while, I ordered a shallow channel constructed, lined with rocks, from the shoreline to my land, with the channel flowing tidally. At my end of the channel, I had a fishpond dug, fifty paces wide by forty long and as deep as three men. As the tide came in, water flowed along the channel and into the pond. When it ebbed, the channel dried up and the pond again became land locked. The pond was then stocked with a large variety of fish, which were to supplement our food stocks at the house. A reed fence was planted where the channel met the pond, to funnel in any fish swimming in the channel from the seaway between Portsmouth and Whale

Island, and a fish weir placed so as to prevent their escape when the tide was up. This meant that we never had to go to the fish market again.

The members of the Knights' Guild knew that if they ever passed nearby our town, as they often did over the years, they were more than welcome to call in and stay for as long as they desired, so long as we or our servants were there to receive them. They also knew that, with the pigs we kept and the few sheep, they would be well fed while they stayed with us. The only payment we demanded from the members of the Guild was that they gave us news of their adventures.

CHAPTER THIRTY-NINE

licia and I spent a lot of the next eight years travelling and working with the Knights' Guild. There were always battles to fight and times at which we had to make at least a show of strength in order to convince towns or their barons or elders to continue supporting the King and his rule.

God be praised, I suffered no serious injury at any of these skirmishes. Although I had been lightly wounded many times. The worst wound I received was an axe strike to the tip of my left thumb, which cut it to the bone. Thankfully the cut was a clean one, so there was no infection and no loss of any part of my thumb, although I do, to this day, carry a small scar there.

There were also many agreeable times in which we took a great deal of pleasure; visiting friends of the Guild, attending Royal courts, fairs, tournaments and many other enjoyable pastimes. Thankfully, these peaceful times far outweighed the few times of strife.

At the end of those eight years, at the age of thirty-three, I had earned enough money to pay scutage, so that I was able to retire from the King's service with honour. Due to that service, I was granted three more hides to make my land in Portsmouth now five hides in size.

I decided that I wanted to plant a small variety of cuttings from Marissa's vineyard. She was still alive at this time, she being only fifteen years my senior. I begged her for a few cuttings, giving her a promise that I would never seriously attempt to make wine from any of the grapes that grew. I told her, "Your wine, as excellent as it is, surpassing even that from the Gascon region, would make anyone with pretensions to prepare his own vintage change his mind, out of fear of failure to match the wonderful taste and quality of your own. Besides, I enjoy eating the grapes too much to make such a pitifully small batch of wine from the few vines I would grow on my land. Any grapes I could grow would at best only produce a small amount of verjus, should I even consider pressing them."

She allowed me several cuttings and gave me instructions on the cultivation of them, so that I had grapes for my table in their season. She even sent one or two men from her vineyards to check on my vines at regular intervals. Any sickly or dead vines were replaced. I was never able to grow enough to make any significant quantity of wine, as I predicted. Besides, Marissa's wine was preferable to any small amount I ever produced.

I was very glad to discover that Gor, my childhood friend, had survived his many illnesses and grown into a well-built man. His archery skills were as good now as any I had seen on my travels.

He had been sent to Oxford to be educated in all the useful subjects needed for administering a household. These included reading and writing, account keeping, preparing of contracts and even the procedures required for courts. His older cousin had paid for him to be sent there when he became old enough to travel that distance on his own. He knew that Gor had not been a healthy child and would benefit greatly from such learning, especially such that would give him a trade which would not involve heavy work.

Besides, Gor's cousin had an ulterior motive. When he had finished his training, Gor could be employed by him as his steward. The cousin would then have a man in charge of his household accounts whom he knew he could trust unreservedly. Gor worked for his cousin for twelve years, before the cousin succumbed to a long illness and passed away. Gor had become yet another man with no service to perform, although he could have taken a position in any great house with the references his cousin had given him before he died.

Soon after we had moved our belongings from the old cottage into our new house, I employed Gor as my steward. He would run my household and be a valuable addition to my resources. Gor administered our accounts for the house with perfect care.

In all the years that Gor was with us, Ælicia and I never had cause to be concerned that we would run out of anything which made our life comfortable. He always made certain that we had sufficient stores for the times that the members of the Knights' Guild paid their visits. Gor saved us from embarrassments of this kind many times, for which we were ever thankful, and we rewarded him often for his service. He was, however, prone to minor fits of emotion when things happened unexpectedly, which threatened to put a drain on our resources. We put up with this, as it was a sign to us that he was personally concerned for our public reputation and welfare.

Sadly, Ælicia and I were never blessed with children, but we constantly enjoyed the playful presence of other people's children in and around our land. They were often amused and entertained by the stories we told of the adventures we had with the Guild. And there were always new younger children to hear the old stories anew.

After Roger the miller died and I was appointed as the shire reeve for the area, I spent less and less time away with the Knights' Guild. I eventually retired from the Guild completely and settled down at home with only the duties of the shire reeve to keep me busy. I also made a personal decision to take over Roger's task of supplying the bread for the Eucharist each Sunday. This was partly because the time I spent in the abbey influenced me in that direction, but mostly because, after Roger had done it for so many years, it had become almost expected of the man in the position of sheriff to do so.

I may not have been as quick as Roger was to be on the scene if anything went awry, but I tried to be as fair in my dealings with lawbreakers as he had been. My training in the abbey saw to it that I was able to forgive readily, but that did not mean I suffered fools easily. I still had my martial training with the Guild to call upon should the need arise.

If anyone thought that I would be lenient on wrongdoers, they soon found to their great cost that the law of the land could be very harsh indeed. Thanks be to the Lord, I had never yet had the responsibility of having to condemn anyone to death or to serious mutilation, but if I caught anyone breaking the law, they knew they were in grave trouble. Besides, there was always the capstan at the mill.

During the times that I had to be away from the village performing my duties as shire reeve, I always took Ælicia with me so that I would never be lonely or miss her company. She was a steadying influence whenever I had to make any judgment on a case. She would temper the law with kindness, advising me with her knowledge of both the law and of the person involved if she knew him. Although she always insisted that it had to be me who made the final decision, I took her advice carefully.

Besides, when she travelled with me, Ælicia could act as my clerk and I could trust her to be scrupulous in her note taking, to ensure that proper records were kept for the King's men when they came to inspect us. We could discuss the case at any time and her memory of what happened was rarely at fault. She also enjoyed travelling with me because she was able to see many other villages and towns in which she was able to sample new foods and trial new clothing styles.

After a period of about fifteen years, visits from the Knights' Guild slowly became more and more irregular, until it was only Master Joseph and Sir Geoffrey who were habitual callers. All our other friends had either retired to their own lands or had died. Thankfully, our villagers were friendly people who gathered often for festivals or celebrations, so that we did not have much opportunity to become bored with our own company. There were many occasions throughout the year for the entire town to congregate and enjoy each other's merriment.

And so life went on. My wife and I were peaceful and content, loving and happy with ourselves and each other. I did not expect our lifestyle to change until one or the other of us passed on to our next life in Glory. Nor did it change – our life continued in this cheerful fashion for quite some time.

Several years later, in 1272, King Henry died, while his son Edward, known as Longshanks, was on Crusade. Allegiance was sworn by the barons to Edward in his absence. He returned from Crusade when he could and was later crowned the new King. There were celebrations all over the land for this grand event. Towns, cities and villages held great fetes and fairs to welcome King Edward.

CHAPTER FORTY

Late one afternoon, not long after Henry, the third of that name, had died, I was settled in my favourite chair in front of our hearth, talking about the day with Ælicia, with a small goblet of warm spiced wine from Marissa's vineyard in my hand. After more than seventy years, she still produced copious amounts of quality wines.

Marissa had been training three of her best workers to make the wines after her fashion and they were quick learners, though at first we doubted that the vintages would be of as high a quality once Marissa passed on. We need not have worried, as they produced better wines now than any that Marissa had done. They had to. Her apprentices soon found out that although she no longer made the wines herself, as she could not manage the work, she could still show her displeasure if the quality of any wine was lower than that of previous years. We were apparently in no danger of having to suffer inferior wines for some time to come.

Ælicia sat in her chair, on the other side of the hearth, embroidering. She was always decorating some item or other for one of the village ladies. It was her way of giving gifts that would be used and treasured for many years. Her fingers were as nimble as ever and she showed no sign of failing eyesight, which was quite common in men and women who did so much close work.

I could hear the sounds of children running and laughing outside. This was a normal enough occurrence in these days of our peaceful life. I thought little of it, except to recall that this was the happy sound that marked the start of the earliest memories in my childhood and now, as I sat here, after a full and contented life, it had come full circle. I expressed to Ælicia that very thought. She laughed gently and nodded her agreement. We had spent many a pleasant hour this way, sitting beside the fire, chatting, on these cold winter afternoons. It was a very pleasant life.

The noise outside quickly became much louder. It was as if the children were coming closer to our door. While the children and their parents were aware that I had given them leave to play on my land, they also knew that they should not come near the cottages or the house unless there has been an accident, or some other emergency. My wife and I preferred our little piece of privacy. However, it seemed that this time they had indeed approached the house.

I reluctantly arose from my seat, half expecting some youngster to start crying at any moment, believing himself to be half dead because he had fallen and skinned his knee or some such triviality. With a broad smile on my face, I told Ælicia, "I shall not be long, my dear. I will raise whichever child is making the most noise from the dead, then return as soon as I can to our conversation."

I opened the door and stepped outside to see not merely running, laughing children, but the most amazing sight I could ever imagine. There, coming towards me on the track leading from the road to my house, was a series of three carts and wagons, surrounded by the children, all of whom were calling out names of plays or songs which they wanted to see and hear. Of the three wagons, only the first was brightly painted, the others were merely common traders' carts. These latter carried large bundles of Heaven knew what, covered with canvas tarpaulins, tied down with thick rope.

Sitting on the seat of the lead wagon was a man I knew. Beside him was the first woman, besides my mother, whom I had ever loved. They were Fynch and Aislinn. Accompanying them were some of the troubadours with whom I had spent so much time and from whom I had learned so much about the wide world. There were three others with them whom I did not recognise.

As they climbed down from the wagons, gently shooing the

children away to make room, I could not help but smile broadly and fling my arms open with welcome. I turned to face back inside the house to call Ælicia to come and see, but discovered instead that she had already come out to stand behind me.

I called to the children, "Go play elsewhere, youngsters, I have old friends come to call. There will be no entertainment today. Perhaps, if you are good children, they may possibly consent to play for you tomorrow. Go now, please leave us!"

As the children slowly and reluctantly drifted away, looking over their shoulders in disappointment, I hugged and shook hands with my old friends and introduced them to my wife. We were laughing and looking, each to see how the other had grown or changed, and I invited them all into the yard behind the house for food and drink.

Questions of all sorts came to my mind. The first I uttered was, of course, "Have you been well?", followed by an insistence that they must tell me all they had done since last I saw them in Dorchester. Fynch laughed quite a bit as he spoke, but I sensed that there was some darkness behind the laughter. He surprised me by introducing Ruth, a Jewish woman he had met near Poole, in Dorset. She was of middling height, slight of figure, with dark hair and eyes. 'Passing fair' would be a less than truthful description of the girl, as she was indeed rather beautiful. I was not surprised that Fynch took an interest in her, especially as she was only in her early twenties.

Fynch told me that she had been run out of that town, as her brother, Simeon, was a moneylender there who had died, with many of the town's population still in his debt. Poole had suddenly become no place for the sister of someone who would remind the townsfolk that their success was mostly due to money loaned by a Jew.

As the troupe were passing out of the town, they had seen her, sitting on the side of the road, sobbing, rather as I had been when I first met them. They stopped to ask if she was in need. At first, she was reluctant to tell them her story, but with Fynch's insistence she eventually told her tale and he kindly invited her to join them. His argument was that, Jews or jongleurs, both are seen as lower-class people in polite society. There would no doubt have been some lively discussion as to whether she should be taken in, but I had not the least doubt that Fynch would have argued strongly to accept a girl as pretty as this one, regardless of the King's official rulings concerning Jews.

While I knew Fynch had certain appetites, Aislinn would not have bedded anyone within the troupe, and Fynch would have been very disappointed not to have the lovely Ruth accompany them on their travels. He would have calculated, to the last farthing, the effect on the donations that a pretty girl like Ruth would have had.

Unsurprisingly, Ruth had soon become enamoured of Fynch. I doubt that it was because he was the smooth, sweet-talking charmer he thought he was. It was far more likely that she knew Fynch was the one who had ultimately convinced the others in the group to make the decision to have her join them. As things turned out, she had been blessed with a beautiful voice. As they were travellers, and she was on the run anyway, it turned out to be a natural existence for her. She did indeed improve the contributions from the villagers and now that I looked at her again, I knew, as did Fynch, that it was not for her voice alone. As they travelled and lived so closely together, it was, I supposed, only natural that one or other of the men in the troupe would have feelings for the girl. It did not surprise me in the least that it was Fynch.

Aislinn was to become one of Ruth's greatest friends – more like an older sister. This pleased me, as I should not have liked to see these two become rivals. Had they done so, the whole group would have fallen apart. Ruth seemed to have a very sweet disposition. As she and Fynch talked, they often, quite unconsciously I am sure, touched each other's arms, stroked their hair, or made some other such gesture of affection. It was obvious that they were truly in love with each other.

Fynch told me that the troupe had stayed in Chulmleigh for a while, entertaining Courtenay, who was well known in that area for his wool trade. He enjoyed the entertainments so much that he allowed them to stay at the castle long enough for Fynch and Ruth to convince the local priest to marry them. She had not long since renounced her Jewish faith to become a Christian. Therefore, she was able to marry Fynch. This had happened just over two years ago. I took another look at her and I thought to myself that it was just as well they were now married. She seemed to be carrying a little extra weight and wore a contented glow. I guessed that the number of members of the troupe would soon be larger.

Fynch then introduced the other new members of the troupe. They were a brother and sister pair, Alexander and Eleanor. He was a singer and dancer, who also performed sleight of hand tricks. She was a dancer and actor. With these extra cast members bigger plays could be performed, better-looking dances could be seen and set up and pack down took less than half the time.

The troupe had become substantially wealthier since I had travelled with them. Their clothes were rather more sumptuous and their bellies somewhat more round. It appeared they were doing well. Hude, however, seemed to have changed for the worse. He looked frail and appeared to have lost a lot of weight.

I asked them all, "What brings you to my house? I am most certainly very happy to see you – I am simply curious as to the reason you came by here."

Fynch's answer was most surprising. "We have received a message from Hugh de Portcestre. It was requested that we come here and put on a show in celebration of the new King. We have not been to the castle yet, we thought to seek you out first. As to how we found you, that is easy. As you well know, you had travelled with us for quite some while, and during the many times we talked, you often fondly reminisced about your family and your hometown. We thought to find you in Dorchester, so we spent several days in that town, trying to find you by giving your description to many people and detailing your talents. However, there was no one there who knew you or knew of you. When we could not discover your whereabouts there, we decided that you had either changed your name or moved on, so we gave up searching for you there."

I felt somewhat embarrassed that they had sought me there, as it was my lies that led them to do so. I interrupted his tale and shamefacedly told him, "I must humbly apologise for telling you a lie. I had no relatives there, I merely had something valuable to protect and felt unsafe after that terrible incident with the lout and his sword, which resulted in my broken hand. I hope you can forgive my not trusting you with my secret."

Fynch smiled, waved away my apology and said, "It does not matter in the least. Anyway, when we found out that we were coming in this direction, we decided to see whether we could find you by asking around while we were here. We did not believe that it would be too difficult to find someone who knew of your whereabouts, if you were here or nearby. All we did was ride into the town, toss a small coin at a young lad and ask after you. He mildly surprised us by saying that you were well known and indeed here, so when we threw him another coin, he was more than happy to guide us here to your house."

I wondered if or when they would ever stop travelling and settle down, so I asked them. Fynch laughed and said, "Our intention has always been to travel as far as we can, for as long as we live. And whenever one of us died, for die we someday must, the rest would simply bury the dead in unmarked graves, shed a small tear or two, and then move on. We would be replaced by other wanderers, though no doubt somewhat less talented."

I admired his fatalism, but told him that I most definitely preferred the way of life into which I had settled. He continued, "Which brings us quite neatly to why we wanted to find you, for there is a very simple explanation. As you can see, we are fast becoming far too old to continue in our trade. We have decided to retire. We, too, wish to settle down, as you have. And besides, as you have likely already noticed, Ruth is soon to bear me a child and travelling on the road is no proper life for a young baby."

CHAPTER FORTY-ONE

I was shocked. Not that Ruth was pregnant, I had indeed already guessed that, but surprised that they wanted to give up the troubadour lifestyle. I obviously could not keep the surprise from my face, because several of them laughed out loud. Fynch continued, "We have had enough of travelling. With all the touring we have done, we know that the better climate is here along this coast, rather than further north and we thought that since you were here – or so we hoped – we thought to settle nearby, with a neighbour whom we knew to be friendly to our cause.

"We are not without our talents for keeping ourselves fed. We are able to learn to grow crops and already make clothes and things, so would not long be dependent on the goodwill of others. Besides, this town looks like it could do with a bit of cheering up. All we need is some small plot of land where we can set up a house."

I discerned from the earnest look on his face and those of his companions that, in this at least, he was not joking. I considered that I could do far worse for neighbours than to have these people living nearby. I told him, "There must be some ground around here on which you may build a house or two for yourselves. I will speak to the other elders of the town on your behalf. I do have some small influence with the council of elders here." I smiled as I said this last. Though he might not know of it, I was well aware of the regard in which I was held by most of the townsfolk. I continued, "In the meantime, you may set up your wagons and tents on the fallow ground behind my houses for as long as you need, until permission is obtained for you to settle here permanently."

He and his friends smiled broadly and congratulated each other on their likely success. I was glad to be able to repay them for their kindness to me for all our time together, and I was looking forward to spending a great deal of time with them, hearing about their travels and adventures. What I did not expect was to hear a tale of woe.

Fynch told me the reasons that they had decided to settle down were not hard to arrive at. "Eight months ago, we were just outside Romsey on the river Test, when there was a sudden flood. It had been raining for about a week, but we thought ourselves safe, camped as we were on a shelf of land above the river. Sadly, during the night, the flood raged down the river so fast that we had almost no warning. We were woken just after midnight by the sound of the rushing water and scrambled out of our beds, grabbing only what we could carry. The wall of water struck our wagons so hard that it took them away, with most of our belongings. Thankfully, most of us were able to get up into some strong trees, but two were taken by the river. They were young Thirn and Leofard. Thirn stood just below me under the tree, his hand stretched out to grab mine when the water hit him. I missed his hand by half the length of my fingers. I was distraught, as were we all, by their loss.

"We never found their bodies. You may remember Thirn – he was the quiet one, more so than even you yourself had been. Leofard was the more boisterous of the musicians. Sadly, he was the best man I had ever met for writing scripts and remembering lines. We will never meet another like him. Leofric, obviously, was heartbroken at the loss of his brother and left us soon afterwards, saying that he no longer had any heart for the life we led. I could not blame him, and we have heard nothing from him since.

"Two days later, after the flood subsided, we found the wagons piled up against a tree. Only one of them had survived reasonably intact, while the rest were smashed beyond recognition. Most of the contents of the wagons were strewn, stolen, or who knows where. We were able to find some few complete instruments or items of clothing and a couple of our weaponry props, but almost everything else was missing or destroyed. Hude tied a length of rope to the one good wagon and we all heaved on it. After some strenuous tugging, it moved far easier than anyone thought it would, but the piece of wood to which the rope was tied suddenly snapped through and struck Hude on his right arm and across his back. His arm was shattered, as were several ribs and his strength has since left him. He could not perform as a strongman again. The rest of us were luckier, as Hude had shielded us, to his misfortune. Once Hude's health had improved he wanted to leave us, because he thought he was no longer useful. Of course, we would not have it. We knew that if he left our troupe, he would likely starve and die. We could not let him go; we love him too much. So he stays with us, doing this and that, but no more strong work.

"After three days of searching, we eventually gave up looking for the lost men. We put our heads together and decided that it was not worth trying to regain what possessions were lost, so we came up with our plan to retire. It was at this point that Leofric left us. We have heard that he has settled in Wales. We managed to make repairs to the one wagon that had not been destroyed and bought two old wagons from a man who had no further use for them. It was then that we decided to come and look for you. And so, here we are."

I told them that I could not be happier to see them and showed Fynch and Ruth to the guest cottage, where they could bed down for as long as they needed until they had their own house built. The rest said they would be happy in their wagons and tents. Ælicia and I had sufficient food and other stores to share with old friends who were in need. My house steward, Gor, would be informed of the guests when he arrived in the morning, provided he did not have one of his customary fits if he saw them before I told him.

Two days later, I accompanied my friends on the short trip to Hugh de Portcestre's castle and introduced them to him. He was very happy to see them and instructed one of his men to show them where they could set up for their performance. The next day, they performed one of their least ribald plays, sang many songs and played dance tunes until the festive guests left, tired but extremely happy. They were a great success, especially if one were to judge by how much they were paid.

Throughout the following month, I spoke to the aldermen of the town and was finally able to convince them that these were good people and should be allowed to settle here. I also made them aware of the value of having entertainers in the town, as they would make our fairs more enjoyable for everyone who came and we could make more money for the town from their performances.

Henry, Roger's son, had taken over both mills and become the only miller in the town after his father died. He had married a small-minded woman who had, sadly, infected him with her narrow viewpoint on life. He was also on the town council and, thanks to his shrew of a wife, argued that these performers were an unknown group who would likely rob everyone blind within the month.

I told the council about the time I had spent with the troupe. I said, "These are honourable people. I spent many months in their company, although they could have left me desolate on the roadside. They taught me most of the skills which I use today and, in exchange, I taught them to read and write. I would give my guarantee for them on whatever terms you would wish. You will have no need to be concerned for their honesty or their desire to become a part of this community." I put forth much more in support of them, expounding their virtues and – while admitting that they undeniably had them – minimising their weaknesses. I knew that these performers could become useful and valuable members of our community, were they given the chance to do so. I told them that even Hugh de Portcestre had made it known to me that he would be content to have them stay here.

Henry was unable to refute my arguments, especially when I had the backing of Hugh. The aldermen agreed with me and the performers were eventually allotted a small piece of ground near the southern tip of the island, at a place called Southsea. Ever since that day, there has always been some sort of entertainment on the site near where the troupe built their first houses.

At first, they had nothing but a small, covered area. This was followed, as they could afford to do so, by a larger pavilion, then a purpose built, permanent entertainment structure. Ever and always, the newer buildings were constructed much larger than the previous ones. Eventually, some of the younger generation of entertainers heard of the riches to be made performing in London and decided to move there in order to join a theatrical group, with a view to eventually starting their own.

I have heard that they were and continue to be, very successful in their art.

CHAPTER FORTY-TWO

The town of Portsmouth prospered as it slowly grew, some of the riches coming from the amusements provided during the fairs. The aldermen never had cause to regret allowing the troupe to stay, although Henry and his wife were never quite happy to have them here. They were always mistrustful of them, but they would never give a reason why.

Eventually, the younger players who stayed here married some of the local men and girls and their families in turn lived, performed, worked, played, and married within the town. They had become proper townsfolk and, apart from those few who went to London, never left Portsmouth for any great length of time. Most of the older members of the original troupe, such as Hude, Fynch and Aislinn, have since passed away – God rest their souls – but the youngest still survive and continue to perform and train new entertainers. Had Fynch lived, I believe he would not have been disappointed to see his friends settle down comfortably in one place.

Now, at the age of eighty-seven – nearer eighty-eight, though I strongly doubt I shall reach that anniversary – I have finished my tale. I have lived longer than Ælfric the doctor, who died many long years ago at the age of eighty-five. Although we were never to meet again, we kept in contact with letters, right up until the very day he died. I admired Ælfric as the wisest man I had ever met, though I was sorry that he never would tell me any more of what he saw in my future. I suppose now it does not matter, as I have already lived through what he might have told me.

I am the oldest person I know and while my life has been long and eventful, I have had many happy years, especially with my wife by my side. My hope is that this story has helped you to understand how people lived, worked and played during my lifetime.

Dear reader, I will take my leave of you now as I am quite tired, as, no doubt, is young Rupert, grandson of my friend Fynch, who has been writing all this for me. Rupert has been visiting me for the last few months, helping me to write down all that I wanted to tell you. I hope he has been faithful to my tale.

I realise that I have not mentioned Rupert previously, but I would thank him now for agreeing to do this writing for me, as my eyes are not as clear as they once were and I no longer read without the aid of a magnifying lens. Nor are my hands as steady as in my youth. My mind, however, is as lucid as ever it was.

My wife has fallen into a happy sleep in the next room. The sounds of children playing outside have died down, now that the sun has set and their mothers have called them all home for their evening meals. Tomorrow, I shall sit comfortably on my chair outside the house, watching life in all God's glory pass by, enjoying the companionship that my loving wife gives me. Soon life will leave me. I suffer from a raucous cough that has clung to me since I caught a bad chill last winter. My health has been slipping gradually ever since. I know I do not have long to live. I am familiar with the progression of my sickness.

My darling wife will be sad when I am gone. I have tried to prepare her for the time when I leave her, but she tells me, "Do not be so silly, my love, you will live for many a year yet."

I disagreed, but did not to argue with her. I will not gloat when I have been proven right. Equally, I would not be sad to be proven wrong. I have lived a long, happy and full life and have gladly taken what the good Lord gave me; contentedly surrendered what He wished to take away. I know that throughout my life, He has given and taken exactly what was needful for me. God has been very good to me. I have made my last Will and Testament and Ælicia is to be well provided for after I am gone. For all the happiness she has brought me, it is only right that I do this.

I wish for you, dear reader, God's gift of peace and that the blessings of all His saints and angels will guard you from any wicked ways.

LIST OF CHARACTERS

Historical characters in *italics*.

Characters in Portsmouth

Adam of Portsea	Nephew of Baldwin
Ælicia	Rolf's wife
Alan	Blacksmith
Alard	Blacksmith, Alan's father
Anne	Wife of Stephen the carpenter
Anselm	Scribe
Anthony	Bowyer/carpenter
Baldwin of Portsea	Held land from *Jean de Gisors*
Bardulf	Rapist
Benjamin	Jew, Money lender/Fisherman
Daniel	Karen's dead husband
David	Weaver
Edda	Rape victim/prostitute
Eustace	Blacksmith
Francis	Brewer
Gor	Young child – given bow, eventually my house steward
Gregory	Blacksmith
Heleward	Scribe with a son
Henry	Miller's son
Hugh de Portcestre	Real name – *Hugh de Port* – Land owner
Jack	Alan and Alard's destrier

Jean de Gisors	Wealthy Norman merchant (1133 – 1220)
John	First son of Troy and Mary
Joshua	Marissa's dead husband
Karen	Thomas the Cooper's daughter
Kate	Beekeeper, Timothy's wife
Marissa	Vintner
Mary	Troy's wife, a jeweller
Matthew	Thatcher
Mog	Sow that attacked Owen
Nicholas	Old man who cut Switha
Osbert	Leather Worker/Tanner
Owen	Thatcher's apprentice
Peter	Scribe
Ralf	Brother of lead character
Ranulf	Father of lead character
Robin	Blacksmith
Rochelle	Stephen the carpenter's daughter
Roger	Miller
Rolf	Lead character
Rupert	Fynch's grandson, who wrote the book under Rolf's dictation
Stephen	Carpenter
Stuart	Beekeeper Timothy's son
Switha	Mother of lead character
Thomas	Cooper
Thurstan	Orange man
Timothy	Beekeeper
Toclyve	Bishop of Winchester (died. 1188)
Tomas	Karen the cooper's son
Troy	A smith's apprentice
Ulf	Archer child – squirrel shot
William	Beekeeper Timothy's son

Abbey Characters

Aubrey	Officious brother in Abbey
Cedric	Old Abbey brother
Daffydd	Abbey brother
Durant	Kind Abbey brother
Johann	Oldest brother in the abbey
John	Spiteful Abbey brother
Mannus	Abbey prior
Michael	Chief Infirmarian in Abbey
Nigel	Clumsy Abbey brother
Samuel	Abbot of Abbey
Simon	Brother who went back to family
Vivien	Master of Postulants in Abbey

Troubadours

Aislinn	Singer, Actress and Dancer
Alexander	Singer, Actor and Dancer
Eleanor	Dancer and Actor
Fynch	Actor – Leader
Hude	Strongman
Leofard	Musician
Leofric	Musician
Louth	Actor
Thirn	Actor
Ruth	Singer – Married to Fynch
Watt	Actor and Handyman

Other Characters

Ælfric	Ancient physician in Affpuddle
Colin	Member of Guild who died in battle
Courtenay	Lord of Chulmleigh
Dagbert	Rolf's servant after being knighted
Geoffrey	Nobleman whose life was saved
Godfrey de Lucy	Successor to *Toclyve*
Hubert Walter	King's Justiciar (died July 13 1205)
Hugh de Warenne	Land owner 1119 - 1148
Nathaniel	Jewish Merchant with Psalter
Joseph	Son of Franklin, Baron of Stone
Walt	Switha's cousin
William de la Colline	Champion of the tournament, also Captain of the Guard for Knights' Guild

APPENDIX

The Knights' Guild of Wessex and Mercia from 779 to 1400

The Knights' Guild in the late Twelfth Century was more powerful than ever it had been before, despite nostalgic stories of the "good old days." The Guild was never very large, but two factors made it far more influential than its size indicated:
1. The knowledge that the Guild would completely support the King, as long as he was on the throne, whoever he was.
2. The skills and influence of the individual members, extending the Guild's fighting force to several times its real size and providing the King with officials and advisers who were especially useful for particularly dirty jobs such as collecting money, enforcing the law and taking hostages.
The Guild's English connections made it quite useful in raising and training local levies (the fyrd) during times of war and rebellion.

The Ancient Kingdoms

There were seven Anglo-Saxon kingdoms (called the heptarchy): Wessex, Essex, Sussex (West, East and South Saxons), East Anglia (East Angles), Mercia (also Angles), Northumbria (north of the river Humber) and Kent. The Viking invasions of the Eighth Century reduced all these to just two: Alfred the Great's Kingdom, formed by joining the southern kingdoms and part of Mercia to Wessex, and the Danelaw (land under the law of the Danes) in the centre and north. Within two generations, the English of the south had conquered the Danelaw and henceforth England would be ruled by one King, whether he be English, Danish or French.

The Knights' Guild was an amalgamation of the Guilds which served the Kingdoms of Wessex and Mercia respectively and, after the time of Alfred the Great, served the King of England, but as separate and competing groups: the Knights' Guild of Wessex and the Knights' Guild of Mercia. The Knights' Guild of Mercia had a particular attachment to Æthelflæd, the Lady of the Mercians, and their alderman carried the axe taken in the Battle of Brunnanburgh in 937 as a symbol of office. The Knights' Guild of Wessex always carried a Dragon Standard for the King. The dragon was the symbol of Wessex.

The early origins of the Guilds are by no means certain. It is unknown whether the body of the Guilds served the King directly or whether the Guilds were retainers of the thegns. It is not known whether all of the Anglo-Saxon Kingdoms had their own Guilds of knights, where the idea first originated, or whether the groups were even called "Guilds." What is known is that the Kingdoms of Wessex and Mercia had their own Guilds serving their Kings by the middle of the Eighth Century.

Two shadows hung over the Guilds for many years. The Mercian Guild defeated the Wessex men near Benson in 779 and the Wessex Guild waited for years for their revenge. It finally arrived when, in 974, the tattered remnants of the Knights' Guild of Mercia arrived at the court of Alfred the Great, King of Wessex. The King of Mercia, Burhred, had fled, leaving his people, including the Guild, for the invading Vikings to hunt down and kill. To be deserted by their King and to have to seek refuge in Wessex was, for them, an intolerable shame.

These two incidents, more than any other, inflamed an underlying hatred between the two Guilds. Apart from occasional duels and riots, the jealousy was most evident in how each Guild tried to outdo the other in their service to the King. Each group was led by a council of thegns, with an alderman as chief thegn. Important decisions were made at a meeting of the whole Guild, known as a Guildmoot.

The Guilds: 1066

The Norman invasion of 1066 was a pivotal point for the Knights' Guild of Wessex and Mercia. After the battles of Stamford Bridge and Hastings, the Guilds were so depleted that they did not have the numbers to continue as separate groups. There was also the problem of how to survive under a new King who was replacing the English governing class with his French followers.

The tradition, as recorded in the classics *Beowulf* and *The Battle of Maldon,* dictated that the Guildsmen should die rather than return home without their lord, or avenge his death as soon as possible. On the other hand, the logic of survival suggested that they should return home and live quietly and unobtrusively as subjects of the new King. Early in 1067, after intense debate and much negotiation at a combined Guildmoot, they did neither. The Frumgar (or Marshall) of the Wessex Guild, backed by all the Guildsmen who had attended the moot, marched into the King's hall and demanded to know by what right he considered himself King of England. William, apparently stunned by such a bold display, listed his right by conquest, the oath of Harold Godwinson and the promise of Edward the Confessor. The reply received no response until William came to his election by the Witan and his anointing during the coronation. The Frumgar knelt and announced, "It is the anointed King whom we serve." An Anglo-Saxon order of King's servants had become an arm of the Anglo-Norman monarchy.

The Norman occupation of 1066 had many other effects besides forcing the two Guilds into one. It confirmed the principles formulated during the Danish invasions that the Guilds served whoever was the legal King. This made the Guild a power beyond its size, if the ruler was skilful enough the use the Guild properly.

Innovations: Late Twelfth Century

The language of the Guild is an indication of changes, either because of innovation or the fact that the governing Guild members communicated with Anglo-Normans and the Anglo-Norman government. The modern word "knight" comes from the Anglo-Saxon "cniht" meaning a young man who was a King's retainer. After 1066, the name was applied to the mounted Norman soldiers, as there was no Anglo-Saxon word for their people of this rank. While the name "Knights' Guild" was retained for the whole organisation, "knight" was also used for one class of members of the group, reflecting the modern use of the word.

Early in the Twelfth Century, the Guild organised its newly granted lands with manors and bailiffs. It would appear that previously the Guilds did not in themselves hold land: individuals did, or the Guilds stayed with the court and had no need of independent support.

"Alderman" and "Frumgar" (first spear), as names for the heads of the Guild, gave way to the more standard "Master" and "Marshall." The Hælthegn, traditionally "thegn in charge of the hall," became more ceremonial and during the Thirteenth Century the real work was taken over by the herald. The use of "stewards" reflected the growing complexity of the Guild administration.

As the Guild ceased to be a purely military force, the importance of the Dragon's Lance grew. A lance was a military unit, a small group who mustered under a pennon carried on a lance. Several lances made a banner, several banners a battle (or battalion). The Dragon's Lance was a specialist group of fighters whose predecessors were the aldermen's huscarls, who worked as the master's bodyguard. There was great competition to determine who in the lance would carry the Dragon Standard. Being young and practised, the members of the lance were also very clannish and quite conceited about their skill, sometimes causing friction with other people.

At the same time, the Guild increasingly provided sheriffs, justiciars and other powerful officials for the King. The Master had always attended the King's court to provide advice, but when barons were Guild knights (either through the upward mobility the Guild provided, or through family connections) they also attended court and supported the Guild interest.

The total Guild military sources consisted of:

- The Dragon's Lance as the Master's bodyguard,
- Guild knights and sergeants,
- Fyrd; two groups raised from Wessex and two from Mercia under Guild gonfanons, often commanded by sergeants,
- Men-at-arms and others, not members of the Guild, but in lances of the Guild knights,
- Banners under the command of knights of the Guild who were also barons. These were not part of the Guild force but operated in concert with, but independently of, the Guild.

Later Days

The working orders of knights such as the Templars became an anomaly as kings gathered power into their own hands. By the Fourteenth Century these orders were dying out or being killed off. By the Fifteenth Century, kings were creating their own ceremonial orders such as the Knights of the Garter.

As time went on, the Guild gathered more and more property. The strict standards of membership were relaxed and its functions became more ceremonial and less functional. The Guild moved away from its traditional support base, which had been the lower nobility and freemen. A rift developed between the landed and unlanded knights, the latter seeing the Guild as a career and the former as a sort of hobby. The noble classes dominated the Guildmoot and eventually drove the commoners out of the decision-making process altogether.

The end came when Richard II was deposed by Henry IV in 1399. Devoid of every principle but a romantic memory of the past, the Guild tried to raise a rebellion to support Richard, but it was easily defeated, disbanded and outlawed. The revolt was a futile gesture which reversed the Guild's governing principle of supporting the anointed King and ignored the political reality behind this, which had seen it through previous changes in the monarchy. Ironically, Richard, whom they were supporting, was already dead when the rebellion began, secretly murdered on Henry's orders.

Heraldry of The Modern Group

The arms of the two Guilds appeared at about the same time as the rise in heraldry, in the late Twelfth Century. It was believed that these were in fact the arms of the kingdoms. While a wyvern was certainly associated with Wessex, its form, and colours as we use them today were not those attributed to it then, and Mercia never displayed a saltire as we do now. The idea of the white mantles that we use these days was borrowed from those that the crusading orders of knights used, as was the use of the titles "brother" and "sister".

In medieval times, when anything new was introduced, it was irrelevant in their psychology. Their world did not change, so once something was in place it was as if it had always been there (see chapter 22 – the missing Psalter). A modern invention such as the Mercian saltire would not have been considered to be a forgery – it was simply filling in the historical gaps.

ABOUT THE AUTHOR

Roy Worrall was born in Portsmouth, England in 1953, and emigrated with his family to Sydney, Australia, in 1965.

After moving to Brisbane, Queensland, in early 1979, he became a postman, a position that lasted for forty years, during which time he acquired an interest in medieval re-enacting. He joined the "Knights Guild of Wessex & Mercia", the oldest medieval group in Queensland, which became the inspiration for *Life's Fortune*.

Roy is now retired and lives with his wife in Mount Nebo, west of Brisbane.

www.ingramcontent.com/pod-product-compliance
Lightning Source LLC
Chambersburg PA
CBHW031947240626
47153CB00003B/891